Turnaround Mill, Sussex in its working days.
September 1950

TALES FROM TURNAROUND COTTAGE

Fairy Stories for an Older Generation

Also by Elinor Kapp

Rigmaroles and Ragamuffins, words we derive from Textiles.
published by Elinor Kapp, Cardiff UK.
Distributed by Oxbow books, 10, Hythe Bridge Street, Oxford,
CX1 2EW
and Casemate Academic, PO Box 511, Oakvile CT 06779 Utah,
US

ISBN 978-0-9574759-0-8 paperback
ISBN 978-0-9574759-1-5 epub

**Ruffians and Loose Women. More words derived from
Textiles.**
Published by Elinor Kapp 2016.
Distributed by Oxbow books, 10, Hythe Bridge Street, Oxford,
CX1 2EW
and Casemate Academic, PO Box 511, Oakvile CT 06779 Utah,
USA

ISBN 978-0-9574759-2-2 paperback
ISBN 978-0-9574759-3-9 epub

TALES FROM
TURNAROUND COTTAGE

Fairy Stories for an Older Generation

by

Elinor Kapp

DIADEM BOOKS

TALES FROM TURNAROUND COTTAGE:
Fairy Stories for an Older Generation
All Rights Reserved. Copyright © 2017 **Elinor Kapp**

Published by Diadem Books
For information, please contact:

Diadem Books
8 South Green Drive
Airth
Falkirk
FK2 8JP
Scotland UK
www.diadembooks.com

**Logo on back cover from a 3D transparent embroidery:
'Ship of Fools.' © Elinor Kapp, 2007**

ISBN: 978-0-244-62531-3

The Persian Poet, Jalāl ad-Dīn Muhammad Rūmi, in the 13th century advises:

"Sell your cleverness and buy bewilderment."

When you are addressing the great themes of Life and Death, as in this book of stories, I can think of no better advice! To sell – and get a good price – for your cleverness can only be a good thing. Then you can let our smiling Windmill turn you around and around and find you a story.

The Winds can take you to be be-wildered, which is to be led into the wild places. Perhaps you will find that you have at last swapped mere cleverness for the true, lasting wisdom of old age.

Dedication

This book is dedicated to my dear family:

To my son and daughter in law, and the grandsons – Dr Rupert Rawnsley, Erika Rawnsley and the boys, Alex and Nate;
and to my daughter and son-in-law and the grandsons, Amanda Foster and Jon Foster and Freddy and Frankie,
Also to the memory of my husband, their father, the late Ken Rawnsley CBE and my extended family who have all encouraged my storytelling.

I wish particularly to dedicate this book to my wonderful aunt, Joyce Lucy Wilkins, who inspired my love both of the Sussex countryside and of stories. She loved windmills too, of all kinds, giving many talks on them. This pen and ink sketch from 1968 of the Mill at Cross-in-Hand is her work:

Acknowledgements

Cardiff Storytelling Circle, under Cath Little and Richard Berry, and many friends in the Storytelling world who have shared with me and listened.

Prof. Charles Muller of Diadem Books, and Gwen Morrison of PublishNation.

Cover picture and frontispiece: Scott Gaunt (scottgaunt.co.uk), with a contribution by Sandra Gajdosova.

Also: my very good friends, patient listeners and advisors:

Alison Walker, Amelia Johnstone, Angie Luther, Anne Rahman and family, Audrey Morgan, Briony Goffin, Caryl Chambers, David Brown, Diana Morgan, Prof. Ernest Freeman, Evie Telford, Helen Wales, Hiroko and Richard Edge, Jacks Lyndon, Jeremy Badcock, John Lewis, Jude Irwin, Kaye Edwards, Dr Kay Swancutt, Dr Lata Mauthur, Lyn Richards, Martin Fenn Smith, Mary and Stephen Ashton of Llansor Mill, Matthew Harwood, Michelle Wright, Miriam and Eliot Baron, Pat Gore, from Canada, The Reverend Pauline Warner, Peter Williams, Sally Humble Jackson, Steph Harding, Steve Gladwin.

Foreword

This is a book of highly original Fairy Tales, though drawing on universal themes. The book is set in a Magical version of Sussex, a County where anything can – and probably does – happen. Here the little River Flitter runs down from the High Weald, through Punnetts Town, eventually to join the sea in Seven Sisters Bay. Strange things happen to people who stay in Turnaround Cottage. It is a converted post mill, which has lost its sails. Now it has become a somewhat mysterious bed and breakfast venue, looked after by a newly retired health worker, Helena Brown. And the Mice! Don't ignore the Mice – generations of active, chatty, cheese-loving, philosophical, Mice.

Though the Mill's main purpose is long gone, the Winds, North, South, East and West, blow the old place around as if it could still grind corn. Now the Winds love telling stories instead and the place may well have just the tale you need, whether you know it or not.

If you stay there – and the prices are surprisingly reasonable – Helena will meet and greet you kindly, to settle you in and to make sure your stay is comfortable. Or will it be? Perhaps occasionally a little disconcerting, let's say, but always well intentioned. What of Helena's own love story, of the visiting Professor she meets through the lettings of the cottage – does that have a happy ending? Ah! You'll have to read right to the end to find out. No cheating now!

You will also meet many of the local people, who are friendly and welcoming. Their own true life stories form a sort of counterpoint to the Fairy Tales tucked in among them. It is not a heavy read; on the contrary, the pantomime-like antics of the evil widow, Arachne le Noir, are a gentle relief, set alongside stories like The Sin Eater and dark tales of the Enchanter and the Shrewish wife.

The stories are safe for children and indeed for anyone of any age, but the book will hold a particular appeal for the older Generation. Indeed any of us are likely at times to be facing up to issues of Life and Death, Memories and Forgetfulness, Bereavements, Illnesses and Healings and inescapable changes of all kinds. There is plenty of joy and laughter in here, all the more poignant against these other themes.

So – what are you waiting for? Turn over the pages, and listen to what the Storytellers of Turnaround Cottage have to say!

TABLE OF CONTENTS

PRELUDE: Gloria, Steve, Rachel and Pearl. Narrator EAST WIND

CHAPTER SEVEN – THE MAGICIAN'S DAUGHTER

POSTLUDE: Gloria, Steve, Rachel and Pearl.

PRELUDE: Gloria, Steve, Rachel and Pearl. Narrator EAST WIND

CHAPTER EIGHT – THE PRINCESS WHO LOVED CHOCOLATE

POSTLUDE: Gloria, Steve, Rachel and Pearl. Helena.

PRELUDE: George Miller. Narrator NORTH WIND

CHAPTER NINE – THE OLD WOMAN WHO WAS LONELY

POSTLUDE: George Miller, Helena

PRELUDE: Old Man, Unknown Woman. Narrator EAST WIND

CHAPTER TEN – THE ENCHANTER

POSTLUDE: Old Man

INTERLUDE – STONE FRIEND Poem.

PRELUDE: George Miller, Helena. Narrator WEST WIND

CHAPTER ELEVEN – THE PRINCE WHO WAS ALL HEART

POSTLUDE: George Miller, Helena.

PRELUDE: The Cyclamen Lodge gang! Carol, Helena. Narrator EAST WIND

CHAPTER TWELVE – GOODY OWL AND GOODY ELIXIR

POSTLUDE: The Cyclamen Lodge gang! Carol, Helena

PRELUDE: Helena. Narrator EAST WIND
CHAPTER EIGHTEEN – QUESTIONS
POSTLUDE: Helena.

INTERLUDE – Old Man as Tom Crow. Resolution.

INTERLUDE – George and Melinda

PRELUDE: Gabriel, Helena, Old Tom Crow. Narrator RIVER FLITTER
CHAPTER NINETEEN – TREASURES FROM THE SEA
POSTLUDE: Gabriel, Old Tom Crow, Helena.

INTERLUDE – Could this be love?

PRELUDE – The Cyclamen Lodge gang! Party at Three Cups Corner
CHAPTER TWENTY – THE MILL'S OWN STORY
FINALE: The Cyclamen Lodge gang. Helena.

LIST OF CHARACTERS

PREFACE

THE OLD WAYS

NEVER FORGET that there are two ways to every road, path, alley or lane. There is a way that leads towards and a way that leads away from wherever you are going – one end for going to, one end for coming from.

The names of these old roads and places sing with their own strange language. My imagination strides purposefully along them, full of confidence. The names alone evoke dreams and stories enough to fill, and fill again the traveller's knapsack.

The roads that pass Turnaround Cottage lead to the South, the East and the West. To the North is Tin Kettle Lane, recalling the days when the Gypsies came, calling for pots and kettles to mend. How many stories depend on the sort of mischiefs and magic the Tinkers bring? No need to look far for plots full of transgression and sly purposes with a waypath like that!

What about the fifth way, the little river Flitter? Coming on its own with a flow of chalky water from the High Weald, the river then circles halfway round the Cottage before joining the South road. Local custom and the Post Office call the South road from there on, 'Flitterbrook Lane'.

The lane is a bold adventurer, marching hand in hand with the charming River Flitter, till they part ways at Flitterbottom. From there on, the South road turns his back on the little Flitterbrook, going on his way alone in ever more drunken zigzags.

I like to think that the little River Flitter, thus deserted, cries all the way down to the comforting sea at Seven Sisters Bay, while the road, faithless lover that it is, dallies with many a crossway and lane, on its erratic course to the town of Battle.

Turnaround Cottage was once a windmill, and has never forgotten this. It welcomes visitors, and loves to have people to stay, but it has one very strange attribute. Now and then, as the wind changes, the Cottage remembers its past life and turns around in the night. The visitors wake to find themselves facing a different view and walking out onto a road they did not expect; a road with a story to tell and a wind which is determined to tell it to them.

Shall we listen to the wind, whispering the first story like soft, distant music? It is a true one, a mystery story, and because of this you learn it from Flitterbrook Lane itself.

CHAPTER ONE

A TRUE MYSTERY, JUST FOR YOU

THIS IS my own story, the true one, of the first house I ever bought, nearly fifty years ago, on the southward slope of the Sussex Downs. My address really was 'Flitterbrook Lane, Punnetts Town, Sussex'.

From the top windows you could see the sea; the English Channel and all the coast between Newhaven and Hastings, and in the right light you could see a silver white line on the horizon, which was the coast of France.

Kneeling in that garden, one overcast day, I buried my wedding dress among the country flowers and creeping weeds, shortly before leaving the house for ever. The dress was white silk velvet, sewn to my own design; a sweetheart neckline, a full sweeping skirt with a bustle trimmed with a single silk rose.

I bought herbs and bedding plants, pansies, wallflowers, winter jasmine and a blue clematis, a few days before I went away, not expecting to go so soon. I spent my very last morning bedding them in, not caring where; maybe over where the dress was already starting its long decay, but I was not thinking of that but of the green fingered pleasure I was leaving for the new owners in a house full of hopes and dreams.

I have never been back, but I have wondered sometimes if my white velvet wedding dress, no longer white, ever rose from the bed, turned over from the soil by a stunned gardener, or marauding fox. What shocks might it have evoked in the finders? A tale of murder perhaps, till no trace of a body was found? A thought of a theft or a tragedy or a ghost story?

Do you think I should go back to that village, to the pub in Punnetts Town, or the neighbours, or even to the house itself, and ask? I dare not!

But you – you who love stories, love mysteries, and have a far better imagination than mine – couldn't you make up a story about the wedding dress buried in a country garden, or maybe a story about who found it, and what effect that had on them?

CHAPTER TWO

THE WIND OF THE DEAD MEN'S FEET

PRELUDE

THE LITTLE VILLAGE of Punnetts Town in Sussex is very proud of its history. The locals suggest it was founded on the spoils of Piracy in the ancient days, while serious historians – who can always be relied upon to spoil a good story – say that it was simply the home of a gentleman farmer called Anthony Pannet, who created a hamlet for his workers in the 17th century.

The locals know better, and they are right!

There is certainly at least one place that upholds the reputation for mystery. No one really talks about it, as they don't want to be thought of as mad and sent to Hellingly Hospital. So anyone who experiences something strange is likely to rationalise it as, "There's something very odd about the

Flitterbrook, you know!" They say it must be something to do with the drains, or the weather, or the stars, or whatever fashionable idea is around. Their friends are more likely to ask if they've spent too much time at the Three Cups Inn.

Some of the old people won't go down Flitterbrook Lane at night, preferring to bypass it by the short cut up Tin Kettle Lane to the downs, or go round the triangle of minor roads leading towards Heathfield, though it's longer and means walking on the main road. They just cross themselves or mutter about not angering 'them' by disrespect.

It is however true that Turnaround Cottage, on Flitterbrook Lane, does have that one strange habit of forgetting it's no longer a windmill and turning itself around at night. Visitors, having come in from the South, expect to go out and find themselves on Flitterbrook Lane, but at those times they will find themselves walking out onto one of the other four Ways.

They will then find that there is a Story leading up or down, to or from, the place at such a time and they seem to have been chosen to hear it. Those who have had that privilege do not gossip about it, but hold what they have been given close in their hearts, if they remember it at all

No one seems to know now who actually owns Turnaround Cottage, but it was certainly once a Post Mill, and several of the locals remember the Miller and his family. Some even worked in it when it was a working mill, grinding corn for all of Sussex. Later, having lost its sails in a hurricane, it became a storage place, then a family home, and a holiday cottage.

One person who always held her tongue about anything she might know or suspect about the Cottage was Helena Brown, a relative newcomer, who had recently retired to live in Punnetts Town. Let's follow her as she stands in the queue at Barclays Bank in the High Street, chatting to a local acquaintance.

"So, you're in the old Wheelright's cottage down Flitterbottom?" said the man. Helena nodded, and added how much she liked Sussex, having been originally from Derby and longing for the warmth and colour of the South Downs. "I'm retired," she volunteered, knowing how country people like to 'place' one. "I was a manager in the Derby Health Authority. We bought the cottage as a holiday place for the family originally. Then my husband died and my only daughter married a Marine Biologist and they went off to live in Spain."

"Ah, Spain!" said the old man sympathetically. "Easy to get to, mind you, on Easyjet and other budget airlines. Benidorm, Marbella and such. A place in the Sun."

Helena refrained from saying that to most of her friends in Spain those areas were not actually Spain at all but strange excrescences of the worst of British exports, the Expats.

"So?" queried the old chap, whose name she didn't know, "Who does own that Turnaround Cottage just above you on the Flitter?"

At that moment the queue moved and it was Helena's turn, so it was easy to be brief as she paid in some cheques. "No one knows," she said over her shoulder, "not even me. It's all handled by the agent. All above board. I'm paid well to look after the place a bit and the agent lets me have money for repairs and things."

"Aren't you curious at all?" asked the old man. Helena felt suddenly awkward. "Not at all," she lied, taking her money and moving away quickly from his sharp blue eyes with a mumbled farewell. She felt uncomfortable, because of course she was curious. Very curious, about all sorts of things to do with her new job, but sure of one thing. Turnaround, whether Cottage or Mill, was a happy, generous place that somehow still ground out the corn of life into golden stories. Helena was sure she sometimes seemed to hear an echo of them, in the breeze round the eaves or the murmuring of the mice within the walls. Helena liked the mice. Generations of them had grown fat and bold on the corn leavings.

Helena returned to Turnaround Cottage a little later, still frowning slightly as she thought about the old man whose name she didn't know and what she felt had been somewhat excessive curiosity.

"What's the matter?" snarled an unpleasant voice. It was the new Visitor, a man with beetling eyebrows. She had arranged to meet him at the garden gate of Turnaround Cottage, to book him in for a night. "Cat got your tongue?" he continued unpleasantly.

Helena forced a professional smile. "Mr Barthwaite, isn't it? Ebenezer Barthwaite, from

Settle in Yorkshire?" She slightly overdid the smile, gritting her teeth, as he gave no more than a grunt and turned to the door, leaving her wondering whether he expected her to bring his case in. She left it there.

When Ebenezer Barthwaite found himself alone and parted from his case, he swore for a moment, but there was no one to hear. He sat down with his head in his hands and gave way to the despair that commonly overtook him on his own. How had he come to this? Once he could have afforded the flash hotel in Eastbourne for the reunion of his Lodge. Now? Well, he'd been lucky on the gee-gees for once and could at least attend, in his old dinner jacket, a bit strained at the waist and green at the seams but it would have to do.

What was the point though? He wouldn't pick up any work and his old colleagues would laugh at him. "Look at old Barthwaite!" they'd say, "He's dropped down the mine, hasn't he? Har har!" He rehearsed to himself the lies he would tell to keep his end up: "....and the Duke himself said I handled that deal extremely well..."

He thought he must have dropped asleep because he seemed to be woken by a mouse sitting up and offering him something. With a long-forgotten courteously he found himself taking a small piece of dry bread from its paws, eating it gratefully (he'd missed lunch), and actually saying, "Thank you." To a mouse! More mice came, with little offerings, crusts, a lump of sugar, a few cherries. One of them tugged at his boot to show it wanted him to get up and follow.

The mice took him up the stairs to a window overlooking the road to the East. It must be a dream, because he found himself sitting on a softly upholstered chair with a wee dram of his favourite malt in his hand, which he knew he couldn't afford. The mice were chattering excitedly and he slept in the chair.

The wind woke him, in the deep night. The curtains were blowing inwards and the wind was chill. It rose and rose, screaming round the eaves of the cottage. It was looking for him, searching him out, freezing his hands till he dropped the glass he had gone to sleep holding, hearing it break as it hit the floor. He tried to pick it up, cut his hand, swore and the wind laughed maniacally in his ear. It seemed to be shrieking his name and he wanted above all to hide from it. *"Ebeneeeezer, Ebeneeezer...!"* it mocked, as he cowered down in the chair.

The mice, who had run behind the wainscot, were squeaking in alarm. One little mouslet had got caught behind the big chair, unable to get home. A latent feeling of responsibility rose in the old man. It was his fault; the mice had been feeding him and got caught in this storm that somehow was meant for him.

He had never lacked physical courage and now he dragged himself from the relative safety of the chair, taking the full force of the demon wind, as it seemed to him, on his back. Picking up the mouslet very gently in a fold of his jacket he managed to hold it out to the paws reaching from a crack in the boards.

On all fours he turned to face this force that seemed to want to tear him from his life and fling him into nothingness. To his surprise, it suddenly yielded, letting him stumble back to the chair. "What do you want?" he found himself yelling and it sounded absurd to his own ears, as he realised the wind had stopped as suddenly as it had started.

He felt strangely warmed and at ease, as the wind spoke and said, *"Wooould yoooou like to hear a sssstory?"*

Now here is where you, the reader, must make an effort to understand what happens when telling people stories. Most will be grateful, quiet and listen with open ears. But sometimes they are frightened, unless they can believe it to be a dream. That is why Turnaround Cottage makes it easy for them to believe that. We like having significant dreams. It makes us feel Prophetic and Important.

What happens if someone is not easily persuaded it's a dream and doesn't like stories? Hard to understand, I know – would you believe there could be people like that? No, surely not? Well, occasionally the Visitors may decide they can cheat Turnaround Cottage. They may stay indoors all day with the blinds drawn. They may stick their fingers in their ears and sing *La-la-la* all the way up Tin Kettle Lane. They may sneak across the garden to the South road, thinking it will all be as normal.

No use! When Turnaround Cottage wants you to hear a story, you might just as well give in, because the story is what you will get. It's the Law of Storytelling; every story gets its own way in the end.

So, what follows is whispered to Ebenezer Barthwaite by the East Wind, blowing to the

West and, if you wish, we can eavesdrop as it blows its wisdom into his ears.

*"Hear now the Story of **THE WIND OF THE DEAD MEN'S FEET,**" whispers the East Wind...*

Do I need to remind you – you who have woken in Turnaround Cottage in the darkest time of the night and found that it has turned around and is facing the Road to the East – that a road has not one, but two ways and two ends? The Wind blows from the East and goes towards the West.

You hear it in the night, the East Wind blowing the small brown leaves, rustling, rustling, rustling, as they pass along, westwards, always westward, or are they soft footfalls, passing, passing, along the way to the West?

That is why it is called the Wind of the Dead Men's Feet, the feet that go sshh, sshh, sshh, quietly along the roads that lead to the lands beyond the seas, to the islands of the Blessed.

Don't go to the door, don't look out of the window, when you hear them passing; the feet of the dead shuffling by. "Sshh, sshh, sshh," they are saying. "Don't speak to us. Don't ask us to speak to you. We are the dead; you cannot turn us back now. Too late. Too late. Sshh, sshh, sshh."

You may hear the East Wind whispering, so low you hardly catch it above the sighing of the rustling souls. "Once in a thousand years someone tries to see them passing, passing, passing, blown before the wind, the Wind of the Dead Men's Feet," sighs the voice, "and once in a thousand years someone comes looking for the Dead. Asking, begging, longing for their return, but they never come back."

THE WIND OF THE DEAD MEN'S FEET

ONCE, there was a Woman whose two little children, a boy and a girl, had just died. She heard the wind passing the door one night, the rustling, shuffling, whispering of the leaves travelling westward and, in her despair, she opened the door and ran down the wind crying out her children's names.

She ran until she could run no more, then walked further than she would have believed possible, all among the rustling leaves.

She found herself, feet frozen and bleeding, in an open space under a twilight sky. All around her were the souls of the dead, but there, at last, in front of her were her own two children. She ran to them and called their names, held their hands, but they looked at her with blank, dead eyes.

"They belong to ussss..." said the East Wind. "You cannot have them. We are walking to the Wessst, to the lands of the Blesssed, beyond the sssea." But the Woman would not accept this. She held her dead children firmly by the hands and begged, pleaded, argued for their return, until the Wind sighed and relented a little.

"You mussst give us something in exchange," said the wind. "You mussst give us the heart out of your breassst."

"You are tricking me!" said the Woman. "If I have no heart I will die!"

"Sssso," sighed the Wind, now a shadowy shape in front of her, "I can give you a choice of a new heart. The shape held out a hand, and in it was a heart made of some hard, white substance, which glowed.

"What is it?" said the Woman.

"It is a heart of ssstone," said the Wind. "If you have this heart you will live for a full lifessspan and many more, but you will have no feelings. You will be free of them."

"How can I bring up my children with a heart of stone! No!" said the Woman. "What else can you offer?"

Again the hand came forward and in it was a heart made of intricate gold chains and links, with diamonds set in them. "With thisss heart," said the Wind, "you will live to a ripe old age, and you will be full of clevernesss, tricksss and deviousnesss."

"How can I bring up my children with a heart of trickery!" cried the Woman. "You mock me! Offer me something better!"

The hand held out to her a Rose, in full bloom, with crimson petals round a deep ruby heart.

"This is your lasssst offer!" hissed the Wind. "With this flowering heart you will be full of warmth, and generosity, but it will not lassst for long. It will support you for weeksss, for monthsss, perhaps even for a few yearsss, but the petals will fall and you will have to return to usss alone."

"Yes! I accept!" the Woman cried, and she felt the cold fingers of the Wind as he reached behind her breast bone, deftly took out her heart and replaced it with the crimson rose.

The force of the wind made her stagger, and then it was gone, blowing the leaves and the souls on towards the west. She stood on a calm dark road. The children tugged at her hands. "I'm hungry!" her son said, and the little girl began to cry. Their mother knelt and they looked at her with living eyes of love and need, as she gathered them in her arms and hugged them to her breast.

They walked on together. The Woman was happy but concerned and as soon as she saw a glimmer of light she ushered the children towards it. Set back from the road was a little hut, and behind she could see dim lights of other houses, a small village. She knocked on the door.

"Go away!" said a creaky, angry voice.

"We are travellers, dying of cold and hunger!" cried the woman.

"What's that to me? Get away, vagabonds, beggars, no-good wanderers," replied the voice.

"I cannot. I am a desperate woman with two children, I beg you for mercy's sake, have pity on us and give us shelter!"

The door opened a crack and an old woman with white hair and a sour expression peered out.

"They call me 'Old Mother Grump' in this miserable village!" she said. "Why should I help anyone?"

The travellers said nothing, but looked at her beseechingly and, with a sigh, she opened the door and motioned them in.

"Thank you! Thank you from the heart for this kindness!" said the Woman and as she entered a single red petal fell and was caught by Old Mother Grump.

The children ran over to the fire and sank down on the hearth, holding out their frozen hands to the warmth. The old woman looked at them sourly for a moment, then the petal in her hand stirred and she looked at it.

The crimson glow seemed to warm something in her and her expression changed as she stared at it. She put the petal in a box in her cupboard, hesitated a moment, then took out a loaf of fresh, warm bread and cut big chunks off it for the children.

Their eyes widened, the colour came back to their cheeks and they smiled up at her. But the little boy, about to eat it hungrily, turned, and gave it instead to his mother.

"No need for that," said Old Mother Grump testily, and she cut off another two pieces. The loaf was almost gone and she sighed, "I'll have to go and beg for some tomorrow, drat it!" she said crossly, almost to herself, "There's nothing in the larder now."

The Young Mother and the children hardly heard. They slept cuddled up together on the hearth, arms around each other.

Old Mother Grump looked at them, her face expressionless, but before she went to her bed she took an old blanket and tucked it around the family.

Next morning, the Young Mother said to Old Mother Grump, "Mother, tell me how I can repay you? At least I can go into the village and see if I can earn some food."

The old woman only grunted, but taking this for assent, the young mother walked into the village. Doors opened a crack and closed again. Faces peered suspiciously behind the corners of curtains. Her children shrank behind her skirts, until suddenly a small girl with jam on her face ran from behind a cottage without looking, pursued by an angry man and fell in front of them.

"She stole my breakfast!" shouted the man.

The boy, always kindly to other little ones, put his arms round the child and comforted her.

"Is she your daughter?" Young Mother asked the man.

"No, she is not! Her mother was my maidservant, but the lazy cow died on me last month. How can I farm if I must cook and clean and look after her child? Such a naughty, wild child too!" he said. "No one in this village will help me," he continued, in an angry growl. "Lazy, workshy, useless idiots! They keep themselves to themselves!"

The Young Mother said, "I am looking for work. If you let me have food I can come in and cook and clean for you in return" – and the old man agreed readily.

She went in, with all three children clinging to her skirts. Quietly getting them to help with simple tasks, in a few hours she had the cottage made comfortable. As they finished, the Young Mother noticed that the Servant's girl was hiding something in her pocket.

"What have you got there?" she asked.

Mutely, the little girl showed that she had taken an apple from a bowl on the table. The Young Mother looked at her sadly, but said nothing. After staring mulishly for a heart's beat, the child suddenly blushed and tears came to her eyes. She muttered, "I'm sorry," to the Old Man, and held it out to him.

For a moment he scowled at her and took a deep breath to vent his rage, but then he glanced at the Young Mother, who was just standing there, saying nothing, and his expression softened.

"I wish I had your patience!" he said. He pushed the apple back into the little girl's hands, and gave her a piece of bread and cheese. "There!" he said, gruffly, "You've all worked hard!" and he gave more cheese and the loaf to the Young Mother, with the rest of the jam, to take back to their lodging place.

A single scarlet petal blew towards him as the family left, and he caught it and stood looking at it for a moment. Then, bidding the Servant's child to go to her bed, he put the petal in a jar on the dresser and took out his pipe.

When they handed over the treasures of food to Old Mother Grump, it was silently taken for granted that they could stay in the cottage with her. They slept together by the fire and washed in the sink, and the Young Mother was happy, occasionally singing quietly about her endless tasks.

From then on she worked for the man and kept his cottage comfortable and clean. She cooked well for him, looked after the Servant's daughter and her own children, and was rewarded with enough food for all of them.

This included Old Mother Grump, who became less frosty and even smiled at times. She taught all three children to care for the chickens of the village and pick berries from the hedgerows. Sometimes she played rhyming games, crooning long-forgotten songs, with the two little girls on her knees.

When their clothes needed washing Young Mother tried to do it, but Mother Grump grumbled and pushed her away. Next day the old woman herself went to the village and came back with some washing to do, from the villagers, and they all did it together in the stream. From then on they were paid a little in outworn clothing, and even occasionally a few pennies or a cut of meat from the farm.

The villagers began to grow curious. They came out of their cottages in the evening and gossiped, first about this strange little family, then naturally enough about their own affairs.

The Young Mother's children and the Servant's little child played in the village square when they could. Hearing their merry laughter the children of the villagers began to appear, first at windows, then hanging round the doors, while the three called and beckoned them to join in games of Last one Home and Grandmother's Footsteps.

At first the other children shook their heads and turned their backs, but the Young Mother called to them too, so gently and sweetly that one day a group of the braver children joined in the play, and soon they were all laughing and running around together.

Young Mother smiled to see her two and the Servant's child so happy in company. She sat by the village pond, in a rare moment of idleness. She felt another crimson petal leave her, snatched by the wind from her breast, and remembered the bargain, but she had no regrets.

Now that the children weren't underfoot all the time, the parents became less crotchety and shouted less. They let them have some simple toys, made at home with loving care.

One of the fathers made a bat and markers and even played Tip with them one day, ignoring the shouts of his wife to come in and help. Next day, she came out flushed and laughing, to join the children, as he washed the dishes.

The days turned to weeks and the weeks to months. Young Mother taught any children who were around in the occasional restful moments of the day; waiting for the soup to cook or the chickens to come and be fed. She taught them their letters and numbers, while Old Mother Grump began to tell them weather lore, wisdom tales, and the use of herbs. She was no longer called by this nickname, for the villagers forgot they had ever thought this of her and called her simply,' Old Mother,' to distinguish her from 'Young Mother.'

The villagers asked their two 'Mothers' to teach them all, adults and children, whenever possible. In return they relieved them of some of the heavier tasks. The other older folk of the village came forward, timidly, to offer their own knowledge, spurned until now.

So, the months gradually turned to a year, one, then two and just into a third. The village was thriving, but what of Young Mother? As the petals one by one fell from her breast, she was slowly fading; a day resting here, a pallor in her cheeks, a slow letting go of her duties, filled in by others quickly for love of her.

Eventually there came an evening when the children were asleep with their arms around each other in the truckle bed and Young Mother was folding their clothes. Suddenly feeling very tired, she fell back on the settle.

Old Mother came over to her and loosened her shawl, then stood transfixed at what she saw. The younger woman's breast was transparent, and she saw the heart of a rose within it. One single red petal, as triumphant as a flag, still clung to the centre.

Young Mother opened her eyes and saw that her secret was out. "I claimed my children back from the Wind of the Dead Men's Feet," she said faintly. "It was the night you took us in. The Wind took my living heart in exchange and gave me a Red Rose in its place, but I knew it would only last for a short time."

"That was a hard bargain!" said Old Mother.

"It was the only way to have a heart that could give out love; the others the East Wind offered would have lasted longer but been hard and sly." said Young Mother.

Old Mother took a little box from her pocket and opened it. "Look!" she said. In it was a single red petal. "The night you came, this dropped from your bodice and I kept it."

"When the last petal drops, keep it too, for the children later. But what will happen to my poor little ones now?" said Young Mother.

"They will miss you and they will grieve, as I will," said the old Woman simply, "But you need have no fear for them. You have changed my life and they will always have a home with me. Yes, and this cottage when I am gone. They will have the whole village to bring them up and care for them as well. You changed us all with your crimson rose heart!"

She turned away for a moment. Young mother smiled and closed her eyes with a sigh. The children stirred without waking, and the boy's arm held his sister closer as she nestled her face into his shoulder.

When Old Mother turned back she saw that the Young Mother had passed on. The single crimson petal was spiralling slowly to the floor and Old Mother caught it in her gentle hand.

Listen to the East Wind as it blows away from the door. Listen as the dead leaves are rustling, rustling, rustling, blown on their way to the lands of Beyond.

"Once in a thousand years you hear the feet passing, passing, passing, blown before the wind, the Wind of the Dead Men's Feet," sighs the voice, "and but once in a thousand, thousand years a woman brought her children back out of the wind."

Again, the Wind of the Dead Men's feet is whispering, whispering, whispering, "What is the price for the life of two children, what is the price for the life of their mother, when the leaves are blowing, blowing, blowing past? Sshh, Sshh, Sshh. Don't look out of the window, don't go out of the door."

POSTLUDE

♪

AS THE EAST WIND finished its story a detached observer would have seen that the tears were trickling down Ebeneezer's slackened cheeks and jowls. But there were no longer even the mice to observe. As if sleepwalking, he walked down the cottage stairs, his feet silent enough not to wake even a mouse. He walked out into the garden at the place where the turn of the Cottage had brought him, to sit for a while under a weeping ash. The scent of lavender seemed to wash over him like a gentle presence.

His eyes, still bleared with tears, could just make out the outlines of trees and shrubs and the neighbouring house. He thought at times that he heard echoes of laughter and even caught glimpses of children playing, hiding and seeking, climbing and rolling down the rockery slopes. Was that the shape of a woman in a long white dress sitting very still beside the door? Surely his eyes were playing tricks?

In the morning Mr Ebenezer Barthwaite had gone even before Helena arrived to check him out. He was on the early bus to Eastbourne, trying to stop the tears which, just occasionally, still rolled down his cheeks. He was trying to rehearse what on earth to say to his old colleagues, something that told the truth but didn't sound like asking for sympathy or a handout. "I've been a fool!" he thought. "Drink, the gee-gees, women. I deserved everything I got. I can only tell them I messed up! Here am I, facing retirement age, lost my family, everything, so all I can show you is an example of what not to do."

The bus rolled on down through Battle, where the Normans beat the Saxons and life as they knew it came to an end. He felt vaguely comforted. "We're still here! We're all the same," he thought, "Two thousand years on, who cares whether you won or lost in that battle. It's enough to be a Survivor."

Helena, coming in to change the bedlinen, was surprised that the bed didn't seem to have been slept in, but the window was open and the curtains blowing in the wind, quite damp.

Mr Barthwaite had left her a substantial tip (it had taken most of his spare cash if she had

but known) and a note in shaky handwriting,
"So sorry madam that I was so grumpy and
rude. Thank you. It was a most memorable
stay."

INTERLUDE

♪

BATTLE ABBEY

Did Harold stand upon this place,
Shielding his eyes like me,
As Hastings-ward he turned his face
To look towards the sea?

And did he see through wind-forced tears
Grim ranks of iron shields,
Where sheep had grazed a thousand
years
Upon these Sussex fields?

Tall trees about this place are ranged,
Peace is returned for strife,
Nine hundred times their leaves have
changed,
Life, death, and back to life.

No pilgrim struggles to this place,
The monks have long since gone,
Only the tourists try and trace
Where England's heroes shone.

Pretending still I raise my eyes
To share the seagulls wheel,

I change their calls to battle cries
And clash of steel on steel.

The sun is warm. Over his earth
The shadows interlace,
I dream a while of death and birth,
With tears upon my face.

I see no ghost, no sound he hears.
The sheep are grazing still,
As they have grazed two thousand years
Upon this Sussex hill.

October 14th 1066
(A poem from Helena's manuscript, kept by the Mice and rescued by George Miller.)

CHAPTER THREE

A RICH AND CHARMING WIDOW

PRELUDE
♪

ON HELENA'S next visit to the Bank in Heathfield she dropped into the cafe afterwards and was pleased but surprised to see her old school friend, Carol, sitting by the door looking out.

"Carol!" she exclaimed. "You never told me you were coming down. Are you visiting your aunt? You promised to stay with me next time!!"

There was no reproach in her voice, just a hint of laughter. They had been friends since the day they met, as frightened 'newbies' at boarding school so many, many years ago.

She quietened immediately as she saw Carol was crying. She knew Carol loved her aunt like a mother – as indeed she had been to the girl, whose parents spent so many years on the Mission field in those days that they had little time with their own children. Something must be wrong!

"I didn't have time even to phone you," Carol said. "The Police found Aunty Mabel wandering round here and they got her into hospital."

Helena put her hand over the other woman's hand. "Oh my dear," she said, "how dreadful. Where is she now?"

"Eastbourne General at first," said Carol. "She's in Hellingly hospital, now; one of the new dementia wards. She's gone downhill very fast even since then. It's a miracle she was managing at home at all, but we think her neighbours were doing a lot for her. She seems to have had a couple of strokes too, her left side and arm are very weak. They found her blood pressure was high, in the hospital. It's come down well with treatment, so they're hopeful she won't have more strokes, but she needs rehabilitation."

"She does still seem to know me," Carol continued, "but this morning she thought I was my mother! They don't think she'll be well enough to come home again. I suppose we realised, in a way, she was getting very forgetful, but didn't want to know, if you know what I mean! "

"That happens a lot," Helena reassured her. "Would you like to stay with me?"

Carol was grateful but felt it would be best if she stayed in her aunt's house, to feed the cat and deal with post.

"But we'll meet every day," Helena assured her friend. "I go up to Turnaround Cottage a lot and it's easy for me to drive on to Cross in Hand."

They parted, after arranging how to meet and what Helena could do to help her friend.

Old Mrs Dunnett, Aunty Mabel to Carol, did not appreciate the nice newly furnished Dementia Ward in the grounds of the hospital in which she now lived. It was called Cyclamen Lodge and, if she had known the older alternatives, she would have been grateful. Unfortunately, among other things they forget, patients tend to forget to be grateful. Although she was treated with kindness, she couldn't settle in.

She made her escape when the newfangled fire extinguishing system malfunctioned, causing a huge flood and the staff were all occupied in dealing with it. All she wanted to do was go home.

Her brain didn't remember anything but her feet, even her slightly weakened left foot, took her on old familiar ways through the countryside, though it seemed regrettably far. An instinct common to hunted creatures told her to hide in the hedge when vehicles passed. There were few on these byways at this time of year.

She rested a while by the roadside, against a wall that still held a little warmth from the weak October sun. She scrumped a couple of apples from a tree whose branches overhung the path, but moved on quickly as a light went on in the house.

When Aunty Mabel reached Three Cups Corner, on the Battle road, where she once lived, her steps didn't falter. Once, many years ago, she had been Mabel Wilkins, daughter of the local Preacher and had run in and out of the nearby Mill all through her childhood, before starting her working life there at the age of 14.

She sat on the step of Turnaround Cottage, smelling the scents of late roses, and was puzzled. It was too dark to see that the sails, or the 'wings', as the sails were known locally, were no longer there, but the cottage itself didn't smell right. It didn't smell of dust and corn. It was cold and a black panic was rising in her numbed body, as it so often seemed to these days, when everything kept shifting around and disappearing like a smoky fire when you need to make supper; people slipping away like the fish when you tried to gut it for father's tea.

Suddenly, just before she was about to give way and scream, bite, kick to keep away the black feelings, there was a stirring, a twittering, a warm musky smell around her, as the mice all crept under the door, to welcome her back. "It's Mabel," the twittering was saying. "Our girl!" They climbed up her dress, over her arms, warming her hands and feet and twittering with love.

She found she could understand every word. How should she not? She was five years old, a shy, only child who understood what the birds, the mice, the grass, flowers and trees were all saying to her, but could never share it with anyone.

So, comforted and warmed, covered in a blanket, a garment, a veritable Robe of living mice, all of them breathing in unison with each other and with her, Mabel Dunnett, *née* Wilkins, remembered who she was, recovered her calm and listened, along with the mice as the mill itself told her a story.

It was, as always, carefully chosen as specially for her, taking her mind back to local events in the cinema and evenings in front of the telly with her husband. She was alert and at peace as the voice began to speak to her and she listened like a child.

This is the Story told by the roguish South Wind, rollicking its way up Tin Kettle Lane to the Pub – listen and share the Story of...

A RICH AND CHARMING WIDOW

EVERYONE in the village was excited about the new owner of Buttercup Cottage at Cross in hand village. None more so than three single men in the village, friends, who hung around the shop and the pub, and now round the Cottage. The widow was rich, charming and beautiful; what more could a man want? They rushed to clean her car, carry in her shopping, and weed her garden.

Discussing it down the pub, the Dog and Knackers, the men, Roland, Brian and Simon, decided to invite her out in rotation, since they were friends and all three had a strict sense of fairness.

These discussions were in the presence of Betty Brown, the buxom Barmaid, who was most distressed at their plans, being a little bit sweet on all three of them herself. But of course the regulars took no notice of Betty, she being working class and them being Sussex posh and ex-public school, except Brian the Chef, who had been to a 'Comp' and so couldn't look down on anyone.

What no one knew, of course, because the widow made sure they didn't, was the various other aliases by which she had been known and the grisly fates that had befallen her first three husbands. "Call me Arachne," she purred charmingly. "Arachne le Noir." Luckily for her it was the sort of village which voted for anti-European Union parties, and where no one spoke French.

The widow's first husband, Dashing Derek from Dorset, rich and aristocratic, had drowned in the pool. The paddling pool, that was. Quite a feat considering it was only three inches deep.

Then there was Foxy Francois, the suave and sexy Frenchman. He was found having fallen from the fifth floor flat. In addition, he had been shot several times, and half eaten by wild animals (just to make sure).

This might have caused more suspicion if it hadn't happened in an obscure Middle European village with an accommodating Police force. (Please note that this shocking racist stereotype is not the responsibility of the Author.)

After this, the widow decided to turn to magic, as being much safer and less trouble. She learnt a sufficiency of magical techniques by attending extra-mural college courses, with credits. Then she took the basics to much greater heights by selling her soul to a number of different maleficent beings, none of whom realised they did not have exclusive rights to her services. This is a very high degree of sharp practice, only known otherwise to Bankers, Hedge Fund Managers, FIFA, and the Devil himself.

Husband number three, Ghastly Gregory from Gloucester, was missed by nobody when he was turned into a wild boar and released into the Forest of Dean. He had been the local club bore in all the pubs for miles around. His new incarnation was a distinct improvement.

In moving away to her new village in Sussex, Arachne had decided to avoid the complications brought by matrimony and try other means of using men to make money for her. The most gullible and charming of the three local men was Roland Ransome, known down the pub as Rich Randy Roland, of Ransome's Racehorses. She had a fiendish scheme to turn him into one of his own horses so she could clean up at the races.

Arachne lured Roland into her house one warm June day and persuaded him to take all his clothes off – though persuasion was hardly necessary. She then turned him into a horse by the application of a herbal remedy and a complex verbal formula, which I have no intention of revealing (though you could try an extremely large sum of money, in a plain brown envelope, care of my Agent).

The reason for taking his clothes off first was, of course, because when a very surprised man finds himself transformed into a horse, it is better that his Boden jacket, Gucci shirt and expensive handmade shoes are not spoiled in the process.

Poor Roland now found himself entered by the enterprising widow into all his own races, using forged applications and a note to his friends about going away on holiday.

Unfortunately, though fiendishly clever, Arachne lacked common sense. She failed to study racing form, and did not realise that if you turn an indolent, sedentary male of a certain age into a horse, what you get is a fat lazy horse, who hasn't a clue how to win at anything.

Roland found himself, most humiliatingly, losing to all the other horses, even the ones who had been doped up to the eyeballs by crooked syndicates, in order to slow them down. This most satisfyingly ruined a number of criminal bookies, but did nothing for Arachne's own finances.

The widow, disappointed of her expected winnings, overworked him ruthlessly. Within a very short time he became exhausted and painfully thin and she declared openly her intention of sending him to the knacker's yard to be made into pet food and glue.

We now leave poor Roland crying horse's tears in his stable and turn our attention to Brian, the second of the single men, as indeed did Arachne.

Brian Pudley, the chef at the Dog and Knackers, was a sweet undemanding man whose greatest love was pastry. He was bosom buddy of Betty the buxom barmaid in an equally undemanding and adoring way. To Arachne, his skills meant only money bags, so she lured him away from his job at the pub, leaving the regulars unfed and Betty bereft.

The absence of Roland had never really been explained satisfactorily. Now Brian was as good as lost too, and Betty was becoming increasingly uneasy. She confided her fears to the third of the pub friends, Simon Wiseman, an unworldly philosopher and theologian.

Physically Simon was tall, extremely thin, and a typical quiet and unassuming scholar, but he was highly observant. He was also the most lukewarm of the three suitors for the widow, and therefore perhaps less dazzled by her. His only real interest in life was tracking down obscure books and manuscripts and bringing them into the light of scholarship.

Since the absence of his friends he had come to value Betty's common sense and soothing presence, so he took her concerns seriously. That very evening they walked round to the back of Buttercup Cottage, and peered in at the kitchen window.

They watched Brian bringing tray after tray of mushroom patties out of the oven. Each time, as soon as his back was turned, Arachne was sprinkling a luminescent green powder onto them. The two horrified watchers could not know that these patties were destined for a rival organisation and were being loaded with colly-wobble inducing poison. However, they could see that something really nasty was going on without Brian's knowledge.

Simon shouted aloud, "What the heck are you doing woman!" and started to climb through the window. Betty shrieked like a fire engine and Roland the horse jumped clean over the gate at the sound. He landed in a pile of horse manure in the yard, sending a spray of liquid muck in at the window and over all the company. He skidded to a stop by Betty, and nuzzled her protectively out of the way.

It was as well Roland did that, as Arachne, maddened beyond common sense at this exposure, raised her wand in her right hand and grabbed the nearest object in her left, which happened to be a bronze standard lamp. It was too heavy for her to throw, but she cast a powerful spell at Simon, capturing him within it. It was quite a good fit, but very inconvenient, as the lamp fizzed and buzzed, showering sparks over everything, as he struggled vainly to free himself.

She turned her wand on Brian and this time was more able to think first, so she transformed him into a cat, rather larger than the average, but relatively easy to control by dropping the waste bin over him. He cursed and swore in cat language and English combined, but could do no more than bang on the sides.

Betty had prudently ducked down behind the window sill at the first sign of trouble – she was used to ferocious fights breaking out on Saturday nights in pubs, though not usually with magic spells involved. Now she bravely pulled Arachne over the windowsill, struck the wand from her hand, and wrestled her to the ground. (I tell you, Saturday nights down at the Dog and Knackers can be quite exciting too!)

Simon the Standard Lamp was fizzing and crackling more and more alarmingly, the sparks shooting high in the air. For him, it was extremely painful and uncomfortable, and his normal academic calm deserted him. He uttered a stream of ancient and powerful obscenities that became caught up in the errant electrical phenomena of his transmutation. A white hot stream of electricity and curses shot out of the top of the lamp, and travelled up so far and fast it struck the grey twilight clouds looming over the cottage. A storm was triggered, and within nanoseconds a huge bolt of lightning struck down into the yard of Buttercup cottage.

A whirling vortex appeared in the dark cloud. The black column caught the widow, spinning her around and around. Betty was once more knocked to safety. Screaming like a banshee, the widow was carried up and away into the heavens, for ever. (Forever?... Hmmm – maybe....)

Betty released Brian Cat from under the bin and the two of them looked at Roland Horse and Simon Standard Lamp in wonder and relief. They all fell into each other's arms – awkward enough with paws and hooves, but have you ever embraced a standard lamp which hugged you back? They were too relieved and happy to care about anything other than that the Wicked Widow was gone. Betty was equal to anything, and within minutes had stopped hugging everyone, put the kettle on and made a good strong pot of tea.

After tea, at her suggestion, the four friends began to explore the cottage. Roland Horse searched the ground floor and outbuildings, stamping a powerful hoof to detect any spaces under the floors. Brian was invaluable at investigating every cupboard and cranny, and the spaces under the eaves. His lithe cat body could be in and out of the smallest opening in no time and he turned out large companies of mice along the way. Betty looked everywhere else – while having to break off to remind Brian from time to time that searching, not mice catching, was the object. Simon struggled along behind her, but he discovered how to turn himself off and on, and his light was invaluable in the darker corners.

At first all they seemed to turn up, apart from the rodents, were quantities of dirty clothing, unwashed dishes and clouds of dust, which distressed Betty a good deal. It was obvious that Arachne had few if any domestic virtues and was too lazy even to use spells.

After a while, Betty became aware that one of the mice, while keeping well away from Brian, was pulling at her skirt and squeaking to attract her attention. They followed the little creature to a room at the back. Brian, thwarted of mouse baiting, scratched ferociously at the wallpaper which fell off in ribbons, as Simon leant forward. His powerful light showed up a mysterious door covered in strange and sinister symbols.

Roland Horse whinnied loudly and pushed through the others. With one blow of his powerful front hoof the door was smashed open, among flashes of green and purple light and an outraged shrieking noise from all over the room. Magic doors are not meant to yield to brute force; it's against all the rules, but I suppose the Widow's spells were already weakened by her transition. Roland stood back, nibbling Betty's hair and looking pleased with himself for the first time in weeks.

Inside the cupboard the friends found many books of useful spells and formulae. Simon was especially excited by them and quickly sorted out those for immediate use to help in their predicament and those to study at leisure. This was indeed a treasure trove for a scholar like him, devoted to the light of learning (though not usually in such a literal way). Betty felt that their lives, and those of others, could be much enhanced by the contents of the magic cupboard, which included many spells for practical use.

As it was late the friends decided to get some rest where they were and set up a camp for that night on the kitchen floor by the fire.

Next day they settled down in earnest to work out what to do. Now that all Arachne's powers had ceased or been taken over, her recent spells could be reversed. Roland the Horse and Brian the Cat discussed it thoroughly, eventually deciding that they actually preferred their present incarnations.

Simon, the Philosopher, however, felt that life as a standard lamp would be too confining and opted to return to his human state. He said he would then be able to look after the other two so that they could enjoy human benefits and a carefree life. By taking over the Widow's expertise in forgery it was a simple matter to create a Power of Attorney, letters of Authorisation and in due course a foreign Death Certificate and Will for Arachne le Noir, all allowing them to continue in Buttercup Cottage as long as they wished. By giving up their magic right of re-transformation they were also ensured of added years, excellent health and an endless supply of suitable food for all three of them.

They continued to spend time down at the pub, where the Cat was particularly popular. He would only allow Betty the barmaid to pet him and spent as much time as he could out of hours curled up in the sunshine on her lap, while she fed him pastry titbits. Horse also joined in, walking down to the pub at opening time and sticking his head through the window by their usual table.

Simon would buy him a pint to sup, causing endless amusement to the regulars and particularly delighting Betty the Barmaid. "He reminds me of someone!" she would say, "Isn't he lovely?" and Horse would lick her cheek and make her scream with laughter.

So we shall leave this quartet of friends, Simon, the Wise man of Buttercup Cottage with his inseparable companions, Roland Horse and Brian Cat, along with Betty the Barmaid.

But what happened to the three of them, and the Mice, or what further adventures might befall them all, is – all together now! –

"ANOTHER STORY FOR ANOTHER TIME!"

POSTLUDE

♪

JUST AS DAWN CAME, Mabel's niece Carol, who had spent the night along with Helena searching the area around Hellingly, remembered what a prodigious walker Mabel had been and her connection with the Mill so many years ago.

Sick with worry, and accompanied by a Community Police Officer, the two women walked up the garden – and there was Aunty Mabel, comfortably asleep on the step, but warmly wrapped in potato sacks and seemingly none the worse for her expedition!

She had a check-up in A and E, but was pronounced as fit as could be expected, allowing for her known previous stroke and dementia. Indeed, the doctor, looking at her notes, said her blood pressure, respiration and neurological check-up were all better than he would have expected from her previous notes and a night out. The professionals listened kindly to her ramblings about her friends the Mice and the story she had heard, but dismissed it all, of course, as her clinical condition.

Innumerable Incident Forms had to be filled in multiplicate for every aspect of the incident, for the health and safety department in their bunker – I mean nice office – in the hospital. This tied up most of the nursing time for the next few weeks, giving Mabel plenty of leisure to plan her next escape, but that is another story for another time.

In herself, Mabel was much happier and more settled. She thought of the old days with pleasure, not loss now, and could often be found chuckling to herself or even laughing aloud, as she remembered the exploits of Arachne le Noir, the evil but ineffectual Witch and her three daffy but lovable suitors!

Carol and Helena, of course, took it all a little differently, but still couldn't quite understand. They arranged to take Mabel out at least once a week and she always chose to visit the mill, if it was available and unoccupied. Well – unoccupied by humans! The Mice were always there and very welcoming even if only Mabel insisted she saw them every time.

CHAPTER FOUR

FROM THE DARK SHADOWS

PRELUDE
♪

THE OLD MAN who had been talking to Helena in the Bank went home to his damp little lodgings after a visit to the pub, his only indulgence. A few evenings later, on a whim, he decided to go home the long way on the triangle of roads, past Turnaround Cottage. His curiosity had been aroused not just by Helena's guarded remarks but because he had begun to think it might have relevance to a long-time puzzle of his own.

"Who am I really? What's my story?" he thought as, glancing around nervously, he slunk up the path to the door, keeping in the shadows. There were no lights on, no car parked nearby; it looked like no one was staying. He was quite good at picking locks but it wasn't necessary. There was a small window in the back, a crack open, and he slithered inside.

"Alright!" he said aloud, with an almost childish defiance. "Tell me! Tell me what my story is?"

There was a breath, no more, of breeze on his cheek, from the open window but no word. Only when he had given up and climbed back out, resting, disappointed and defeated on the garden seat, did an answer come, inexorably. A sound of creaking panicked him, till he realised it came from a child's swing that he didn't remember seeing in the garden before, but there it was. *Creak, creak, creak* it went rhythmically, so that as he listened, almost in a trance, it translated itself into words. His story! Told at last, though only as a fragment that tore into his heart like a piece of jagged metal.

FROM THE DARK SHADOWS

A Fragment...

THE COLD BREATH of the North Wind assaulted his ear, whispering venomously as if even nature disliked him. "Listen now and hear about the Dark Shadows," it said and he heard and saw Her come into the garden. How could he ever have forgotten?

She came silently out of the half-light, almost invisible as always in her grey robes, veiled and swift of foot.

"At last!" he whispered, stretching out his hands to her, "So long! Is it really you, my one true love?"

"You said I was," she replied, "and you thought me beautiful once, but so much has happened, so much time has passed!"

She raised her veil and he stood, struck to the heart by the face she showed him. Time and suffering had marked lines across her beauty, cancelling out her youth.

He could not conceal his shock, or speak. After a moment a tear gathered in her eye. In it he saw his own reflection; an old man's face, a body bent and worn.

His hands fell, his manhood shrivelled, he groaned helplessly.

She dropped her veil. "Goodbye!" she said, turned and was gone

"No! Wait!" he shouted.

In his mind it was a young man's voice, but all his ears heard was a croaking like a crow.

"Wait! I'm sorry... *cawk... cawk... cawk...*"

A light wind stirred the branches above the glade. No one stood there. Only a big black bird, head down, dragging its wings.

Only a gust, stirring the grey branches, a trace of a perfume he could no longer smell.

POSTLUDE

♪

THE OLD MAN, suffering, knowing he had asked for the knowledge but was as far from any redemption as ever, shuffled back up the hill to his lodgings. He did not cry, for all tears had been dried up for many years.

"How long?" he groaned, "how long?"

CHAPTER FIVE

ELIOT'S SCARF

PRELUDE
♪

HELENA walked up the path to Turnaround Cottage at teatime one day when the nights had drawn in so that it was already dark. The Cottage had been let rather less frequently through the early winter and Helena rather missed having contact with visitors. In fact she had been told by the Solicitor who arranged such things that the Cottage would be shut over Christmas and New Year, for a month or two, but she would still be paid.

As Helena walked up the hill to the Cottage, she saw a young man waiting for her there under the porch light. She smiled and waved to him and he returned the greeting.

"You must be Nathaniel?" she said in her pleasant voice from which nothing could quite remove the northern tones.

The young man had been looking a little serious, even sullen, but when he smiled Helena's practiced eye could see that those expressions were only the way his features fell at rest, giving an impression of poor humour.

She also guessed at a certain shyness of temperament, which was confirmed when he strode forward, offering a tentative but sweet greeting. The smile lifted his long flexible lips and showed a one-sided dimple of considerable charm.

"Yes. I'm Nathaniel Jenkins," he confirmed, "but please – everyone calls me Nate. It's a bit of a mouthful otherwise!"

Helena took the offered hand, smiling back. She loved meeting these new people and welcoming them to the Cottage and to her adopted Sussex countryside.

She took him straight in to show him the little kitchen, sitting room, bathroom and bedrooms, finding him a towel and stocking up the tea and milk as they went, not having had time on the day the last Visitor had left. All the time she was chatting to him, listening too, and speaking of the garden as seen in glimpses through different windows.

To the South from the bedroom window over the front door he could see the way a rough grassy slope led down to the stream whose turbulent waters were sparkling in the late afternoon sun. Between the trees a silver-grey sheet marked the sea, in fact the English Channel, proud mark of our island status.

From the opposite window on the landing were the Downs, part of the High Weald as it was known, rising to the North over a view of the vegetable patch and the bins. He thought he could just see the next house up Flitterbrook Lane to the East in passing, half hidden in a grove of trees and wild brambles.

Helena stopped at the big window in the sitting room facing West, justly proud of the small ornamental trees and shrubs in a little green lawn, set out with herbaceous beds and a rockery, even a bench and a swing. It was late for most flowers but there were shrubs waiting in winter stillness, late roses still bravely blooming and Michaelmas daisies in flower by the gate.

Sure enough, by the time she left him, having refused the offered cup of tea but without offense, she knew a lot about him; that he had just got his second higher degree and had been head-hunted by a big computer firm. They had sent him to the Sussex coast to talk preliminaries of a merger with an American giant. How torn this made him feel, between exploring the world and staying in Sydenham, outer London, near his parents, who were getting towards retirement and, as an only child, he worried about them.

She knew that with a little more encouragement he would have been telling her all his history, his work problems and his love life, because she had a great ability, honed by years in the NHS, of drawing people out. That was why she refused tea and returned home quite soon. It was not her job to offer therapy and she was well aware of the importance of boundaries.

Nate pottered round for a while, drinking his tea from the biggest mug he found; a rough pottery frog with bulging green eyes, because it reminded him of the Managing Director of Dynamic Microelectronics, Mr Rumbelow, and made him laugh.

He would like to have shared a little joke with that nice lady who had signed him in, but in her absence he said to no one in particular,

"Meet Mr Rumblebum, and bow down to the biggest green turd in Britain!"

Then he sighed and sat down on a shabby red brocaded armchair that had seen better days but been worn by umpteen bottoms over the years to ideal comfort for a tired and lonely bachelor. He took out a photo of the young woman he was not quite sure was his girlfriend and as he looked at her oval face with the big laughing eyes, his own eyelids drooped towards sleep as he murmured her name.

"Jilly," he said, "Jilly, Jilly!" It seemed like the sound of the stream outside that he had not noticed till the silence.

"Come with me!" pleaded the little River Flitter. "Come with me tonight – down past Rushlake Green and Foul Mile and into the Cuckmere at Upper Dicker, through Arlington and Wilmington, through Birling Gap and we will meet the sea at the Seven Sisters!"

"The sea?" he found himself murmuring. "Will it take me over there? Over the ocean to California? To Jilly?"

And it seemed to him that the little river voice said, "Yes, yes, yes, that's where you will go. To Jilly, Jilly, Jilly!"

He woke in time to eat a simple microwave meal, read a favourite book of Azimov's from his own extensive library of classic science fiction and go up to bed in the tiny bedroom right at the top of the Mill, looking out to the sea.

He remembered, as his eyelids fluttered closed again, that Mrs Brown, or Helena as she'd said to call her, had mentioned that you could see the coast of France from the top window in a good light. He really must look to see in the morning.

In the dead of the night he woke. Coming downstairs he grabbed his coat against the cold and walked out of the door with a sensation of turning, almost as if he was on a boat. He expected to see the sea in the moonlight but somehow he seemed to be facing up towards the Downs, so had to go round the little path, in the dim gleam of moonlight, till he saw the wonderful silver sheet of the sea.

"I'm dreaming," he thought comfortably, as the voice of the river Flitter came again.

"We will go down together!" the Flitter seemed to be saying. "Hold my hand and come with me to the Big Water. Down through Rushlake Green and Foul Mile and into the Cuckmere at Upper Dicker, through Arlington and Wilmington, through Birling Gap to hear the Seven Sisters tell you a Tale. Please say yes! Please say yes."

Nate was not to know that it would have made no difference if he had not said yes, since the River Flitter could be just as insistent on telling a story as the Winds and the Cottage itself. Luckily he loved stories, of all and any kind, and listened in a trance sitting on a convenient bench as the river continued...

"Listen and I will tell you how Eliot got his scarf and more than he bargained for. This is his Story..."

ELIOT'S SCARF

ELIOT LIVED in a wooden hut at the very top of a pebble beach, under a cliff golden with gorse, where at very high tides the sea nearly reached the door. Indeed, when the storms and the spring tides came together it was touch and go whether the hut might be overwhelmed – the waves would reach out and touch his door with their foaming fingers, and then go back to where they belonged.

After the storms Eliot would go out and gather up what the sea had brought him. Lots of rubbish to be tidied up, but also there would be all sorts of marvels for a practical man. He would add things discarded from the village and farms to his sea-harvest. Shells and bones, hollow sticks, metal pipes, bright tins and plastic, fabric and flower pods. He collected anything that could make sounds by being hammered or hit, struck or squeezed, blown through, fine-tuned and fiddled, rubbed, ratcheted or rippled, for Eliot was a musician and maker of instruments.

On Saturdays and Sundays he went into the town, to meet with other people, to chat, laugh, drink, play and sing in the market and the pub, and to trade his work for his simple needs. He was well liked, but no one knew him well. It was said that he had once been married, but his wife had tired of living in a hut smelling of seaweed and full of bits and pieces, and had run off many years before with a travelling salesman.

One freezing winter, Eliot caught a cold, and couldn't shake it off. His normally pleasing baritone was a frog's croaking and his head felt as if a gong was beating in it as he went walking along the marshes near his hut.

He came across an old woman, known as Goody Elixir, a neighbour he knew slightly, standing watching the sunset, a covered basket on her arm.

"Your music sounds rough today, friend Eliot," she said, "You should go warmer in this weather."

She reached a hand out towards the scarlet and purple clouds, and pulled at something, with a little twist of the wrist.

"What are you doing, Goody Elixir?" Eliot asked.

He could have sworn her hand came down full of purple thread, but she tucked it quickly under the cover of the basket, and didn't answer directly.

"You need a warm scarf, Eliot," she said again.

He laughed, "What use would a scarf be? I'm out in all weathers, soaked by the rain, sprayed by the sea."

She answered, "All the same, I'll make you one. 'Warm Throat; No Need for a Coat', as we say." She smiled at him and Eliot was touched by her kindness. He had hardly known her before, other than that she also lived in a small cottage almost on the beach, up towards Birling Gap.

Goody Elixir added:

"My friends the Mice will knit this scarf,
Their tales will give you many a laugh,
Your cold will soon be gone away,
and you will sing throughout the day.
Come by my house tomorrow night
and get my gift to put you right!"

Eliot thanked her most sincerely – "A kindly gift, Gives one a lift!" he improvised in return, and they parted laughing.

When he looked back, Goody Elixir was still staring out to sea, but he could have sworn that where there had been a line of acid green light near the horizon there was nothing now but the pink clouds.

Eliot soon had his scarf, and a wonderful curly confection of pastel wool it was too. Colours of sunset, pink, peach, rose, melted into each other in each row, and an edging of purple and a single row of green made it truly amazing. Certainly from then on his cold entirely went and he had no more of them. His rich baritone rose once more from the beach as he worked at the instruments, with a backing sound from the sea in its varied moods, loud crashing like tympani alternating with gentle regular sighing sounds like hearts beating together.

Spring came to the countryside, where the path edges were rich with sea holly and lavender, and one day he and the evening breeze were playing at the edge of the water. It was his favourite time, when he would lay out all sorts of things; strings of shells on sticks, hollowed out stalks and bones, metal drums, and plastic skins, and the breeze would blow into and around them, with a music as soft and bright as the early spring weather. Lazy little waves would wander up to his feet, listening, then go back down again, with a "Sshhhhh" and a sigh.

Today the breeze was a little rough. It tugged at his scarf and tried to unwind it from his neck, making him pull it tighter and button it into his coat. He thought he heard a soft, silvery voice from the water, saying, "I want it! Bring it to me!" and again, "I tell you, it's the sunset made into a scarf and I must have it!"

Before he could hold onto his scarf, the breeze had whipped it out of his coat and sent it sailing over the little waves, dropping it into the deeper water, where it was immediately pulled under.

Whoever had it didn't reckon with Eliot's quick reflexes, or his determination. He threw himself into the water, sank down, and opened his eyes. He could see a blur of colours, but the scarf was just out of reach. Instead, he grabbed for the next best thing, nearby, a mass of rippling greenish gold. He took it to be seaweed, but as he surfaced he found himself pulling a girl out of the water by her long golden tresses.

"OW!" said the girl, with a soft silvery voice. "How dare you? You're no gentleman!"

"And you're no lady!" said Eliot indignantly, "Stealing my scarf like that! Give it back to me!"

As he spoke he realised two things. Firstly, what he had said was literally true. She was definitely not a lady. She was naked from the waist up, and below that she appeared to have a long fishy tail, swishing about angrily under the water. Secondly, she was deliciously beautiful, and very desirable.

He held on to her rather more firmly, shifting his grip to her shoulder and trying to unwind his scarf from her neck. He felt righteously justified in holding on to it - after all, hadn't Goody Elixir and the Mice made it especially for him?

He noticed that under the water the scarf appeared to be made of light, rippling and flowing, fractured into a thousand lovely shades, as the sunset is reflected at the horizon. Where he had brought part of it out of the water, it turned back to wool; somewhat soggy and stuck with bits of seaweed, but definitely his scarf.

Of course she struggled to keep it, and with him pulling it around his own neck, the inevitable happened. They came very close together, breast to breast, and Eliot kissed her. He always swore afterwards that she kissed him back, for a heart-stopping moment. Then *WHAM!* The end of her tail came up and fetched him a great slap on the cheek. She slipped from his grasp, scarf and all, and was gone.

Surprisingly, as Eliot waded back to the beach, he didn't seem all that upset, particularly considering that he had just learnt, first hand, what it was like to have a slap in the face with a wet fish.

He was thinking carefully, and he even smiled and whistled a little tune as he dried himself and had his supper. However, he was extremely cross with the evening breeze, and made it clear that it was in disgrace, refusing to play with it for several days, until it flattened itself out on the beach and sobbed a little. The small waves, frightened, threw up handfuls of the most amazing tropical shells, never before seen in those parts, as a peace offering.

A plan formed in his mind, and he shut himself in his hut for several days, with the curtains drawn tight, so that even the most importunate breeze could not see what he was up to. But he came out at evening to play with the waves and wind as before, and – now that he knew what to look for – he was certain he could see the flowing colours of his scarf, well out of reach in the deeper water by the rocks, and a glimmer of green-gold hair. He tested the weather, checking it would stay exactly so, calculated the tide, and bided his time.

Soon, he knew he was ready. Come evening, the little breeze came off the water as usual, and found at the edge of the sea a most astonishing Music Machine. It was like nothing he had ever made before, such must have been the power of Love that inspired him. It had a collection of bells and pipes, and when the breeze blew into it the sound was like seabirds calling, like church bells under water, like the sound of love itself.

Silver vanes, set at an angle, turned, at every little puff of wind, releasing spheres that dropped, chiming, against water pots. Necklaces of shells tinkled, and the breeze in the pipes whispered and sang. So enchanting was the sound that it was impossible for the breeze – or anyone else who might happen be out there – to realise that Eliot was not with the Music Machine. It was entirely set up to work alone in the wind.

So where was Eliot? Well, of course he had swum out hours earlier, unobserved, and was waiting, holding onto the rocks, deep in shadow, until the moment when the evening breeze should come and set the music going. Sure enough, as the breeze strengthened and the sounds swelled, Eliot could see a faint glimmer of sunset-coloured wool, edging towards the beach. And now, the mermaid was the wrong side of him, in the shallows.

It was the moment for which he had been patiently waiting, and he pounced. Now, he held her again in his arms, and her protests were very half-hearted. She didn't smack his face at all, and the scarf wrapped itself around them both, and held them in a loving embrace.

They felt as if they were wrapped in everything they could possibly need to keep them healthy and give them a long and happy life, together. Wool and the Light of Sunset are, indeed, known to be the best possible things to keep close to the skin for their sound, life-giving properties.

So, after a while, Eliot asked the mermaid to marry him.

At first she cried, and said, "It's impossible, Eliot. You would drown if you joined me to live in the sea, and my tail would dry out if I spent too much time out of it."

Eliot dried her eyes. "Nonsense!" he said, "Marriage is all about compromise. I will build you a waterbed in the hut, where you can keep your tail nicely wet, and you can live with me all week. At the weekends you can visit your friends and family under the sea, and I will go to the village."

So that was just what they did, and no couple could have been happier. She loved the hut, with its smell of seaweed and his things everywhere – after all, it was much tidier and cosier than the ocean bed from where she came.

Eliot did not forget how much he owed to Goody Elixir. He gave her a music machine of her own, with a note saying:

"Oh thank you Goody, you're such a kind friend!
Your caring for all never comes to an end.
I'm in your debt for the rest of my life –
You cured my cold and you found me a wife!"

Eliot also continued to play and sing in the village at the weekends, and if he overheard anyone saying what a shame it was that he had such a lonely life, he would smile inwardly, and keep his own counsel.

Who ended up wearing the scarf, you ask? Ah! All good marriages should keep a few secrets from outsiders.

POSTLUDE

♪

It was still very early, only 3 o'clock in the morning, when Nate found himself, somehow, back on the comfortable red armchair, with his phone in his hand. "Just the right time to phone Jilly," he thought. "It'll be around eight in the morning there; she'll be awake and at home."

Jilly Hoffmann, who he had met when they were both back-packing round South America, how many years ago? Was it four? Or five? They had been inseparable on the trip and had parted in tears, swearing to keep it going, but it was hard, as she went back to her job as a telephonist and her parents in California and he to his higher degree and the cold little bedsit in Sydenham.

They had met again, when either could afford the fare. He had met and liked her dad, with his balding hair in a pigtail and loved the sweetness of her mother, in dropout hippy skirts, still beautiful, with the fey manner, of those who have lived it up in their youth.

Jilly had met his highly conventional parents, who stifled their horror at the family photos of Jilly's childhood in a California commune, and showed her the stiff Sunday pictures of an utterly respectable family over roast dinners, from the youth of their Nathaniel – as they preferred to call him. Jilly had won both their hearts, in spite of themselves and they thought of her, secretly, as the daughter they wished they had.

Nate had no idea why he wanted to phone Jilly so badly, nor what he wanted to say. He had only a hazy memory of some sort of entertaining dream that had made up his mind about something. But what? He really couldn't say.

"Compromise!" he muttered, "It's all about Compromise!"

"Oh! Hi there Jilly? How are you?" he asked. "Listen, listen, Jilly. I want to ask you... I've got some leave coming... Can I come over to you? We could have a holiday. It's been too long without one... What? Orlando? Yes, if you want. Orlando, Disneyland, the Moon – whatever you want Jilly! I'll always give you that!"

After a surprised and happy Jilly tore herself from the phone, Nate settled down to sleep again, a big grin on his wide mouth and a lock of hair flopping over his forehead, making him look like a carefree teenager.

His dreams seemed to be filled with the rippling of water sounds, running, chuckling, murmuring "Come with me! Come with me! – down past Rushlake Green and Foul Mile and into the Cuckmere at Upper Dicker, through Arlington and Wilmington, through Birling Gap to the Ocean at Seven Sisters Bay!"

He slept well, but late into the morning and was only just up, having breakfast, when Helena came round. This time she sat down and accepted the big green mug full of tea, enjoying the joke of its likeness to Nate's boss – indeed the mug was called Mr Rumbebum from then on! She could see by a sparkle in his eye and a new firmness in his step that he was full of some news he wanted to share with someone, anyone.

"It's this girl," he explained and produced Jilly's photo. "We've been friends for a while, but she lives in Los Angeles and it's a long way. I sort of wasn't sure she even really liked me, enough... enough... Oh, you know!"

"To be a serious girlfriend?" suggested Helena with her sweet crinkly smile.

He grinned in return. "Yes! I mean my parents seem to like her and I... I think... I think I... *love* her!" He spoke with the surprised recognition of a shy young man who has only just been able to admit this even to himself. Indeed, before we criticise his slowness in this area, let us admit that many men of much more mature years have trouble with the sincere 'L' word, when it is bandied about with so little meaning nowadays.

"How lovely!" said Helena, indeed with true delight at the hope of a romance. "When will you be seeing her again?"

"That's it!" cried Nate. "I was listening to the river and somehow I made up my mind I must go and see her as soon as I can, and tell her how I feel. I rang her up in the night – it was morning there. I said I'll arrange to take my holiday and go out there as soon as I can book a flight. She was thrilled, and started to cry.

"I think it was a good sign; she said it had been so long since we saw each other and something about letters not being enough.... Who knows? There may be jobs going there;

lots in computers. She could come here perhaps... I don't know. It's all about compromise, isn't it?"

"Yes," agreed a smiling Helena, as always her romanticism tempered with practicality. "Yes... Love is all about compromise."

INTERLUDE

♪

ON THE BEACH

Look! Where she danced
in pale sea foam
A mermaid's purse lies on the sand.

Iridescent flowers of the sea
dissolving,
sparkle in the sun.

Through green glass
and torn sea lace
We glimpse King Neptune's richest
                          palaces.

The waves sidle up to the rocks.
Smack! Pull! Push!
The doors never open

CHAPTER SIX

A CHEESY STORY

PRELUDE
♪

ALTHOUGH the Cottage had been closed for the Winter, Helena still visited frequently to check it over, make small improvements and keep it ready. All transactions were conducted through a firm of Solicitors, R and E Jenks, who had a tiny office above The Sweet Polly Parrot cafe in Heathfield High Street, which they also owned. There was in fact only Mr Peter Jenks Esq. his father, Edmund, having passed away many years previously.

When he was offering Helena the job, he assured her that it was all above board and though conducted always through his letters to and from a poste restante box, he was happy with that. In reply to a rather anxious query from Helena, he told her that, in the event of his own retirement or passing away, his simple task would devolve onto the younger firm of Filbert and Tonkins of Tunbridge Wells.

Though elderly, he was a sprightly gentleman and Helena accepted, along with a quite generous monthly salary, that it was all above board and he would be likely working for a long time to come. The salary was a very welcome addition to her small NHS pension. Whoever owned it was very reasonable, so she was always able to hire extra help for cleaning if necessary or for maintenance and repairs.

A firm of gardeners from Heathfield came over regularly, so she could do the sort of choosing and planting flowers and simple tasks she liked to do. The garden always looked good whatever the season, providing flowers for the Visitors and Helena herself if she wished – an express clause in the agreement, so whoever the owners might be, they obviously liked flowers.

Helena was glad that the winter was over. Truth to tell, she had been a little lonely without the Visitors, though she was getting to know the local people rather better now Christmas was over.

Her Son in Law, Jon, had been offered a period of teaching and research residency in Florida for the Winter and the University had paid for her daughter, Jocelyn and the baby, Rodney, to go too, with a sabbatical from his own college in Madrid. It was a wonderful opportunity for them, although it meant there was no way Helena could see them, certainly not to spend Christmas or New Year. She swallowed her disappointment to write very positively to them, as indeed she truly rejoiced in his success and their happiness, but she missed them terribly.

Her friend Carol had invited her up to Derby for Christmas itself and she had, in the end, a good time visiting Carol's many relatives and her own old friends. Even so, on this cold Winter's day she was pleased to be back seeing to the Cottage, which as expected had a dusty and neglected feel as she opened the front door.

Immediately she was aware of a noise, coming from the sitting room, a sound of squeaks and shrill alarm. She opened the door and immediately a smell of mouse fear, dust and decay assailed her nose.

The mouselets were rolling about the floor of the sitting room, clutching their tiny tummies.

Helena was horrified when she came in, but as the mice had become so tame she picked up the biggest and noisiest one – about the size of her little finger – and went to ring the Vet's assistant.

"Hello Rosie," she said. "It's Helena. I've got a little problem to ask you about. It's er... um... like this. A friend of mine has a pet mouse and it seems to have a stomach ache."

It had suddenly occurred to her that, nice as Rosie Cullen the vet's assistant was, now was not the best time to try and explain about the Mill mice.

"Has your friend been feeding them cheese?" asked Rosie.

Helena remembered seeing a very old half eaten cheese sandwich on the floor. It appeared to have been disinterred from some crevice and gnawed. "I think so," she said. She felt almost guilty that she had not thought of the Mice as needing anything, but indeed, they had survived for generations without outside help. It was the invasion of Visitors, with strange exotic new foods that had caused the problem, it appeared.

Rosie told her to tell her friend that cheese, contrary to popular belief, was very bad for pet mice and she should keep them away from all dairy products. Having made sure that the pet mouse's symptoms were not those of the thousand and one contagious and horrible diseases that pet rodents can pass on their human owners, Rosie read her friend a lecture on sentimentality towards animals in place of proper understanding and care.

Helena expressed suitable – and genuine – contrition, and Rosie softened, and said to tell the friend to keep the pet warm and feed it nothing but water for 24 hours. The mouselets and their corporate parents, indeed the whole colony, appeared suitably chastened too.

Helena put on the heating and made old rags into little beds in the warm, providing clean water. The mice appeared pleased, but wanting something more. The little mouselets and their parents were not only looking at her imploringly, and squeaking, but she could understand that they were actually begging her to tell them a story!

A CHEESY STORY

IMPROVISING quickly, Helena began, "Well, there was this little colony of mice who lived in the Town, and they were always hungry." She thought that the mouselets were saying, "How can any mouse go hungry? Especially in a Town?"

"Not all mice are lucky enough to live in a place where they get enough to eat," she replied to them quickly. At the back of her mind was a voice saying something like, 'Helena, are you mad? You're talking to the MICE for heaven's sake!' But she ignored the voice and continued, warming to her theme.

"Well, when you don't have enough to eat normally you sometimes do something silly. These mice saw a Falling Star in the sky and knew it meant they could have a wish. Did you know that?" She smiled at them and many little heads nodded solemnly. The whole colony of mice had come creeping out from the wainscoting at the prospect of a new story.

"Those town mice started to argue. Some wished that they could have as much food as they could eat, but others wanted a brand new house, like this sort of house, that humans live in. They started to quarrel and neither group would give way!"

She paused, dramatically, and dozens of tiny voices squeaked in unison, "Who won?"

"Both!" continued Helena. "You see, that meant that whatever Power it is who grants wishes now had a problem! There was an obligation to fulfil both of these wishes. After a moment of suspense, there was a long churning sound and, suddenly, those mice found themselves all living in a house made entirely of CHEESE!"

At this point in the story, Helena looked at the mice and paused theatrically. There were further mouse noises, in which Helena understood the younger mice were saying how wonderful that would be and the older ones shaking their heads and uttering Dire Warnings in a vague sort of old person – or old mouse – way.

Helena clapped her hands for silence, and they all quietened down at once.

"At first it was great!" she said. "Cheese for walls in all the rooms, cheese beds and chairs, cheese curtains and soft white cheese pillows and cushions. After a while though, it was not so good. How can you cook on a fire made of cheese? How can you eat off a table made of hard cheese, and − above all − what are you going to eat?"

You could have heard a pin drop as the mice absorbed the enormity of the predicament. Never mind that they themselves had no use for tables and chairs and beds, for they knew they had a problem. One mouselet, a really brainy one, who would go far, held up a paw and said, "Could they eat the house?"

(He did go far! He ended up in the Public School over at Tunbridge Wells and became a terrific scholar and know-it-all in Halls, or at least under the tables there, picking up the crumbs of Scholarship, but that's Another Story for Another time.)

"Yes indeed!" said Helena, "Well done Herbert!" She had no idea if he had a name, but he was known by it from then on.

"Yes. They nibbled away at all the furnishings, the roof, the doors and eventually started on the walls. SO" − she added with a dramatic flourish, "What happened then?"

In the dramatic pause the silence was most impressive till one little mouselet burped and that broke the tension. Gales of mouse merriment swept the room,

"No more House!" they all cried in unison and rolled about, laughing until they were all hiccupping and breathless. An amazing thing if you have never before been lucky enough to see and hear a company of mice in such a state.

Helena called them to order again. She had completely forgotten that it was not possible to be having a talk with a party of mice, and was fully into Health Advisor mode.

"Now!" she frowned, looking serious. "What you must know is that those mice were very lucky to survive! Cheese makes mice very, very ill, if they eat more than a careful small nibble of it."

Some of the older, grey-furred mice were nodding their heads sagely; this they knew, but could they get those flighty mouselets to heed their elders and betters? No sir! Now perhaps they'd listen, and pay heed to other crumbs of wisdom too!

"You must always ask before you eat anything you don't know, and it can be very dangerous in Town, so don't go there on your own!"

The mouselets, came over and patted Helena's feet, with contrition and gratitude. They kissed her with their whiskers and nibbled oh so gently at her ears, and covered her in unconditional love.

Herbert, the newly named mouselet, suddenly chirruped up, "And I propose that we have a new Proverb, 'Never build your House out of Cheese!'"

There was an awed silence and then all the mice gave way to gales of laughter and chanting of the new proverb. Indeed it went down in mice lore from then on, becoming as common sense as the adage 'Don't build Castles in Spain' for a pointless fantasy...

POSTLUDE

♪

THE REST of the mice scampered off, as Helena's eyes closed and she drifted off to sleep in the armchair. Startled awake later, she walked down to her own cottage through the owl light, hearing the chuckling voice of the River Flitter: "You told them, didn't you, dearie?" it seemed to be saying, and she thought what a wonderful dream she had just had.

CHAPTER SEVEN

THE MAGICIAN'S DAUGHTER

PRELUDE
♪

ON HELENA'S NEXT visit to the Bank in Heathfield she looked out for the old man, with a mixture of anxiety and interest. His nosiness and something slightly creepy about him raised her anxiety, but also triggered a feeling of sorrow for him. He seemed lost and lonely.

She was, however, well aware of her own habit of looking after lost sheep. While it might be excessive to say they could turn out to be wolves, they were occasionally not as docile as they seemed. After all, if you think sheep are harmless, you've never seen a Derbyshire ewe face down a dog!

Helena looking around but didn't see him, though she noted with pleasure the town sign of the old woman with her basket, letting the spring cuckoo fly free, because it told a story and she loved stories. Daffodils were blooming round the base of the sign and she could almost imagine the painted cuckoo slipping off the sign and heading back to Furnace Wood to frighten the charcoal burners.

The old man had slipped behind the sign, out of her line of sight.

Helena was still smiling as she took her faithful little Ford Fiesta back on the short road home, noting the signs of spring in the bright, clear morning sunshine along the way. The Hawthorn hedges were already in flower and she added a spray of the white blossom to the feather goose she had as a charm hanging in the back window of the car. There were celandine in the verges and fat mauve buds on the Wych Elm at Cade Street.

A few lettings of Turnaround had gone by without incident. Helena had become more alert to those visitors who seemed to have experienced the strange ways in which the Cottage worked. She would sometimes ask innocent seeming questions that allowed her to glean some insight into a story or its effect.

The mice were much bolder, but only with Helena herself. Carol who had spent some time with Helena, as a return for Christmas, had reluctantly returned home to Derbyshire where her large extended family of siblings and nephews and nieces were missing her.

Carol had agreed to go back home only if she was able to come down as needed, particularly as Aunty Mabel had settled in so much better, but occasionally seemed to evade all attempts to hold her in Cyclamen Lodge. Aunty Mabel's much loved cat, Percy, had been given to a family down the road, but Carol had not dared tell her this yet, and dreaded the inevitable question.

A little family had taken Turnaround Cottage for a long weekend, Friday to Sunday. It was not so common to have families, who usually wanted a larger place and to be nearer the beach and the bright lights of Eastbourne, Hastings or Brighton. However, the Cottage was cheaper than most accommodation and cost even less out of season, like this. It was not too far for the Sales or Conferences in the towns, or for at least one day out at the seaside.

Such had been the reasoning of Steven Johnson when a small windfall had allowed him to take his little family for a weekend away. He had unloaded the car and gone for a rest in the sitting room, having worked right up to their departure.

He tried to have a nap after the journey, but worry at his responsibilities kept him restlessly moving around in the red brocade armchair, thinking about his, still relatively new, mixed family.

He was sure he and Gloria Gunnersford, his girlfriend, were still very much in love, but had to admit he was finding it relentlessly tougher living together than either had expected. Even after three years Gloria's health had not quite returned to normal following the birth of their daughter, Margareta, known as 'Pearl'.

Gloria's older daughter, eleven-year-old Rachel, by her ex-husband, was getting early into teenage stroppiness. She had not accepted him in place of a father in those three years and was still often jealous and resentful of little Pearl. Understandable, as the family counsellor had told them, but still very difficult.

Steve tried to be understanding, but it was difficult for him, given that Pearl was his first, indeed only child. They talked occasionally about having another baby, and about getting married, but sometimes he felt frightened at what he was taking on and uncertain if they could make a go of it after all.

Gloria's ex hadn't helped; he had a habit of appearing randomly at long intervals, showering Rachel with gifts and then vanishing immediately. He certainly had never sought official access or custody and their rare rows usually related to his appearances.

As Helena went up the hill to Turnaround Cottage she saw the van again and two little girls playing in the garden. It was too early for most flowers, though the Forsythia bushes held spiky yellow flowers like a promise of rays of sunshine and there was Milkweed round the dustbins and back door.

One little girl was very young and was more than satisfied with picking daisies to make a little play garden; the other looked to be around 11 or so, with a bored almost teenage air already. She was ostentatiously ignoring the efforts of her younger sister to get her to join her game.

Helena introduced herself, giving her warm pixie smile to both girls. "I'd like to have a word with your mother," she said.

"I'm Rachel," said the older girl. "I'll get her for you." She pushed past her little sister, almost knocking her over in a pretended accidental way. Gloria stepped out from the open kitchen door, where she had been within hearing range and sighed helplessly as Rachel took offence and stormed off behind the bins in the North part of the garden.

The little girl remained oblivious of all this and placidly shared her daisies with Helena. "My name is Pearl," she confided. "It's really Margareta, but mummy says I'm as precious as a pearl!"

"I'm sure your mummy's right about that and lots of other things," smiled Helena.

A loud and rather rude "Harrummph!" from behind the bins suggested some dissent from this view. Helena saw that they had everything they needed, shook hands with a sleepy dad and went on her way, leaving this slightly fragile reconstituted family to a fractious evening.

The following evening Helena was around when, tired and even more fractious, they all returned in the van from a day trip to Hastings which it didn't take much to see had been disastrous.

Gloria had a migraine and retired to bed. Steve had to get supper and manage the bedtime routines for the girls. Even Pearl, normally so placid, felt the tensions and was tearful and difficult, insisting that her mother be roused to kiss her goodnight. A late at night argument the evening before between the parents had done nothing for the adult relationship either.

In other words, it was one of your absolutely typical bog-standard family holidays!

Later in the night both children were awake and cried out at being in a strange place. Gloria took them down into the sitting room and made milky drinks, cuddling both girls. To their surprise, but somehow without any sense of fear, they heard a little voice from a small group of mice who crept out from the oak wainscoting in the corner.

"Could we all listen to a story?" said the mice, as one. Without waiting for a reply they climbed halfway up the curtains and drew them back with a flourish.

"East Wind", they called, "Come and tell us a Story!"

Again, it seemed perfectly normal to Gloria and the girls, to hear this and say an enthusiastic "yes please", echoed by Steve, who had missed Gloria and come down to join them.

Steve was the only one to go near the window and notice that it appeared to look out at the little grove of trees to the East and the neighbouring cottage, instead of the lawn and the view of the Channel. He forgot about this as he settled down with the others, all snuggling up in a hug under a blanket like a larger version of the Mouse group, also listening intently

ELOISE, THE MAGICIAN'S DAUGHTER

ELOISE was the daughter of the Magician and his wife, Rhiannon, who lived in an old cottage near Rushlake Green.

She was just four years old and was mostly very good. However, on this occasion Rhiannon had gone away to Llanberis in Wales to look after her own elderly mother and Eloise was only going to have her father to look after her at home.

She woke early and decided – just like that – that it was going to be a Naughty Day. The wind was in the East and anyway she just felt like being naughty.

At breakfast she let the cat, Black Malkin, in from his night prowling around All Saints Church and other very exciting places and let him drink the milk from her bowl of cereal. The magician had to throw the cereal away and let her eat a honey sandwich instead. Round one to Eloise and Malkin, who winked at each other.

All morning she played with her toys and had a good time. She was too busy trying to do spells she had seen her mother do to be naughty and her father was keeping an indulgent eye on her in case she actually managed some inconvenient magic.

Luckily she didn't! But at lunchtime Eloise refused to put any of her toys away. The Magician had to magic them into place, one by one. It took much longer than if he had done it by hand and he was very cross. Eloise didn't care.

After lunch, Eloise dug up lots of plants from the garden and made a flower bed in the middle of the kitchen floor. She found mauve Aubretia from the garden walls, a few yellow primroses and a lot of weeds in exciting shades of green.

It was fun! Eloise and the kitchen got covered in gooey, slimy, sticky mud. There was mud on her face, mud on her dress, mud on her shoes and even mud in her hair.

The Magician, who had been out of sight round the corner of the kitchen, doing his accounts on the Computer and finding it much, much harder than by magic, was extremely cross. He sent Eloise into the garden and cleaned up the kitchen. When he called Eloise to come in for a bath and bed, Eloise said, "Shan't!" and – Oh my goodness! – SHE POKED HER TONGUE OUT AT HIM!

By suppertime he had just about managed to wipe off the worst of the mud, bit by bit. Eloise turned herself into a Tiger and climbed up into a fork of the apple tree. "You can't make me go to bed," said the Eloise-Tiger. The Magician turned himself into a big green Elephant and picked her off her branch gently with his trunk.

Eloise turned herself into a little white Mouse. Horrified, the Elephant-Magician let go and backed away, trumpeting loudly.

Then the Magician turned himself into a Cat and took the Eloise-Mouse between its paws, with the claws carefully sheathed, and purred to her, soothingly. Black Malkin swore and spat and retreated to the garden in a huff.

Suddenly, there was a horrid burning pain in his paw. The Eloise-Mouse had turned into a Wasp and stung him. The magician said a few rather naughty words himself and thought hard, till he came up with a plan.

The Eloise-Wasp swooped up and down in the air and turned somersaults. She loved the feeling of the sun and the wind around her wings. She glided down to where Malkin was peeping round the kitchen door and zizzed so loudly in his ear that he jumped eight feet in the air and hit his head on the door lintel.

Oh look! There on the table was a honey sandwich, just the thing for a hungry Wasp. It was too big to eat it all up as a Wasp, so Eloise flew down and turned back into a little girl.

Wham! The sandwich turned back into the Magician. Holding her firmly, her daddy bathed her, stood over her while she ate a real honey sandwich and cleaned her teeth. Then he put her to bed.

"I love you, daddy," whispered Eloise. "Can I have a story?"

"I love you too," said the Magician and started the story – "Once upon a time there was a little girl who decided to be naughty all day because the wind was in the East..."

"The wind will be in the west tomorrow," said Eloise, sleepily, "and I will be very, very, very Good."

Then she fell asleep. So did the magician.

POSTLUDE

♪

THE FAMILY enjoyed their hug and loved the story – even Rachel forgot to be sophisticated and superior – as two very sleepy girls were carried up to bed, Pearl asking wistfully, "Does it mean I can be very, very naughty too?" Luckily they were both asleep before an answer was needed.

CHAPTER EIGHT

THE PRINCESS WHO LOVED CHOCOLATE

PRELUDE
♪

EVERYONE slept well and enjoyed a relatively peaceful breakfast. Unfortunately it didn't last. Their second day out was, if anything, even more fraught and quarrelsome than their first. Apart from a serious difficulty in finding ice cream, a loo, cups of tea or the car park, Rachel had a massive sulk because she was not allowed to buy a provocative T-shirt even though she offered her own pocket money. She had to compromise with a Banksy rat saying, "I'm up and dressed, what more do you want?" – which was not nearly transgressive enough.

Rachel stormed off to her little shared bedroom, barricading herself in and preventing the usual bedtime for Pearl. It was with a sense of desperation that her mother settled down with Pearl on the sofa and were joined by Steve. No telly even, to pass the time.

In the bedroom, Rachel was being subjected to love-bombing by the Mice.
(Mice-o-phobes look away now!) They sat on her bedside table and made funny noises till they got her attention, then daringly came near and kissed her with their whiskers till she began to laugh.

"Do you like Chocolate?" said one of the older Mice. "Of course," said Rachel, amazed that anyone, even a mouse could ask such a question. "Why are you sulking then?" asked the mouse. "I'm not sulking!" she cried, offended. "It's just, oh... it's just that Pearl had more chocolate than me today."

"No she didn't. You had identical bars," said the mouse, bluntly. Rachel was furious. "You're very stupid. That's why it was unfair – I'm older than her and much bigger. I should have had more than her!"

The mouse considered this carefully. "I'm not sure if that follows," he said. "Do you know something? We mice had a whole big house made of cheese once. Would you like a house made of chocolate to eat all the time?"

Rachel began to giggle. "You are so stupid!" she cried. "If I ate my house I'd be homeless."

"Well then," said the mouse, "would you like a different story, about chocolate, specially for you?"

Rachel nodded and the mouse said casually, "Call your dad in and we'll ask the wind again."

Rachel tried to say grandly "He's not my dad", but even to her own ears it sounded petulant rather than dignified and she called out to Steve and went downstairs obediently with the Mice. After all, that was very different to obeying the boring old grown-ups.

Gloria and Pearl smiled welcomingly, all disputes forgotten momentarily, and they all curled up on the sofa with Steve. The Mice opened the window curtains and the cottage turned around to let in the East Wind.

The following story is the second Story the East Wind told, for Rachel and Pearl, the family of Gloria Gunnersford and Steven Johnson.

THE PRINCESS WHO LOVED CHOCOLATE

ONCE UPON A TIME there was a Princess who loved chocolate. One day, sitting by a spring, she was about to eat a bar of the best and most delicious chocolate you can imagine when it slipped from her hand and sank beneath the bubbling water.

Out popped an ugly frog. "What will you give me if I get your chocolate bar back for you?" he said.

"Anything you want!" she cried, for in the grip of a chocolate addiction one is desperate enough to say things like that.

The frog dived in, and very quickly reappeared with the bar in its webbed green paw. The chocolate was unharmed, being wrapped in the best grease proof, water-repellent paper (although sadly not a biodegradable, planet-friendly, green container, because this story takes place in olden and less politically correct times).

"Here you are," said the frog, as the Princess grabbed it and began to munch. "I want you to take me home, let me share your place at table and your supper, and then put me on your pillow at bedtime." The Princess was mortified, but a promise is a promise, so she took him home, introduced him to the King and Queen, and did as he asked.

In the morning it was a great shock to wake up and find the frog still there, but he said to her, "Don't be upset. I'm not really a frog, but a handsome Prince – I'm such a good actor that I can be whatever you want. Which would you prefer, me, as a handsome Prince to marry, or a lifetime supply of chocolate?"

Well, what a dilemma! The Princess closed her eyes and debated with herself earnestly for, oh! all of 10 seconds, before saying, "A lifetime supply of chocolate!" Then she added, "Please" – because she was very well brought up.

"Bravo!" shouted the Prince. She opened her eyes, astonished to find him still there, and now looking like a really handsome Prince.

"You have passed the test," he continued. "You can have both, though you may have to buy the chocolate yourself sometimes, as I'm often rather skint."

So they were married and lived happily ever after (though it was a little tricky at first, explaining to her parents the presence of a handsome Prince in her bedroom).

And the moral of the story is: –

YOU CAN NEVER GO WRONG IF YOU CHOOSE CHOCOLATE!

POSTLUDE

♪

PEARL was sucking her thumb and nodding off at the end of the story and Gloria carried her off upstairs. The little girl could be heard murmuring 'chocolate' all the way up.

Rachel asked about the technicalities of making chocolate as she was pretty sure Steve wouldn't know much and she could keep her (imaginary) lead over him. Unfortunately he knew quite a lot about it and she was therefore One Down and bored with it.

She decided to tell Steve about the Prince being in the bedroom. "I know why the Wind said that! It's because you shouldn't be in bed together till you're married." She paused dramatically, and added: "You and Mum aren't married!"

If Steve felt any embarrassment as she might have hoped, he certainly showed none. Rachel continued, "Are you going to marry my mum?"

Steve's response was a cautious, "What do you think, Rachel? Would it be a good idea or not?"

"Would I have to be a bridesmaid?" she asked.

Steve crossed his fingers and replied, "Only if you wanted to be."

"Could I wear what I want? Even jeans and the T-shirt I wanted to buy?"

"Yes, I don't mind." said Steve.

"What about Pearl? Can I dress her up too in anything I want to?"

Terrifying visions of what attire Rachel might devise for her little half-sister, from matching crocodile outfits to The T-Shirt, made Steve qualify his reply with a diplomatic, "– well, if you have the choice, shouldn't she have too?"

Even so, he knew it was pretty well game set and match to Rachel. He might have a lot of difficulty explaining all this to Gloria and her relatives someday.

Or maybe not! As Rachel curled up beside him on the sofa, she put her hand in his and he heard a little voice mutter, "G'night dad."

Gloria came looking for him and they carried their deeply sleeping older daughter up to bed. As she slept, Steve sat up beside her for a long time. "I may be just a Frog and not a Prince", he thought, "but I think we can make a go of our own Story."

As if sharing his thoughts, Gloria stirred in her sleep and held out her arms. He sank into them and kissed his soon-to-be-wife, smiling as he fell asleep entwined with her in a place of magic that is known to all lovers.

CHAPTER NINE

THE OLD WOMAN WHO WAS LONELY

PRELUDE
♪

HELENA briskly worked her own type of practical magic on the cottage to turn it around domestically for the next Visitor. She had liked the little family very much and smiled at the stories the two girls vied to tell her after breakfast the day they left, about mice and chocolate and a wedding with crocodiles in it and more chocolate.

The family had been happy and grateful, full of praises for the Cottage and Helena's care, writing in the ever hopeful Visitors' Book, which not everyone remembered to do.

Helena had given Gloria a bunch of Tulips, just out, from the garden. All the plants were beginning to stir and stretch, or at least that was the fantasy the family and she shared.

Rachel even mimed being a daffodil opening out, to show the budded stems what they should be doing. She and little Pearl went off in the back of the car, wriggling and play fighting amicably, waving to Helena till they were out of sight.

All around Punnetts Town the trees were greening up nicely. Later that same day, an old Mercedes came along purring, the driver admiring the same early signs of Spring and feeling the lift in the air that this gives. The verges were full of celandine and snowdrops and there were African lilies showing as an orange splash in a garden he passed. The car turned gently off the B 2096 before the village and took the turning to the right just after the pub, as instructed.

The driver, Emeritus Professor George Miller, looked anxiously at the oil gauge. He really didn't want to top it up again before going to the Public School in Tunbridge Wells in the morning and he was well aware that the car could really do with a replacement engine. No chance at the moment, he had to be realistic; he was already almost in the red again this month.

He had the cash for his night in Turnaround Cottage in an envelope ready in his pocket. It had been much cheaper than any of the hotels in Tunbridge Wells and he was intrigued by the address, Flitterbrook Lane, Punnetts town, that he had seen in an obscure advert in a magazine.

He had cut it out – 'An unusual retired and converted Postmill under the edge of the Sussex Weald. If it likes you, it can be rented by the night or by the week. (We have never found anyone who it doesn't like.) All amenities. Two bedrooms, bathroom, sitting room and kitchen. Gardens all round. Many unusual features which may (or may not) reveal themselves to you. Incredibly beautiful views of the Sussex countryside, changing all the time.'

With luck the school Bursar would give him a cheque straight after the talk he was giving. It had been luck too that had given him this opportunity. A retired Professor of English Literature, specialising in Religious and Children's Fiction in 19th Century Britain, didn't get many opportunities like this. The Frank Brinton Memorial Lecture, no less, at one of the best Public Schools in the South East.

An old Alumnus had recommended him, after a tipsy and uproarious evening in which, wearing a metaphorical Professorial hat, Professor George Miller had compared his own dissertation 'Charles Kingsley's The Water Babies as an agent of Social change' to War and Peace – to the detriment of the latter!

Not that he'd be repeating that as a talk. 'Just don't mention the War,' he thought and as he pulled up just down the lane he was smiling to himself. Consequently his creased and weathered face was seen at its best as he stopped beside a woman walking down the road.

Helena, returning from the village shop, certainly thought he looked both distinguished and rather nice, and her eyes crinkled a smile in return. Perhaps it was his fairy-tale mind-set of the moment that made him think she looked endearingly like a pixie, though her real age was apparent in other ways.

"Excuse me!" he said to her. "Can you direct me to Turnaround Cottage, please?"

"I wonder – are you perhaps Professor George Miller?" she asked in return. "The cottage is just a little further down this lane, round the corner. You're almost there."

He smiled fully at her then, and put the car gently into gear so he could let her guide him round the corner, to see the Cottage on their left, set in a lush summer garden.

"This is certainly the right place for you!" Helena smiled at him. He looked a little puzzled and she added quickly, "Sorry! You couldn't know – Turnaround Cottage used to be a Windmill, in fact a Post Mill" – and she explained how that worked. "You can just see where the sails went," she concluded as he was getting out of the big car.

She was admiring the lovely lines of the old Mercedes, while truth to tell George was secretly admiring her trim ankles. They were getting on so well that she said casually, "I suppose the years of grinding corn are why there are still generations of Mice in the cottage" – and equally absentmindedly he said, "You could use poison or traps I suppose..."

"Oh NO!" Helena was horrified and spoke quickly. "I promise the Mice won't be a bother to you! I couldn't do that to them!" she said, almost tearfully. She was looking at him now, he thought, rather as a kindergarten teacher might regard King Herod.

George looked at her curiously, more used to women who either screeched and affected to be frightened on seeing a mouse, or went about their disposal with jackbooted efficiency. Twice married and twice divorced, with a couple of affairs in between, he regarded himself as someone who understood women.

He felt a deeper interest stir in him over this woman though, who somehow seemed to have the same oversensitivity and vulnerability that he had himself, but that he was used to concealing so successfully. His reply about disposing of mice had been purely a reflex of the armour plating behind which he habitually hid his feelings.

Helena showed him round in her usual routine, but her sparkle had somehow gone and she looked, he thought, more her age. What might it be, he wondered? He guessed, from her recent retirement, that she was probably in her early sixties, like himself.

He had forgotten the pretty ankles and the pixie smile. He wanted to go to the loo and he wanted to sit down with a wee dram – or sensibly, a cup of tea first – and relax after his journey, not be made to feel bad about a parcel of rodents.

Helena was concentrating on opening and shutting doors with slightly more emphasis than usual and this was successful. Not an ear, not a whisker, not a mouselet, was in evidence anywhere. All was clean and neat. George, who lived in a typical type of squalor of an academic kind, with books and papers everywhere, rather liked the orderliness and the cottage layout.

He was particularly thrilled by the glimpses of cottage garden from each window, though Helena's presentation of them lacked its usual enthusiasm. She was too afraid of an errant mouselet appearing to risk lingering and soon went down to her own cottage at Flitterbottom.

George, perhaps a little too used to rapt attention from the fair sex, was a little piqued by this, then forgot her as he made himself tea from the cupboard she had replenished and sat in the garden on the sloping lawn to the South, enjoying the late summer sunshine.

To his delight he saw, mysteriously, the gleam of almost golden light in a line across the horizon of the water to the South; that must be the English Channel, he thought, and he knew he was looking at the Coast of France, presumably Brittany. Had he but known it, as he drank from the big green frog mug, he was thinking elevated, meaningless Rumblebum-type thoughts.

His mind had recently been preoccupied, not entirely beneficially, with big cloudy dreams of shutting out the miseries of the recent past and of redeeming himself in the eyes of his family and The World by emigrating. Forget the bitterness of his last divorce, the acrimony and the alimony. Go and make a New Life in the South of France – just like the youngest prince in a fairy tale or the disgraced aristocratic younger sons.

"There is a tide in the affairs of men, which, taken at the flood, leads on to fortune..." He murmured these words to himself and it was as if a hollow echo came from within the belly of the green frog mug: "Omitted, all the voyage of their life is bound in shallows and in miseries..."

'I must get away,' he thought. 'Live somewhere else. Become a new Me. I don't want to be bound in the shallows and miseries for my remaining years.' 'Affairs of men?' he mused again. 'Yes, I've had enough of them! Why did none of them turn out to be my Soulmate?' and he lapsed into a self-pitying reverie about his unlucky choices in love, to cover his unease.

For the first time, in this quintessentially English garden, he wondered why it was only in a foreign land he could think of 'finding' himself again? Meanwhile Helena had returned to Wheelright's Cottage full of depression and self-dislike, not actually that unlike his own mood. 'Why do I always seem to say the wrong thing?' she was thinking.

Only a vigorous and efficient attack on the beds and the dust in her home could dispel her feeling of somehow, once again, having said the wrong thing, sabotaged her chances with a man who she had to admit had attracted her greatly. Of course he wasn't a Mouse-murderer, it was her oversensitive and over-talkative personality that was the problem, she thought.

Returning later that night from a visit to the nearest neighbours to Turnaround Cottage, Bert and Norah Doveport, for coffee, Helena saw the light on in the tiny sitting room of Turnaround Cottage and had to resist the temptation to knock on the door under the pretence of checking if George had everything he needed, something she would normally not dream of doing. She resisted the temptation and went on down to Flitterbottom.

Had she but known it, George at that very moment was leaning his head on his hand, abandoning the book he had been trying to edit, and allowing himself a reverie about the woman who had shown him the way here, wondering what she was really like. He gave up after a while, unsatisfied with himself and his life and retired up to the bedroom.

From the window there he could once again see the line, silver now in the moonlight, which was the coast of France, marker of his future dreams. 'That's the Further End of Nowhere!' he thought playfully, 'Not a real country at all.' As the clouds obscured the moon and the line vanished like a mirage or a dream he felt a curious sense of relief, an escape, as if it represented another mistake, a burden rather than a new adventure.

He stood so long motionless at the window that Herbert Mouselet, always one of the boldest especially since his heady success with the new mouse proverb, had inadvertently crept out just by his feet.

George was by no means anti-mouse; his earlier comment to Helena had been a reflex attempt at solving someone else's problem, so he was careful to move very slowly.

"Hello!" he said, tentatively. Herbert squeaked in alarm. In fact he said distinctly "Cogito ergo..." and then burped loudly. George, though naturally startled, replied politely, "You're welcome."

Herbert's response was a polite, "Oh to be in England, now that (*burp*) is here," as he came nearer. The little Mouselet could not run away, even if he had wanted to, as he was dragging behind him his most precious possession, a slightly tatty sheaf of handwritten paper which he could not bear to abandon. A protective view that George and all true lovers of literature would applaud.

"May I see your manuscript?" said George politely. He was in that hinterland between sleep and wakefulness known as the hypnagogic state, so that the mood of slight melancholy induced by memories, hopes and – it has to be said – his favourite malt, sipped in most evenings, also played a part. Herbert held the edge of the papers out towards him in his miniscule paws and George took it almost reverently.

It was a handwritten collection of what appeared to be poems and was much too heavy for any mouselet or even mouse to be able to carry. George had only seen Helena's handwriting once, on the letter accepting his booking of Turnaround Cottage, but if he had not been sure, *Helena Brown* was signed on each sheet.

With a pleasant acknowledgement to Herbert and to the other mice who seemed to have crept out to join them, he read a few of the poems aloud, as poetry is normally best read, and thought they were rather good. Being sleepy, he then laid the manuscript on the dressing table and retired to bed.

As he prepared for sleep, the Mice, reluctant to let such a good playmate go – one who read or told stories to them being particularly prized – they explained to him that in the past they used to eat any papers left around, but they had recently realised that this was a mistake and a particularly clever Mouse had taught them all to read. (Anything taught to one Mouse becomes known to all and passes down the generations as they are a collective.)

In fact, you could say that they had taken a little too literally the famous instruction, 'Hear, Read, Mark, Learn and Inwardly digest', by adding to it – 'and then burp it up again.'

They loved the words and were beginning to find it was better to preserve them whole than simply to rely on burping them up occasionally. George was giving them a little talk on the Right Uses of Literature and encouraging this enlightened approach when sleep overtook him.

He could not have said at what point he woke and, as if sleepwalking, found himself by his bedroom window. The Cottage had turned again and there was no line of sea and land, but the view of the back gate, the bins and compost heap and the dark bulk of the Downs. The North Wind found its way round the braided edges of the red brocade curtains and said in his ear:

'Listen to hear a story which will introduce you to your own Soul, George Miller. Your friend, Turnaround Cottage, has adopted you tonight and will grind an answer to a question you do not even know how to ask.

'Learn then to understand the Loneliness that takes your Soul by her throat and threatens to squeeze the life out of her. Listen to how someone once recognised the same desperation you feel and what answer she was given...'

THE OLD WOMAN WHO WAS LONELY

ONCE, there was an old woman who was very lonely. "Oh, if only I had a husband who I could care for and who would care for me," she sighed every day. "I feel so alone!" Indeed there came a day when the loneliness swept over her so strongly that she cried out aloud, "I don't care who or what he might be; I would marry him, whoever asked me!"

Three nights later there was a knock on the door. A tall man stood there, face and body masked by swirling grey and white clothing, or was it mist?

"I am the husband you have asked for," he said. "Will you agree to a betrothal, a sure promise of marriage?"

She started to protest that she didn't know who he was, but he cut her short.

"My name is Death," he said, "but you agreed to marry anyone who was sent to you, and I will take you with me to my Castle for the wedding itself."

Well, the old woman was so lonely that she said she would marry him, but asked for more time. Death agreed and told her to be ready for his next visit.

She looked round at the bareness of her cottage and started to make things for a dowry. She made clothes for herself, serviceable and plain. She made warm things for a husband who would never wear them and toys for children she would never have.

After a year and a day, there was a knock on the door, and there was Death again. "I'm not ready," she protested. "Look at all the things that aren't finished!" So Death agreed and went away again.

After a year and a day, he was back, but once more she protested she was not ready and he went away again.

The third time, after a year and a day, she had finished all she could think of to make, and she was tired. She rested until the knock came on the door, and then let Death in.

"What shall I do with all the things I've made?" she asked him.

"Leave them," he said. "You won't be coming back here."

"What about locking the door?" she said. Death shook his head and she wrote a little note and put it on the table, that anyone who came should take what they wanted. Leaving the door open, she went out with him, to where a great grey horse waited.

Death swung her up before him and rode away so fast that in an instant, it seemed, they had left the familiar fields and farms behind and were riding deeper and deeper into a dark forest. Branches whipped her face and body. She cried out and tried to escape, but he held her fast. The twigs whipped her so hard she could feel the blood running down her face and body.

It seemed to go on forever, but suddenly, they were free of the forest and running across a dazzling desert. The sun shone on the white sand pitilessly, even though she tried to close her eyes against the light. Death suddenly swerved and bent her first one way and then the other. She cried out again, then realised that he was avoiding arrows, shot at them from every direction. She could hear them hissing like snakes as they went past, occasionally grazing her, so that again she felt the blood running down her skin and soaking her clothes.

Suddenly again, the grey horse stopped and reared. They had come to the shore of a wide and restless sea, stretching to the horizon. Death held her closer and the horse waded in, deeper and deeper until it was swimming and she was almost submerged and drowning. The salt water soaked her clothes and washed away the blood, but oh how it stung in her myriad cuts and bruises!

At last she felt the horse climbing onto sure ground and opened her eyes. They were in front of a towering castle. She saw high walls, turrets and windows, gleaming in the morning sunlight as golden as the dawn itself.

"This is my home," said Death, lifting her off the grey horse, and leading her up a magnificent staircase into a great hall. Ahead, the old woman saw a figure coming towards her as if to welcome her. It was a woman, young and beautiful, with skin as pearly as dew, clothed in rainbow colours of the finest fabric.

She stretched out her arms and smiled and so did the woman, but when she moved forward, her fingers met glass and she realised that it was a mirror.

"That can't be me!" cried the woman, "She is young and beautiful, not old and careworn!" She looked down at her arms and body, and touched her cheeks, for of course we can never see our own faces. Sure enough, all the blood and signs of age had been washed away. She appeared to have soft young skin and was dressed in a rainbow of beautiful colours.

As she looked up again, amazed, but now recognising her own reflection, the mirror dissolved away and she could see shallow steps, leading to a great throne. So much golden light came from the figure on the throne, that she could not have described it in any way except that her heart was filled with awe and love.

"I am the High King of all the Universe," said the man on the throne. "I heard your plea, and I sent for you to be my Bride. You consented, but I need to hear it again from your own lips, my beloved."

When she began to stammer in surprise and shock, the King spoke again:

"A King cannot go out to fetch his bride; he has to send a proxy who will arrange the betrothal and bring her to him." He turned his golden look towards Death. "I sent you, my servant, to bring her to me. Surely you explained it all, and exactly who she was marrying?" he said.

Death shuffled his feet and looked extremely sheepish. "Well... not exactly, Sire," he said. Then he added defensively, "It's a bit of a boring job you know, riding around all the time, getting shot at, and that, and never having anyone of my own. Perhaps I wasn't quite as open about it all as I should have been!"

And the woman who had once been old, understood at last that she was the Bride of the Golden King, Chatelaine of the Castle and most of all, was totally loved and no longer lonely.

Reaching up on tiptoes she pulled Death down to her and kissed his cheek. She said to him, "Indeed you told me everything I needed to know, and you brought me here safely, which is all that matters. Thank you!"

Death turned and stumped off down the steps. He rubbed his cheek thoughtfully for a moment, then went off to look after his horse, smiling to himself for once.

The woman turned back to the Golden King, who held out his arms to her, laughing. She ran up the steps to him and was enfolded in the golden mist, for ever with her Beloved

POSTLUDE
♪

IN THE MORNING George found he had inadvertently fallen asleep on his knees with his head on the bed, almost as if he had been praying. He was feeling very cold and sore even after a hot shower in the tiny bathroom.

He collected his necessaries, clothes and papers into his case in a hurry, not realising that Herbert Mouselet had stowed away in his spare boots and the mice had added the Manuscript of Helena's poems so the Mouselet would have a warm bed and something to read.

Helena came round quite early to see if George had slept well. He thanked her and said it had been an excellent night, but he didn't enlarge on that, still astonished at the story – half sure it must have been a dream and unwilling to mention Herbert Mouselet and the Poems, in case of further misunderstanding.

"I think the Mill is a delightful place to stay, Helena, if I may call you that?" he said.

"Of course," said Helena, "Please do. I presume I may call you George?" They both laughed at the unexpected formality, both sensing that any little tension from their first meeting, the previous afternoon, had gone.

George felt very easy with her and said, "I'm not quite sure when I will be free to come south again at the moment, but I will of course book. Perhaps I could take you out for a meal and a concert, if you like music?"

"That would be lovely!" she replied enthusiastically, assuming correctly that he meant Classical music. "But do allow me to cook you a nice meal!"

They parted with mutual warm feelings. George hesitated momentarily and then leaned forward to kiss her cheek, which she presented with alacrity. Another little social hurdle overcome successfully and they parted on the best of terms and – perhaps – with a few secret hopes.

George reached the school in Tunbridge Wells where he was to stay for the night before his return to the Scottish Borders, in good time to join the boys in some of their lessons, judge a poetry competition and get ready to give his lecture.

He left his case open in the assigned boring little bedroom he'd been given. Boring, that is to say, by comparison with Turnaround Cottage and its mysteries! He was called down to meet the Staff by one of the boys, and went straight away, leaving his open case on the bed, the clothes draped over the lid.

He therefore didn't see little Herbert Mouselet climb fearlessly out and start to investigate his new home. Herbert really was the courageous voyager who had taken "the tide of fortune" at the flood and deserved fame forever.

Incidentally, Herbert lived long and happily in the School boarding house, safely protected by successive waves of sixth formers who had finally learnt Care and Compassion in their long and risky trip through adolescence – that voyage which we would all like to be spared, but not with such longing as our relatives wish they could be spared from us. (Some of us never truly emerge from this voyage!)

George's talk and presence at the Dinner was a great success and he had a wonderful time. He took the opportunity later that evening to send a letter including the manuscript, as follows:

"—Dear Helena, You will be glad to know that my talk was very well received. I do not know how I inadvertently packed this fascinating collection of your poems in my case on leaving Turnaround Cottage, but I return them forthwith. I hope you will consider possibilities for publishing or sharing them in some way, dear lady. I think they are well worth a wider audience.

"I thoroughly enjoyed my stay in such a beautiful part of the country and in such a warm and welcoming house. I do hope I will be able to repeat the visit in the near future. It would be a great pleasure, also, to hear more of your poems, which have touched me deeply by their simple yet intensity of feelings.

"Yours etc, George."

George Miller wondered, as he concluded the letter, to what extent his feelings were touched by her poems, or by the recollections of those beautiful hazel eyes, crinkling endearingly with emotion or laughter, or those delicate ankles that promised hidden delights beyond the visible confines of her short skirt.

CHAPTER TEN

THE ENCHANTER

PRELUDE
♪

HELENA had seen the creepy old man again once or twice in the distance at Heathfield Market and – in spite of her usual impulse to help everyone – had found herself carefully avoiding him.

The old man bought his meagre basket of vegetables and returned to his cottage, near Three Cups Corner, speaking to no one, not even the stallholder. His name does not appear on the electoral roll and there is no apparent tenancy for the cottage.

Shall we call him A (for Anthony) Nonymouse? No! I think that sounds too friendly. We don't know him yet, and like Helena should be wary. I might call him Tom Crow and you can call him what you like, or nothing at all.

Later that evening he made his way, as if unable to resist, back to Turnaround Cottage. The building was dark; it appeared there were no visitors tonight. Disappointingly there were no windows open at all, not even a crack he could squeeze through. "Open up to me!" the old man snarled.

It remained quiet. The cottage seemed poised. Waiting. Was it laughing at him, frustrating his long search deliberately? He picked up a stone from the path, and pulled back his arm, aiming at the window, waiting for a sign, a resistance, a fight – then he could smash his stone through the window. No one would hear, not even that proud bitch down in Flitterbottom who couldn't even give him the time of day in the market.

The only thing that changed was so gentle he wasn't sure at first. A low sweet humming sound, lower and lighter than bees, or electricity pylons. It swelled and ebbed away, never quite lost, an enchantment of warmth, an answer to questions not yet asked; it wrapped around Tom Crow.

'The Humadruz,' he thought, 'I'm hearing the Humadruz!' Awe and wonder swept him. He thought he could smell violets and lilies in the twilight garden as he sank to his knees on the grass.

The top of the cottage turned around to face him; he could hear it creaking above the buzzing of the Humadruz and see how the frontage resembled a face, a friendly, kindly face.

The stone fell from his hand and was picked up by a woman, sitting behind him. Was she the woman he had loved so much, his own True Love, before the great betrayal? He could not tell; she kept her face turned from him, and she was holding the stone close to her ear.

The woman leaned down and pulled some of the grass, exposing the heavy soil.

"Do you know what this is?" she said. "It is clay, good Sussex clay and this mill was built of it. You need to be as caring as the earth that grows the corn, as tenacious as the clay of its bricks, as strong as the tower that carries the sails, as faithful as the sails themselves, as loving as the wind that turns them around, and as powerful as the gritstones that grind the flour. You must live your strength and your faith and your love through all of time."

She turned to face him, He had no choice but look into her eyes and face his betrayals, over and over again, and her betrayals, over and over again too. For love is always betraying or betrayed and it is nameless.

Where it needs to be caring and tenacious and strong and faithful and playful and powerful, it is selfish and fleeting and threadbare and unfaithful and unloving and weak!

Was it his fate to face again the eternity he had spent loving her as well as the eternity he had spent without her?

He had no choice and he fell almost senseless on the grass, for who can bear such dark reality, even under the shadow of a Mill that grinds the corn of life?

In that moment he could see shadowy shapes, of a woman in a long white dress and veil and children playing, and he turned his face into the earth so as not to see them, as the East Wind spoke his own special story into the old man's unwilling ears.

So shall we listen to it too, in the silence of the night? To hear about all betrayals and all lost loves, as the Bride dies and the children weep in the garden, where the heavy sails have turned, turned and turned again to face the East?

THE ENCHANTER

THE ENCHANTER lured the Princess into his tower. "Come, my beauty," he said. "Nothing to frighten you here. See all my pretty things. Here's fame and money and power and delight and you'll be the Belle of the ball!" he said.

Somewhere the bell tolled and for a moment, just a moment, she hung back. Too late she realised his perfidy and wept, screamed, rattled the door. Too late!

"Now you're all mine!" he cried. "See what pretty things I have for you!" He cajoled and persuaded and camped by the door, he himself unable to leave for even a minute, fearing her escape more and more as the months went by.

He fed her and sang to her, gave her more gifts, sent up with her food on a rope. He gave her everything except her freedom. In the end he slept for brief periods, always alert, one ear open for her movements day and night.

The Princess looked out, bored and fed up with her life. A Prince, passing by, struck by her beauty decided to fall in love with her instantly, as she looked down from her tower.

"Are you going to release me?" said the Princess. The Prince stepped forward and bowed, with a flourish of his hat. It was a game to him. What was it to her? He cared not at all!

"Of course, my beautiful Princess. my own True Love, my Soulmate!" he cried, with an even deeper bow.

"He'll do," thought the Princess. With a cry that could have been misinterpreted as ecstatic love, she threw down the rope made of her sheets that she had been plying together for just such a scenario, and scrambled down into his arms.

They were away before the Enchanter awoke and hurled himself after them, with a cry of frustrated rage and humiliated pride.

So the Princess and the Prince lived, as they had done before, bored and deceitful and full of worldly wealth, but in true poverty even so. For those who misuse love are living dangerously. Sooner or later they will each betray the other and will cry out in outrage at the perfidy.

True Love is not to be fooled and not to be bought. It does not open doors, it is not a commodity, nor does it solve all your problems, cancel all your debts and bring you long life and happiness all by itself.

So! What of the Enchanter, tied by his obsession into guarding so porous a prison? Tell me, asks the Wind – which of them was really the prisoner then – the Princess, or the Enchanter.

Again! the Wind asks us – And what of the Princess and the Prince? Married from lust and self-love and boredom. Will either of them ever be truly free?

POSTLUDE

♪

THE OLD MAN woke cold and damp on the dewy grass, in the small hours and found his way by owl light back to the place where he lived but could not call home. He seemed in those moments to have been wandering for centuries, for millennia even, with nowhere to call home.

Something had broken in him. He hoped it was his pride but feared it was his heart.

There was a long period of silence and sorrow in the garden. The old man slept, face down in the earth. The stone he had not after all thrown in anger, rested, discarded beside him and he dreamed. In his dream the woman he had loved and the stone were somehow made one.

INTERLUDE
♪

STONE FRIEND

"SHALL I BE YOUR FRIEND?" said the Stone. "Your Stone friend?
"Did I choose you, or did you choose me, Stone Friend?" he asked her.
He sat with her in his hand, slept with her by his pillow, carried her all day.

As she rested against his ear, mineral on shell-flesh,
He heard her whisper in his dreams,
"I was once part of a great mountain of stone," she said.
"How was it?" he asked her.
"It was good, good, good," said his Stone Friend.

In his dreams he heard his Stone Friend chanting,
"My mountain lasted a million, million, million years,
It froze and thawed, froze and thawed.
Water crept into spaces, ice stretched, ice melted, cracks grew,

Water crept into spaces, ice stretched, ice
melted, cracks grew,
Water crept into spaces, ice stretched, ice
melted, cracks grew."

"Suddenly, the mountain split. We thundered
down the plain,
As many rocks as there are stars in the sky."
"How was it?" he asked her.
"It was good, good, good," said his Stone
Friend,

In his half-sleep he felt the rush of water over
a bed of rocks,
Or was it bodies, rolling, melting, rotting –
pebbles and bones rolling, rolling down to the
great sea?

He dreamed again, and heard his Stone
Friend say,
"I was ground down by water, smashed
against rocks,
jostling and crushing and scraping till I
became as I am now."
"How was it?" he asked his Stone Friend,
"It was good, good, good," she said.

"For many ages I was part of a stone cairn,"
she said.
"We guarded a King. Men came and went,
came and went, came and went,

Then the water returned and swept it all away."
"How was that?" he asked.
"It was good, good, good," said his Stone Friend.

He told his Stone Friend, "I took you from the water once,
Now I am leaving, where shall I put you?"
"You can put me in the earth, on the mountain or in the water."
Said his Stone Friend.

"I'm going to miss you. Doesn't it matter to you?" he asked,
"Are you going to miss me?" he said
"Yes, I will miss you," said his Stone Friend
"But I will miss you because I had you, and
it is good, good, good, good, good!"

CHAPTER ELEVEN

THE PRINCE WHO WAS ALL HEART

PRELUDE
♪

HELENA replied to the letter from George quite promptly. She had found him interesting and attractive and felt that it was appropriate to reply in a straightforward way, without letting herself get into that mind-set that so easily besets the single woman, of being unsure whether to be honest and say a straight yes, or to delay so as not to be thought of as too keen.

So she wrote back and asked when he would like to come, as she would look forward to cooking him the promised meal. George promptly rang her and they talked at some length about all sorts of general things, and then agreed on a date. She ascertained that, while he did not want to put her to any great trouble he was really pining for a proper roast meal and fruit pie, of any sort, to follow.

She rang off with a happy smile, already working out the best menu and recounting the whole thing to the Mice when she was cleaning the cottage next morning.

"I think perhaps good English Beef," she told them solemnly. "It's not quite the season for farm lamb and chicken is a bit too ordinary."

The mice preened their whiskers in assent. "What sort of pie do you think?" she asked them again, and a faint squeaking allowed her to smile and say:

"Yes, I agree, good Sussex Apple Pie can't be beaten, but we'll big it up by adding a surprise ingredient." The Mice seemed more than satisfied with that.

When George came again to Turnaround Cottage for the promised meal with Helena he was much encouraged by the friendship she showed him and was delighted to be able to tell her that the Tunbridge Wells School had been very pleased with his performance at the Lecture.

"Do you know," he said enthusiastically, "they've actually asked me if I would take some special scholarship classes occasionally. Probably also some exam marking. That would be a nice little side-line! I could do it by post."

"How lovely," Helena replied, equally enthusiastically. "You must have made a really good impression in such a short time. Isn't that good! Now, would you like some more of the roast, or are you ready for afters?"

George looked into her smiling eyes and felt his heart turn. "Thank you," he said simply, indicating he'd love some more food. "Your roast dinner is unparalleled in my experience."

He continued, "I love this cottage too – you have a fine eye for furniture and decor. Is that really an 18th century desk?"

Helena was very pleased, as she loved her bargains and was proud of her eye for colour.

"No I'm afraid not," she smiled, "but it's a dear little thing – an Edwardian reproduction. A *Bonheur du Jour*, almost an antique now. It cost me a whole month's salary, when I was young!" And they both laughed.

George said, "I wish I'd known you then!" and Helena blushed. They looked into each other's eyes, grey meeting hazel, and time seemed to stop, until the silence was broken by the little carriage clock, chiming the hour before it could seem awkward...

Indeed, the dinner was excellent. Helena had given it her best and the roasties, the gravy, and especially the Yorkshire pudding were well up to the praises applied to them by a hungry and grateful George.

"My Yorkshire pudding's not a patch on my own father's," Helena confessed, smiling. "He was a Yorkshireman, born and bred, so his was the best in the world. He always said it could never be the same anywhere else, unless you imported the air from Yorkshire to help it rise!"

By mutual consent they delayed the dessert for a while and chatted, arms resting on the table, confiding more as the wine went down. Under Helena's sympathetic responses George admitted that he had only very recently come out of a bruising romance that had lasted a couple of years and cost him his marriage.

He told her a little about his past, saying, ruefully, "Two marriages ending in divorce. A stupid affair that I should have had more sense about and that hasn't lasted. I could be called damaged goods really."

He meant it to sound light hearted, but the underlying sadness made Helena murmur dissent to this, gently touching his arm and turning his ideas, by her questions, to his more successful life story.

He had three higher degrees, plus his professorship to talk about, drawing her out too about her life and family. Above all she was pleased at finding out a little about his children. He had three, all doing well and two married, so that he was also a grandfather five times over. "I can't come anywhere near that," Helena laughed, telling him with pride and pleasure though, about Jocelyn, Jon and her grandson, little Rodney.

The pudding, too, when they got round to it, was a success. She had used the bright red Ashdown apples, grown nearby, at their very best at this time of year, and added generous slices of quince. Served with Haagen Dazs vanilla ice cream it topped off a meal fit for a king – at least that was George's expert opinion as he finished off the wine!

After supper they relaxed with music and as he was still inclined to confide in her about his past, she listened with tenderness rather than suggesting any hint of criticism, registering that he was at the stage where he might feel he was over it all, but was in reality very raw and vulnerable and liable to mess his life up even more if he didn't take care.

So after their most enjoyable evening and listening to his choice of music from her collection of cd's, Mozart's Piano Concerto number 23 and some Haydn, she gently but firmly limited the kissing to something friendly rather than passionate because, greatly attracted though she was to him, she did not want to take advantage of his vulnerable emotional state.

Going back up the hill at midnight to sleep in the cottage (one of the perks of her wardenship was a certain number of free nights for guests) George was not sure whether to be glad or sorry to be on his own, but he certainly felt happy and comfortable with her and very grateful for all her kindnesses. In his experience women were not often kind without any hidden agenda, but he sensed that she was genuine through and through.

Helena was, as so often, fighting off the inclination to beat herself up about having been too open and outgoing, simultaneously with having been too standoffish and slow. However, she went off to sleep feeling on the whole very happy and satisfied with their time together.

Had she but known it, this reflected very much George's own view of the day.

As he undressed in the little bedroom, sleepy with good food and wine, he half hoped, half feared getting a story. As it happened he slept extremely well and when he woke it was still a little early for breakfast, so having got himself washed, dressed and shaved in the little bathroom he went down to the sitting room and sat in the red brocade chair to see what, if anything, would happen. "It's almost like waiting to have my fortune told!" he reflected to himself.

Nor was he disappointed, except that this time the Mice did not come out. It was daytime and they were all sleeping deeply under the eaves and in between the floors packed together and breathing as one.

Nonetheless, it could be that even in their sleep they took in a sense of warning in the Story that George was told, a warning about Enchantresses that he was totally to ignore sometime soon. Where women were concerned he had indeed ignored such warnings on at least three occasions, to head shaking from his Doom-Prophesying cousin Patricia in Canada.

With a slight jerky motion and noises of stops and starts the Cottage turned round again. The West Wind that had been chasing the clouds across the Uplands of the High Weald now stopped its sport. It cut through the garden, barely stirring the herbs so that the building could be turned to face the view to the West with the flower garden and the swing.

She blew suddenly onto George's cheek. Truth to tell he had almost fallen asleep again as he jumped and heard the West Wind say cheerfully – "Wake up, sleepy head! Here for you George Miller, is the Story of…"

THE PRINCE WHO WAS ALL HEART

ONCE UPON A TIME there was a Prince of a Kingdom, in a country known as 'The Nearer End of Somewhere', who was so kind that his people said of him, "He's all heart!"

Now this may be a very lovable and appealing thing in itself, but when he was due to inherit the Kingdom it did not prove to be so. If asked to judge between two people who were arguing, he sided with both and neither were satisfied. He would cry at every sad story a petitioner told him and give them money, so in no time the Kingdom was bankrupt.

Worst of all, when an evil Enchantress heard about this she lost no time in leaving her home in a country called 'The Further End of Nowhere' which was very bleak. Her intention was to take over this country of his, which the Prince was completely unable to prevent, being too full of heart to defend himself or his people in any way. Just before the Coronation that had been supposed to make him King she demanded he marry her and make her his Queen.

When he refused to do this, she raised her magic Wand and called on the powers of darkness. Suddenly, the Prince was nothing but a heart with two little eyes, ears and a mouth at the top and no limbs.

"They call you 'All heart,' young man," she cried, "and that is what you will be from now on! You must leave here at once!"

"Have mercy!" cried the Prince, "at least give me some legs to walk with!"

The Enchantress looked at the table and contemptuously threw him a pair of chicken legs leftover from supper.

They landed by him and attached themselves to the base of the heart. On these inadequate limbs the Prince limped off into exile to seek his fortune.

He had gone a long way and the legs were bending and breaking, so he stopped by a field to rest. There on the fence he saw a head with no body attached at all.

"Stop!" cried the head. It had rolling eyes, a wild expression and quantities of thick wiry hair, waving and curling round its head.

"I am a Philosopher!" said the Head, "Or rather, I was one once, till my dependence on my head alone, with no heart to guide me, allowed me to fall into the hands of an evil Enchantress, who did this to me!"

On discussing their problems they realised they had both fallen prey to the same fate. Then, as they lamented together and wondered how they could even get around – since the chicken legs were now bowed and splitting, unable to take even small steps – another strange creature came walking past.

It had the body of a fine strong man, legs, torso, arms. Everything except it had no head and an open hollowed out cavity where its heart should have been. There were just a mouth, ears and eyes in the top of the body.

"I heard what you said!" cried the man, "I too fell into the hands of that evil Enchantress. I was a very strong man, the strongest in the world and I relied on that to get everything I wanted, with no heart for other people and no brains to see danger. She made me like this and threw me out!"

Well, it did not take the Head long to work out that if they were prepared to cooperate the Body could carry both the others, and they could at least become mobile, feed themselves and perhaps search for a Solution to return them to their previous lives.

In fact his clever brain and memory knew what they must do. The evil Enchantress had taken out both her own heart and brain many millennia previously, substituting clockwork facsimiles and putting the real organs in a locked box buried in her old Kingdom, the Further End of Nowhere, with the intention of keeping them safe and herself therefore immortal. They must travel there, find the box, open it and she would die, automatically restoring them to their previous state.

This strange creature, not quite human, now appeared like a rather tall and extremely strange man, or alternatively a very small and misshapen giant. But the amalgamation worked in practical ways and they set out as fast as possible around the edge of a terrible and dangerous swamp which lay between the two lands, the Nearer end of Somewhere and the Further end of Nowhere, reputed to be guarded by a very Hungry Wolf.

Indeed this was proved right because they heard a woman's pitiful cry of "Help! Help me!" and, as they came to the very edge of the swamp they saw the woman herself, near the path, pinned to the ground and about to be eaten by the Very Hungry Wolf, who was licking his chops in anticipation of the feast. They could hardly see what she looked like but her golden hair streamed across the muddy ground and she appeared to be young.

"Help me!" she cried out again, "Oh please, whoever you are, help me, save me!"

The Strong man said, "I'm sorry. I am not strong enough against that Very Hungry Wolf. I cannot save you, for all my strength."

"We must pass on because we have a vital errand," cried out the head of the Philosopher. "The odds are extremely high that we would all be killed uselessly in trying to help you, and what would be the good of that? I'm sorry, we must leave you to your fate, I'm afraid!"

The Prince who was all heart could not bear that, but he could see no way that he could persuade the others, nor had he any freedom of movement himself, nor powers of persuasion like the Philosopher.

"Stop!" he shouted at the Wolf. "Look here at me! Am I not a much better and bigger meal than that girl? Leave her alone and I swear I will stand here and you can eat me!"

"You can't do that!" shouted the other two and the Body made to start running away. But the Heart slowed itself down so that the other two could not move, indeed it would have rather let them all die than refuse help to a sufferer in danger of death herself.

The very hungry Wolf let go of the girl and closed in on this larger and more toothsome meal. All would have been lost, but the girl, freed from his paws and unnoticed now, had sat up and was holding out a cedarwood box.

"Stop wolf!" called the woman, commandingly. The Wolf stopped, frozen at the sight. The Heart started to beat again but slowly, as the young woman said:

"In here is what you Three men have been looking for. If you had not turned from your way to save my life you would have failed in your quest for it is the brain and heart of the evil Enchantress.

"I am Soul and I am Eternal. I was there when the Enchantress worked the magic that made her invincible and ageless. I heard her cry out the spells that took her heart and brain out of her body to keep them safe in a silk handkerchief in a box of sandalwood, inlaid with gold and bound with three bars of steel.

"She bound the Smith who made the box in the fire in his own smithy, but I released him secretly when she had gone.

"She buried the box in a secret place, guarded by a viper, a scorpion and a weasel, in the Further End of Nowhere, many millennia ago.

"Alas! She saw me watching her and until three days ago I was bound with spells, tied in a silken rope and laid under the earth for many millennia, until the time should be right.

"When you three came together and decided to seek out the box and destroy the power of the evil Enchantress I woke up and was freed from the magic. I knew the time had come.

"I sat and sang three songs until the viper, the scorpion and the weasel – the powers of cruelty, greed and deception – were lulled asleep. I carried the box to the smithy and the Smith said, for gratitude and love of me, he would break them for me. The steel bands burst and the box rose up into my hands.

"I brought it with me and here it is. I repeat again – if you had not agreed with me to turn away from your quest and save my life, because of your Kindness of Heart, you would not have found it.

"Of all things in the world to counter the powers of evil, the best are Loving-kindness, Wisdom and Steadfast-strength."

She brought out of the box something wrapped in a pure white silk handkerchief and unwrapping it, held up a ruby heart, in pristine condition and a similar silver brain, scarcely used. The heart was glowing red and warm, beating and alive, while the brain quivered gently giving off a soft luminescence.

This action was received as a signal by the evil Enchantress from her new kingdom in the

Nearer end of Somewhere and a terrible, but distant, cry started. It was the Enchantress herself and it grew louder as she swept across the skies to protect her own and destroy her enemies for ever...

As the young woman called Soul held out the heart and brain for them to see, the Very Hungry Wolf, who had remained almost forgotten in the shadows, leapt over the box. Snap! Catching the heart and brain of the Enchantress in his powerful jaws, he swallowed both in an instant and vanished back into the dark, not quite so hungry.

From high above came an awful, wailing keening sound as the Enchantress fell dead from the skies, to be swallowed up in the Bottomless Swamp.

At the passing of this evil woman, a strange change came over the Creature made up from the three young men. They began to merge truly into one. Each now seemed to offer a part that was missing or rudimentary in the others.

The strong man's body accepted with humility that strength was not enough on its own. The Philosopher accepted with humility that all his rational reasoning would have been worse than useless without the wisdom that comes from a loving heart.

The Prince's heart swelled and beat firmer in pride at its ability to fuel the whole; the brain worked out many numbers to thousands of decimal places and wrote the plays of Shakespeare in five minutes just to show it could, and the strong man danced and pirouetted till the very air seemed to dance around them. They all laughed aloud for joy at this success in their quest.

The change of the three into one person was very moving to see. At that moment of release from the spell that had bound all of them, each spontaneously sacrificed a measure of individuality and independence to form a coalition, a Trinity, that would benefit each other, all in cooperation rather than conflict.

Soul looked on with great pleasure and delight. "Now you understand!" she cried. "Each of you on your own is crippled, incomplete, sad and lonely. United in one, even with the sacrifice you had to make, you have all power and potential.

"Each of you wished it all, selfishly for yourself," she cried out - "Yes, even you, Prince! You wanted to be the most generous, the most loving, the best, but that was still Pride."

"I acknowledge that," the new Man said, hanging his head and allowing the last trace of separation to melt away, as did the other two, all freely acknowledging their unity and oneness. A blue light swept through them all and they became truly one new person and yet each one was perfected in that unity.

What had seemed to be a somewhat small Giant, now showed himself to be a rather tall man, of perfect proportion and great beauty, sweetness and courage.

The final insight was given to him, as he turned to look at the woman who had named herself 'Soul'. She smiled at him, holding out her hands and he fully realised how incredibly beautiful she was.

"I recognise you now!" he cried. "You are the final part of me, which must always be integral yet always separate. You are my Soul and I will never be whole till I have succeeded in persuading you to be my Bride. Please, please, my dearest soul – marry me so we may become truly one!"

"You have understood my name and so know who I truly am!" said the woman, blushing rosily at what he was saying. "Yes, I am Soul and I am yours for the asking." As she leaned up and kissed him it was obvious that she would not take long in the persuading. In his response it was also obvious he would in no way delay either.

So they were married and together ruled the country at the Nearer End of Somewhere well and fairly, because to do that requires a partnership of Body, Mind and Heart, infused with Soul.

However, you must never forget that the Nearer End of Somewhere is a measurable distance from the Further End of Nowhere and between them is a bottomless swamp, in the process of detoxification, but always needing more Love and patrolled by a Very Hungry Wolf.

POSTLUDE
♪

THE WEST WIND fell silent. The Cottage had turned back and George was ready for breakfast. He could hear faint stirrings and chirpings from under the floorboards and called a greeting to the Mice as he left.

George strolled down Flitterbrook Lane to Wheelwrights cottage, where he judged it be about breakfast time – correctly. He was beginning to feel almost at home as Helena saw him from the kitchen.

"Good morning, George," she called out cheerfully, welcoming him in, and pressing a cup of tea into his hand. "How did you sleep?"

George answered a little non-committaly, feeling somewhat shy of admitting that strange and almost mad things had happened in broad daylight. Helena sensitively let the matter rest, though she was sorry afterwards and hoped to hear later if he had been given a Story.

They kissed very warmly and then she sat him down by the fire.

"Would you like a full cooked breakfast?" she asked and George replied, "That is just so tempting! I absolutely love a full English. I know how well you cook now too, but I think I'd better be good and just have part of it this time."

"Let's both have scrambled eggs on toast then," said Helena, much cheered by the hint that this wouldn't be the only occasion they might eat together.

Helena's scrambled eggs were quite intriguing, as she put in tasty chopped marigold petals from the late blooming flowers in her garden, with a trail of them in a pattern on the plate.

"A lot of our flowers are good in food," she said, "so long as you choose carefully and avoid things like deadly nightshade of course. Though one of Aunty Mabel's friends swears that's good for pain in small doses, especially toothache!"

"Well," said George, "I suppose if you get the dose wrong you've got a permanent cure for your bad teeth. Sometimes when it's bad enough I guess one wouldn't care!"

Later on they drove down to Hastings for a quick visit. Helena drove, as George would be leaving at teatime to drive to Tunbridge Wells and visit the School, before returning to the North again.

They had a lot of fun. George insisted solemnly on trying out the Penny Arcade and wearing a Kiss Me Quick hat. They bought beef-burgers on the pier, in what George described as 'a light Sussex breeze' and Helena 'a howling gale'.

She held tightly onto his arm as they made their way back out of the wind to a secluded seat to eat their lunch. Helena laughed and screwed up her nose after she accidentally squirted tomato ketchup onto her face.

George, wiping it off expertly with his hankie, smiled down into her hazel eyes, admiring again how deliciously they crinkled when she laughed. She didn't seem to care at all about her dignity or her hair being blown around and tousled by the wind. George felt an almost irresistible wish to tousle it some more, but the wind changed and his Kiss Me hat blew off, pursued by Helena; and so the moment passed.

All the same, when they got back to Punnetts Town and had a very quick cup of tea before his departure, they seemed both to be happy and to feel that they had the sort of good understanding that doesn't need putting into words.

"There's a Haydn Concert coming up soon in Tunbridge Wells," said Helena.

"We could go to that together," replied George, enthusiastically, then added, "It'll be advertised I expect. Could you find out when it is? Then I can ring up to get the tickets, if it's a convenient date. Count it as a 'thank you' for the lovely evening we've just had."

Helena assented with pleasure. "I'll give you a ring," she said as he got into the car, after a brief hug and a kiss.

She stood outside watching him drive off, waving till he rounded the corner, as he too saw her in his mirror and tooted his horn as he turned.

CHAPTER TWELVE

GOODY OWL AND GOODY ELIXIR

PRELUDE
♪

CYCLAMEN LODGE, in the grounds of the old Hellingly Mental Hospital, was really a very nice and comfortable place to live, about as far from a traditional Dementia ward as you could get. It was therefore not the fault of the Sussex Health Authority that some of the long-stay patients there had a tendency to wander off when they could. Most were locals, country born and bred and like Aunty Mabel, being very used to walking long distances, living independently and having firm opinions as to what was good for them.

Since this might include old Country remedies such as Henbane, also known as Devil's eye, or stinking Roger, for toothache, and the use of cobwebs to staunch cuts, it is not surprising that some of them were quite a handful for the (as always) inadequate number of staff who could be employed.

Many of those who did work there tended to be local too; they stayed and trained extensively and often became very fond of their charges and inclined to go the extra mile for them.

One such was Joe Price. He came from a loving and rather chaotic family, originally based in Heathfield. His Nan and uncle and an aunty had all been nurses at Hellingly. His own mum and dad, however, had taken a different path, owning a small electrical hardware shop, but had recently sold up and retired to Hastings. Not a long distance in miles, perhaps, but a big upheaval for a local lad who had lived at home with them until now and tended towards shyness.

He did not however lack an ambition to better himself and to learn. Not feeling academic enough initially to aim for College, he was living in the Nursing Residency, though at nearly 30 he was a little older and steadier than most of the student nurses in training at the hospital.

According to his Nan, Joe had a heart of gold. He had been close to her, as both his parents had been very hard working and she virtually brought him up. Joe had found it very hard when she had passed away rather suddenly, three years previously, just before his birthday.

Maybe that was why he quickly took a shine to Aunty Mabel, but again, that's too simple. He was equally good with all the charges in his job, covering a number of more conventional wards as well as Cyclamen Lodge in his varied shifts.

One big burly chap, Arthur Brassington, was a particular cause for concern, just by reason of his size. He was normally a polite and well contained old man, but his severe form of dementia led to sudden episodes of paranoia in which he could be aggressive. Even in these he showed a lot of good – if inconvenient – feelings, as he was convinced that the war was still on and that the Germans were attacking Sussex from the sea.

Luckily, even in these extreme bouts he had an innate chivalry for women, so the combination of Joe, whose wiry strength and skills belied his slender physique, together with a couple of female nurses could usually be relied on to manage him remarkably well and patiently, without having to resort too often to doctors and prescriptions.

He also tended to have auditory hallucinations in which he could hear the air raid sirens at inconvenient times. This early afternoon the lunch had barely been cleared away when he insisted that the siren was sounding and that all must take cover, personally trying to usher everyone within sight behind sofas and under armchairs.

If not properly supervised some of the other patients were inclined to obey George, so impressively did he present himself. Dolores Entwhistle, a good friend Mabel Dunnet had made in the weeks since she had been admitted, would have obediently climbed under the nearest safe piece of furniture in spite of arthritic limbs, but luckily the staff were there to prevent such things. Aunty Mabel also scorned such defeatist behaviour.

"Nonsense, Arthur!" she said calmly, staying put with her treasured cup of coffee. "Don't let the side down! Must defeat the Nazis you know, not give them the satisfaction of hiding."

She herself was aware of his delusions and thought of him as a nice but dotty old fool.

However, Dolores and some of the other Oldies had been brought up on this kind of fighting talk, so they saw nothing unlikely in the idea that Hitler was actually in the room, observing them through a potted plant and must be Defied.

Arthur, who claimed he had been a Colonel in the War and Knew Things that were still Top Secret (though unfortunately he could not remember them) was immediately recalled to himself and stood up.

"That's right, dear Lady," he roared. "That's the spirit. Carry on!"

Joe, keeping a careful eye on the scene at the beginning of his shift, was well aware of Arthur's secret – he had not been a Colonel or anything like it in the army, but a very lowly rank indeed, about ten steps further down the ladder.

Shh! We shall leave him his secrets for now, though they may be revealed later! Everyone has secrets and who can say that his job in the Royal Sussex Loamshire Regiment was not just as essential, if not more so than that of a Commissioned Officer?

He certainly looked the part, with a large bristling moustache and a weather-beaten plummy complexion. Joe was happy to address him respectfully as Colonel Brassington – which had a nice ring to it and raised the tone of the Lodge.

The staff were kind and conscientious – for the most part – but life there among their charges was lively and unpredictable. Even in quite advanced dementia a sort of sense of solidarity sometimes made for friendships. Aunty Mabel, as everyone seemed to call her, was in quite an early stage and made friends easily, so she, Dolores and the Colonel, formed a somewhat unlikely trio.

'Colonel' Brassington had been a widower for a good many years and his only son was abroad, so he had virtually no visitors and had become far less lonely since Aunty Mabel had been admitted, particularly as Helena kept her promise and visited quite often, as did Carol who came South from Derby when she could.

Dolores Entwhistle, a Sussex girl born and bred, combined sweetness of character with a vulnerable diffidence which made her defer to both Aunty Mabel as a mentor and have a deep respect for Arthur who reminded her of her father, lost at sea many years ago and still venerated by the family.

Joe, who had sat through many 'Memory Sessions' with all the patients, was inclined to think, from the family albums and other memorabilia, that Dolores' father Terrence Entwhistle, might have been an alcoholic and a bully and they had been better off without him, but of course he kept these thoughts to himself.

This afternoon it was imperative that they kept the Colonel onside, as it were. The Powers that Be had decided to arrange for the little group of Mabel, Dolores and Arthur to be taken by staff on a visit to Turnaround Cottage, if staffing levels allowed.

This was in the hopes that a properly arranged and permitted trip would prevent the determined attempts by Aunty Mabel to get there, on her own and with her friends, that had been happening almost weekly. Though she was much happier than when she first came in, it had to be admitted that Aunty Mabel could be a bit of a handful.

They were supposed to have three responsible adults for an outing with three patients. Joe was in charge, and Rosie Cullen had also been co-opted – in her role as Police Liaison Officer rather than Vets assistant. Rosie was a relative newcomer to this area, rather shy, self-consciously plain, but with a strong moral compass and a – hidden – sense of fun and the ridiculous, which had instantly created a bond with Helena.

Rosie had taken on her community role very recently. She had already met Aunty Mabel and Carol and was enjoying her first taste of army life with the Colonel and Dolores. She had been looking forward to the outing and hoping to get to know Joe, whose dark good looks and easy manners she already secretly admired from ward meetings.

Norah Doveport was Rosie's distant cousin and the nearest neighbour to Turnaround Cottage on Flitterbrook Lane. Rosie knew Helena slightly through this link, and had given that useful advice on the cheese-sick mice a few weeks earlier.

It happened that Carol was down in Sussex that week, on one of her treasured visits so she of course came along too. Knowing also that Helena would be waiting to let them into Turnaround Cottage, the decision was taken to let the trip go ahead.

Helena had taken the precaution of asking for permission from the mysterious owners of the cottage. A note sent via the solicitor elicited the reply, presented verbally, that she was very welcome to take visitors there at any time, at her own discretion regarding security; nor did she need explicit permission each time.

"I did hear," Joe was saying, "that one year – it would be, oh all of ten years ago – when this old Mill had been derelict for years, that it was done up by a local shopkeeper who hoped to let it all year round, but it never really 'took'."

"Was that the same as the present owner?" asked Rosie who knew less than the others about local life, though she was learning fast.

"No," Joe replied, "No one knows who then took it over; that was quite recent, just before Mrs Brown came to the Wheelwright's cottage, down Flitterbottom. That earlier year I'm talking about, nine or even ten ago, it hadn't really been let hardly at all. The owner was pleased when it was rented for the whole winter season by a pair of witches."

Rosie laughed and he added defensively, "That was what they all said round here. They installed a great big cauldron in a corner of the sitting room. Got permission and all. Calor Gas. Of course they removed it after six months when they moved on, but there's still folks won't sit in that corner or in the red chair. Says it gives them the willies!"

Rosie Cullen smiled at him, not sure whether to believe his story, but very much liking his accent and manner. He caught her eye and burst out laughing too.

They all went off together, Joe driving the ten-seater hospital Hyundai van. They arrived in good spirits and were welcomed at the door by a beaming Helena, who greeted them all warmly, like the good hostess she was.

She had told the Mice firmly, to stay out of sight on pain of no stories for a week. It was a fine day and both staff and the Oldies enjoyed walking in the garden. Everyone was on their best behaviour and – mercifully – the Colonel seemed to be taking time off from his demanding task of Keeping Hitler Away.

Helena had prepared a fine tea, with scones from the village bakery. Norah had donated a special jar of her homemade strawberry jam and cream from the dairy. They were sitting around, almost filling the little sitting room, while a strengthening breeze began to stir the curtains.

Afterwards, each person's recollections varied and it was long, long after that anyone spoke of it or checked out what happened.

Although he was well aware of his responsibilities, Joe believed he must have nodded off and dreamt. Helena knew much more, but held her tongue and kept a careful check that their three charges were sitting still and safely enjoying the story.

Because, of course, a story there was! You just try stopping Turnaround Cottage when it wants to tell you a story and now listen to the East Wind as they sit looking out of the window at the usual view of the copse and the little River Flitter.

GOODY OWL AND GOODY ELIXIR

ONCE UPON A TIME there were two very good friends, old ladies called Owl and Elixir. They had worked for many years at making magic, of the white variety – mostly – and preparing healing concoctions. Generally speaking, they were regarded as Wise Women, though it must be said that a few people were more inclined to think of them as interfering, naughty, and an infernal nuisance.

Although they lived at opposite ends of the country, they visited each other regularly, and communicated by mysterious means through the aether. They had been retired for some years at the start of this story, and what a retired Wise Woman does is a bit of a mystery. Perhaps they never really retire, and their sense of humour tends to get a bit blacker with much use.

One day they were both relaxing together in Turnaround Cottage, which Goody Elixir had secured at a bargain price for the winter season. (She was given permission to install her cauldron, which of course added usefully to the central heating.) Goody Owl had flown down to visit her friend, in her owl form, and as usual they had spent the time eating (a lot), drinking (in moderation), laughing (immoderately), and Goody Owl had been telling her friend stories, something they both enjoyed enormously.

Goody Elixir's cauldron was capacious, always on the go, into which all the stories, laughter, and even sometimes the emotions, around in the cottage tended to drop, and be absorbed into the liquid. It had started out as soup, but so many colourful words and ideas had dropped in that it was constantly changing, as jugs of it were siphoned off and strange liquids added. For a long time now it had only been used as a source of dye for all the threads and fabric in which Goody Elixir delighted. No two things ever came out of the pot the same colour or shade. Long after it had been dismissed as unfit for human – or even Wise Women – consumption as soup, it was still on the go.

Unfortunately, there were occasions when Goody Elixir forgot it was meant to be a dye-pot, and absentmindedly ladled some of it into the teacups or added it to the stew, so eating in the cottage could be a slightly unnerving experience; odd things tended to happen.

On this occasion, it was time for Goody Owl to go home, and Goody Elixir, stirring her cauldron, said, "Oh wait a moment! You have told me so many wonderful stories, that I must give you a present to take home. Flying is cold this time of year."

She dropped a bundle of mixed threads into the cauldron and waved a hand over it, adding a few mysterious words. Goody Owl thought they sounded like "Oh Bloody Hell, the boiler's on the blink again, and the mixture's gone cool!" but that doesn't sound like a spell, so perhaps she was mistaken.

WHOOSH! Out of the mixture exploded a large, squawking bundle of bright feathers. It was a magnificent hen straight out of one of the best stories. She was covered with black and gold feathers, and had a crest and wings of copper-colour. Her claws were purple, and diamond-sharp. She flew round the room like a tornado looking – it can be presumed – for a particular grain of corn, with her wicked, bright eyes.

ZIP! She swept over their heads, raking their hair with her claws so that they had to duck. Zap! Over went the tea things; a china teacup and a small silver cream jug toppled into the cauldron (where they later created a great deal of trouble, but that's another story altogether).

Goody Owl grabbed the hen as it swept past on another dangerous reconnaissance mission over the table, and the two of them waved their hands and muttered further imprecations, to which it is better we do not try to listen.

The hen turned into a beautiful scarf, curly and soft. It was in shades of deep red and copper, and had a purple frill along the edge. Goody Owl wrapped it three times round her neck against the cold, and the two women exchanged affectionate farewells before she flew off into the night.

That is all to the story really. The scarf kept Goody Owl warm and well, and was much admired by her friends.

Just occasionally, when Goody Owl was dealing with a particularly tiresome Jobsworth of a local councillor, or someone being deliberately obstructive about her projects, the scarf would slither from her neck. It would shoot across the floor; there would be a flash of purple claw, an anguished "OW!" from the person who was being difficult, who would then find a nasty deep scratch on some tender portion of their anatomy. In no time the scarf would be back round Goody Owl's neck, looking entirely innocent, as indeed, so would be her own expression.

No-one ever complained – what on earth would people say if they did?

So, just remember to be a bit careful when obstructing the wishes of wise old ladies. They can sometimes have short tempers and an unfortunate propensity to make strange things happen. Entirely against their own wishes of course – it goes without saying that they themselves are entirely benign.

POSTLUDE

♪

THE GROUP was uncharacteristically silent and, as often happened at the Cottage, Helena took over in an unobtrusive way,

"Well!" she said, brightly, "I almost nodded off then. What a nice restful afternoon. Cup of tea or coffee, anyone?"

People hastily agreed and chose, while Helena vanished into the kitchen and Rosie collected up the orders. Helena had skilfully given a lead to those who might not want others to think them crazy, while hanging on to the enjoyment this little story had given them.

Our three friends, Mabel, Dolores and Colonel Arthur (as the ladies had taken to calling him, in a nice mixture of friendliness and formality) were talking about the story openly but in their own little group. Rosie had joined Helena in the kitchen, Joe had gone to find the loo and Carol, with an enigmatic smile on her lips, was keeping her own counsel.

She and Helena had confided a lot in each other recently. Strange stories about the Mice and the Visitors who underwent amazing experiences overnight, for the two women to speculate about. Having been at boarding school together was a great bond, for nothing seemed too strange or too intimate to find some form of expression. And of course a good deal about a certain attractive Professor had been discussed between them in considerable depth.

Helena had been complaining of toothache, but she gently waved aside Dolores' suggestion of Henbane tea from her extensive lore, passed down from her grandmother, who had been a Wise Woman in Rye. Dolores looked pained. "It's perfectly safe!" she said, "and it's only used in extreme cases and with great care. But it's marvellous when nothing else works!"

Helena smiled her crooked pixie smile and thanked Dolores warmly, before moving into the kitchen to join Rosie. She took a tea towel to help with the washing up.

"I'm not taking henbane!" she said quietly to Rosie as they washed up the teacups. "It's deadly nightshade, isn't it?" As they were out of sight and hearing of the sitting room, Rosie could say out of the corner of her mouth with a wicked twinkle, "Instead of one of Dolores' grandmother's remedies, how about I take the tooth out for you with the instrument I use to castrate the piglets?" The two women subsided into giggles, carefully hidden over the washing up bowl so no one's feelings would be hurt.

There was, however, one other very strange thing, which rather endorsed the idea the locals had sensed – that Turnaround Cottage was – "You know? There's something a bit, 'other' about the particular corner of the sitting room where the cauldron stood."

Joe now returned to that corner and to the red brocade chair. A pretty china teacup and a small silver cream jug seemed to have appeared, as if by magic, right in the centre, though Joe swore he couldn't have been sitting on them without noticing.

As Helena could be certain the objects did not appear in the inventory in her care, she felt that they should go back to Cyclamen Lodge for safekeeping. No one seemed likely to claim these objects. Even the cream jug was only silver-plated and of relatively low value.

Ever conscientious, Helena enclosed a little report to be passed on by the lawyer, but silence continued about the found objects and the solicitor said that though technically they should be handed in to the police station for six months, he saw no reason to do this, in view of the low value and a note being kept by himself.

Aunty Mabel's friend Dolores had taken an extraordinary liking to the teacup and had already insisted on taking it back to Cyclamen Lodge, where this normally very passive, almost overly obedient old lady had become a fiery defender of her right to keep it at all times. Woe betide a Carer who accidentally let someone else use it from the communal kitchen, or handled it, in her view, carelessly.

Helena gave the jug to Rosie, with a little laugh, saying it was about time she thought about stocking up her bottom drawer. Helena had meant it as a joke, not even sure that a modern young woman like Rosie would 'get' such an old fashioned concept. To her intrigued surprise Rosie blushed a becoming shade of pink, her plain features becoming quite pretty for a moment.

All the participants agreed that the outing had been a tremendous success, and the

Authorities on receiving Joe's glowing report agreed it could certainly be repeated some time. Everyone slept very well the following night and apparently Hitler, defeated in an exercise worthy of true Historical Glory, according to Colonel Arthur, retreated back over the Channel for several weeks. A relief to all parties.

CHAPTER THIRTEEN

THE STRAY

PRELUDE
♪

IT **WAS** a pleasantly warm afternoon and Carol had come down to Sussex to see her Aunty Mabel and take her out for the day from Cyclamen Lodge. As it happened, her friend Helena was not available, though they intended to meet up later.

Not surprisingly, after a trip to the seaside at Brighton, a wander down the Lanes and a number of small purchases as presents, both Aunt and Niece were glad to look out for a cream tea on the way home. Carol was feeling her years too a bit since retiring from her job as occupational therapist in Derbyshire, though she still kept her hand in with some community work.

The presents were for their numerous joint nieces, nephews and great nieces and great nephews, whose birthdays demanded a certain amount of ingenuity. There was always cash of course, but Aunty Mabel was 'old school' and wanted to give them appropriate gifts, while her failing memory made it rather a difficult task.

Having dissuaded her from getting the twins, Anthony and Belinda, a toy Noah's ark with all the animals, jointly – after all, they were rising 30 now and working in separate towns – Carol took the road to Punnetts Town to go past Turnaround Cottage, since Aunty Mabel always felt happy and at ease there, and usually her memory improved a little as a result.

They seemed out of luck when they parked and walked a few paces up the hill. The cottage was evidently taken, with some washing on the line, but as they prepared to return to the car a plump woman with a brightly smiling, lined face, brown hair in a bun and wearing a dirndl skirt and apron came out of the kitchen into the garden and greeted them in friendly fashion.

"Gut afternoon!" she said with a strong German accent. "How are you? I am so pleased to be seeing this very nice so-English village! Can you giff me a historical lesson please?"

Carol, always friendly, was of course also at ease with people in general because of her work.

"What can we tell you?" she replied in stumbling German, which was a mistake, as it unleashed a flood of words that neither Carol nor Mabel could understand, but gathered was an invitation to share English tea with her.

However Elsa (as she was called) could speak good English and was very glad to return to talking it and to making her new friends welcome. In truth, Carol wondered if she was perhaps a little lonely in a strange land.

So it proved in fact. The tea materialised in a short time and – lo and behold – it was full of lovely warm scones, made miraculously in the tiny cottage oven, plus plenty of local cream and jam – as recognised by Carol who was becoming quite a connoisseur of the different delicacies, sold through the WI and the indefatigable Norah Doveport.

Elsa introduced herself more fully as Elsa Zeibig from Austria, in fact from the Tyrol, hence the homemade dirndl skirt. She proudly showed them other pieces of her traditional outfit, which included a necklace, also made by herself, of beads from a deer's antlers, exquisitely carved and her own smocking design on her bodice. She was a little older than Carol they found, a retired farm worker and a great enthusiast for all sorts of crafts, being also heavily involved in puppet making and Storytelling. She and Carol had a lot in common and chatted away while tucking into a very good tea.

Carol told her something of the history of the cottage as Turnaround Mill and Aunty Mabel's part in it, while the old lady smiled beatifically, completely absorbed in the joy of scone, butter, jam and cream – all essential and in that order and never let anyone tell you different!

Easter was late this year and Elsa was over in Sussex for the holiday break and a Craft Exhibition in Brighton, with a strong Viennese theme. She had seen a little advertisement for Turnaround Cottage in an international craft journal and was intrigued by the sound of the cottage. It was also attractive because of the reasonable price, even though it had meant taking buses in and out of Brighton. She had spent a few uneventful days and was due to leave the following day.

Aunty Mabel was having one of her lucid intervals and – in a potentially embarrassing moment – said to Elsa:

"You will be told a story here, you know? You're always told a story by the Winds and the Cottage, specially chosen for your life!"

It might have passed off quietly except that Carol coloured a little and Elsa was immediately intrigued, questioning, "Stories? I love stories. What sort of stories, and how do you mean, the wind tells it? What puppets do you use – are these hand puppets or marionettes, or perhaps rod puppets?"

Before Carol could answer there was a strong breath of air that blew the sitting room curtains into a full bell shape with a delighted voice saying:

"Oh Elsa, you have asked the Question and it means we must give you an answer. Bless you, bless you a thousand times for letting us speak and tell you a story specially for you, though it is an English story and therefore in a strange tongue!"

Elsa looked surprisingly unsurprised, as though she was used to strange events surrounding stories, which indeed she was, as anyone who uses puppets will tell you. They are strange and uncanny creatures to mix with – and that's just the puppeteers!

Carol, relieved at the turn of events, but somewhat shell-shocked at being told a story alongside a stranger in broad daylight, nonetheless settled Aunty Mabel into the comfortable red brocade chair, mutely indicated to Elsa where to sit and sat down herself, somewhat on the edge of her chair, as the Cottage turned to show the Northern outlook and the back gate where Tin Kettle Lane led up to the Sussex Weald.

The North Wind, for it was he, announced:

"Elsa, beloved stranger from over water and land. Hear a story that shows we are not puppets, nor subject to fate but make our own story by diligence and kindness, as you have always done, dear child. And so have you, Carol and Mabel, equally beloved by all, yet sometimes overlooked in your value to the world.

"Hear now the Story of…"

THE STRAY

MADELEINE had just come to live in a pretty cottage at the side of a winding road near the village of Warbleton. On this fine morning she had come out to check on the weather, having planned a happy day gardening, to celebrate her recent retirement.

To be honest, she knew little of how to go about this and it seemed it might be rather a lonely occupation. She had not been living in the village long and had come from a high rise flat in a busy London suburb, without a garden. In fact she had never had a garden, her childhood having been spent with a father whose civil service job took them round the world, constantly moving on. A great and exciting life, but also, in its own way, lonely for an only child.

It seemed that it took time to get to know the neighbours here in Sussex, when they might be nearly half a mile up the road, so rather than asking the locals she had visited a busy Garden Centre near Heathfield.

"I need a few things to look after my new garden," she had said, naively, to the gnarled old-timer serving her, so he had taken full advantage of the opportunity to supply her with lots of tools and a couple of brightly illustrated – and expensive – books. Not for the first time she went home thinking wistfully how much happier her life might have been if she had not been widowed early and never found another life companion.

She thought fleetingly of her much loved Stewart, a warm and humorous Scot who had seen something irresistible in the shy pretty young secretary to his firm and married her. Ten short but blissful years together, somehow no children, before a fast growing brain tumour had invaded their dream. Within a few short, desperate months he had been taken from her, holding her hand to the last.

The years since then seemed almost a blur as, somehow, on this bright morning she found herself going back in time as if it was all recent, remembering it all in a way she had not done for years.

"Oh, I wish, I wish, I wish!" she found herself saying aloud, not even knowing what she wished for, other than company. Unexpected tears suddenly squeezed out under her eyelids. It was just the move, the being tired and the loneliness without the job. She had lost the daily companionship of the 'girls' in the typing pool – most of them over fifty! And promises of visiting were not the same.

This morning the birds seemed to be singing particularly loudly, so different from the growling, clashing, whirring traffic of South London, and she took a moment of quietness to listen fully to the song, a celebration of morning.

Madeleine loved birds. In her small high up flat they were quite often blown onto the window box on the sill, bedraggled and exhausted, something to do with air currents around this particular corner. Tiny London Sparrows, normally cheeky as barrow boys, but beaten down and exhausted till they were more like the homeless tramps on the street corners.

Madeleine had rescued countless such little Passers-by of the Air as she called them, bringing them inside just long enough for them to dry off, re-groom themselves or be gently stroked dry, fed and released again quickly, to fly off with a flirt of the tail and a sweep of the wings. She loved the small contact with their fluffy little bodies, the same shape and feel as her old fashioned powder puffs. She loved the swooping feel of a breath of wind from their wings as they rejected her, flying off energetic and restored. They were her children going off into the huge world she had once known.

She even liked their independence and lack of gratitude! They were unaware of her as an agent of rescue. She thought sometimes that she herself must seem to them a frightening ogre that they had inexplicably defeated, so maybe they flew off believing themselves to be great Heroes who had Fought Against the Odds and Survived! The idea made her laugh and feel like an unknown angel, a good role.

Occasionally she felt more like a darker angel when she had to bury the few who didn't make it. She had to go down the five floors, by the stairs if the lifts were out of action, to a tiny, dry little patch of earth, cat-pissed grass and weeds, known ironically as 'the garden.'

This morning she was reflecting that it might have been better to wait and see what other local gardeners could tell her about suitable tools and flowers before buying any manuals, but all thoughts of this vanished, as she saw a large unkempt shape lying on the path near the kitchen door.

It was a very big dog, frantic with fear, unable to move any further, tongue protruding sideways from slack, dribbling jaws. It seemed almost dead, with ribs sticking out under the thick, matted and bedraggled fur. It seemed to be an old English sheepdog with mixed white fur, coloured with salt and pepper patches.

Horrified, Madeleine rushed over to him, speaking soothingly and being careful not to touch him till he was ready, as if he were one of her little birds. Indeed, incongruous as it might seem with 80 plus pounds of dog, that was the exact feeling she had for him.

The dog showed no signs of fear or animosity though. He wagged what seemed left of his tail and attempted, pathetically to rise, but flopped back, froth oozing from his mouth.

For fully fifteen minutes Madeleine concentrated on talking to him quietly, stroking parts that did not respond with pain and withdrawal and reassuring him with all her being. Then, keeping a wary eye that he did not try and stand she told him she was going to get him food and water and ran into her kitchen, just by the path. She was back in less than a minute and it seemed he had understood, as he was resting, turning his head towards her trustingly.

She gave him warm water, initially dripping it into his mouth from a wrung out piece of cloth, then he was strong enough to raise his head and lap clumsily from a bowl, spilling most of it.

His fur was matted and there were sore areas. She had brought out a bland cream and the kitchen scissors, so she was able to cut away great knots and clumps of fur. Then she very gently anointed the bad areas. It hurt him, as evidenced by a few whimpers and inadvertent withdrawal, but he never growled or showed his teeth. It was as if he, unlike the birds, saw her as his angel from the start and trusted her willingly, gratefully.

After a long time of this she got a chair for herself and a cushion to ease his head and started him on some meat broth, hastily made from some of the mince that should have been her supper.

Most of the day seemed to pass in this way. The dog grew stronger by the hour, standing and shaking himself, timorously at first, then getting livelier and more bold. He still kept close to her hand though, howled when she tried to go anywhere, and looked up at her with his adoring brown eyes.

He would not consent to go into the house, even with her. Later on, towards evening, he was strong enough to come for a very short walk. Just down to the road, at the sharp bend and onto the safe little crescent of green grass leading to the stream, well away from any traffic.

No one could have anticipated therefore the tragic coincidence of events. Just as they reached the middle of the grassy area a revving of an engine split the peace like a chainsaw of noise. A car, accelerating carelessly, too much, too close, skidding as its wheels left the road, right across the grass and the car was upon them.

Madeline had no time even to scream before this powerful metal monster reared out of the dark. The dog, roused to almost superhuman strength, knocked her out of the car's path, so that she fell, unhurt, into the soft mud and rushes by the brook.

Alas, not so for the dog. It took the full force of the car's drunken trajectory. The driver, who could not be identified through the windscreen, swerved again even more violently, his wheels re-attaching to the earth, then he was back on the road with a screaming of rubber, hurtling out of sight. Madeline had no chance to take his number or even identify the car's make.

She staggered to her feet and found the dog, so recently and briefly in her care and knew at a glance she had failed to save him. As she sank down away from the road, pulling him into her arms, sobbing uncontrollably, it came to her that it was the other way round. He had completely and selflessly saved *her* life.

There was a pool of blood at her feet. The dog's fur and her hands, her face and her clothing were all soaked in his blood. She cared nothing about that, but sat for a long while with her arms firmly around the soft warm body, sobbing in horror and wretchedness.

Eventually, Madeline stopped crying. She had been resting her hand on the dog's bedraggled fur but now her fingers closed on nothing. The body was gone!

She looked at her hands. No blood! She felt her face, looked at the ground. No speck of blood, no fur. Nothing on her skirt other than a few smears of mud.

She searched the crescent of green grass, the copse by the brook, the verges. Nothing! The dog's warm but lifeless body had most certainly completely vanished, leaving no trace.

Dazed, she walked back into her cottage. By the fireplace a strange man was standing. Over 6 foot and sturdily built he had a mop of untidy white hair and a dazed expression. "Who are you?" Madeline asked, too miserable to be alarmed.

"I don't... I d... d.... don't know!" he stammered. "I'm so sorry. I just got lost... lost my memory. Who am I?"

They sat and talked. Madeline tried to relax for a while, exhausted and he seemed to understand. He even tried to make her some tea, so she then roused herself and made it for both of them. He found a packet of biscuits by the tea caddy and insisted she needed them.

Madeline rested again, soothed beyond measure by this little kindness and they talked for a while more, about nothing in particular, really.

He was worried because his memory had still gone. It seemed his head hurt too and appeared to be bruised, so Madeline bound it up with some ointment and gave him a painkiller. She said they should both take it easy for a while and there was no hurry, but they could perhaps later on take him to the police station, to check if he was missed from anywhere.

He was gentle and sweet, and still concerned to be no trouble. Eventually, he fell deeply asleep on the sofa and she covered him with a rug and dozed for the rest of the night in her armchair beside him, her heart eased.

Next morning she fed him and they talked some more. She found him some suitable temporary clothing, jogging trouser bottoms and a loose shirt, with an old jacket and as she helped him dress, looking into his brown eyes, a warm feeling came into both their hearts and they kissed. They never did get round to going to the Police Station, just stayed happily together and no one ever came looking for him.

He didn't get his memory back either, so she named him David. They often wandered down the village to the Black Duck, hand in hand for a pint and made a lot of friends. Eventually they went away on holiday and said they had got married. True or not, they remained happy living in the present, and his lack of memory of any past was more of a blessing than a hindrance.

He had a few odd habits – don't all husbands? – but in a little while she was barely aware of them. After all, a lot of people don't like cats. On coming in after a shower of rain he would shake himself vigorously and there'd be a sort of pong for a moment. Also, he was very proprietorial over one particular flower bed near the kitchen door and insisted on being the only one who could tend it. Madeline didn't mind. After all, every old dog needs to remember where the bones are buried.

POSTLUDE

♪

THE LISTENERS were silent, as the wind ceased and for a few moments they said nothing either. Some tears were shed, particularly by Elsa. Dusk had just started to fall as the story ended and the wind subsided.

Carol noted, without surprise, that the Cottage had returned to facing South and got up to pull the curtain across.

Elsa spoke tremulously, "That was a gut story, Ja? It was specially for me?"

Carol stepped over to her. Elsa stood up and the two exchanged a warm hug. Then they both spontaneously turned and hugged Aunty Mabel, who was pleased but inattentive, having already forgotten the story and discovered the last of the scones. She was covering it with jam and cream and settling down again to eat it.

Carol and Elsa looked at each other and both spontaneously burst out laughing at Aunty Mabel's absorbed expression and the jam around her mouth, making her look for a moment like a naughty child. Carol wiped it off tenderly and both ladies smiled at each other again, as Elsa came to help the old lady up, knowing that they would all be friends from now on.

"I too live alone," Elsa said as she prepared to help Aunty Mabel to the car. Carol noted she had no rings on her fingers.

"Me too," she answered the unspoken question, "I have lots of lovely nephews and nieces..." Carol's voice trailed away momentarily and Elsa nodded sagely.

"Is not the same, ja?" she said. "Is a gut life, but not the same. Sometimes we all need little stories. You vill come and pay visit to stay with me in beautiful land of Tyrol, ja?"

"Ja!" replied Carol happily, as they exchanged address cards. "I will come tomorrow morning too, to take you to the station." Then they drove off into the deepening dusk.

INTERLUDE
♪

NEW HORIZONS?

IT **SO HAPPENED** that George had arranged to go out the very same evening after the phone call he had made to Helena about the concert, with a friend who was visiting from Manchester. Indeed, this was Nigel Stubbs, the same old college chum who had got him the invitation to lecture at the Public School in Tunbridge wells recently and with such success.

Of course George said nothing about Helena or Turnaround Cottage, but was proud to be able to tell Nigel about the invitation to do some marking and occasional lecture sessions at the school. His old friend was cock-a-hoop at having been so useful and naturally they went out to the pub and indulged in a good many wee drams.

Being rather drunk, George remembered and mentioned his almost-forgotten idea of going to live cheaply and successfully in the South of France. Nigel took this up with the greatest enthusiasm for the whole idea of going abroad to live, full of praise for this solution to all his friend's problems.

It appeared that Nigel went often to Saint Tropez and waxed lyrical about the climate, the opportunities to save money (not to mention to spend it!) and the exciting women you could meet there, balm to a bruised heart and dented ego.

By an extraordinary coincidence, that they both made much of, Nigel was due to fly out on a cheap midweek ticket very soon. He was insistent that this was a sign and that George should get a cheap ticket and come with him straight away. George somehow found it impossible to resist this mood of excitement and bravado and agreed.

Waking with a sore head and gippy tummy rather late the next morning, George did not in any way remember this until an excited Nigel phoned and reminded him.

"I've got the tickets, Miller old boy," he appeared to be saying much too loudly into George's fuzzy ear.

Indeed he had! Unreturnable too. Nigel was so pleased with himself that he would not listen to any protestations a hungover mind could produce and swept on to list all the pleasures they would have. A week in the South of France certainly did sound more fun than one decorous concert and George couldn't cope with saying no.

This of course left him with both the aching head and the even worse task of sending a conciliatory letter to Helena, crying off from the very evening out he had so gladly booked.

As he puzzled over how he could be reassuring about a future date, he realised that more hung on this than he had fully thought through. He became aware now that it was most unlikely that he would be able to pursue a new courtship, nor perhaps would he want to, if the Answer to all his problems lay in a New Life in a new country.

"If only I had fallen in love with Helena!" he said to himself in excuse. "That would have solved everything!"

He had found her very attractive, warm and kind; a lifelong friendship had already seemed to develop, but it was not the overwhelming 'knock me off my feet, stars in the eyes' romance which was the only way he could associate with the experience of 'being in love'.

What he had found in Helena was an almost inexpressible friendship, deeper and of a sort he had never known before. He would not have hesitated to call her the best friend he had ever had – and had indeed said so to her in a letter and on the phone. It did not really occur to him that this could be the beginning of a love deeper than a new life in some Lala Land. Indeed, in some way, he was secretly frightened at just how deep such a love and commitment could go, if he once allowed it in.

Helena was the secret Soulmate of his dreams, symbolically leaning out of a window with her hands extended to him – and he somehow now turned his head away and hurried on by.

He had quite forgotten that all those wonderful, intoxicating feelings of being totally in love had worn off pretty quickly in both his first marriage and the affair he had after it. Even his second marriage, which had been happy, had somehow not lasted in the end, and had been punctuated by passing romantic feelings for other women, never explored and all inappropriate.

Nor was he able to recognise that when he had met and got to know Helena his feelings were still frozen and bruised by the very recent break up of that disastrous affair which had been instrumental in ending his second marriage. Indeed he and Laura had only irrevocably broken with each other a bare six weeks before he had first met Helena. He was not even over the trauma of his divorce either, really missing his wife and desolate at the grief he had caused his family.

George was certainly in no state to fall durably in love with anyone, but he did not reflect on this at all, nor that in those circumstances the peace and gentle happiness he had found in Helena's company were worth any amount of saccharine Hollywood-style 'Romance'.

"I'm not really good enough for a charming, intelligent woman like Helena!" he said to himself, consoling his conscience with the thought that he was anyway a lousy sort of person and she'd be better off without him.

Shamed and wretched as he was, there was even an element of self-punishment, of self-exile in the way he accepted that, mistake or not, he had cast the die and was now committed to exploring this new life abroad. He consoled his conscience with the thought that he and Helena could still be friends at a distance and that this would be enough, while guiltily being aware that this was hardly what either secretly had wanted nor would it be practical if he hurt her and rejected her at this stage of the friendship. But the pull of the new overcame all.

So the guilt he felt meant that the letter came out with more than a hint of bravado and rodomontade in it, and was overly brusque in its silence about any future meeting, a silence as good as a dismissal.

Helena certainly felt this, as she read his letter in the porch of Turnaround Cottage, where she had intercepted the postman to save him his journey down to Flitterbottom. This is what she read, and reread many times, with tear marks gathering on it, hoping each time it would be different and have something more to read into it, as women have always done.

"Dear Helena,

"You have been very kind and tolerant of me with all the currents of change that have rippled through my life lately. In my quest for stability and a new start I have been driven to seek new horizons.

"It is a time when opportunity seems to knock louder than ever before and I am so afraid of losing this opportunity for a new beginning: as Shakespeare says:

"'There is a tide in the affairs of men. Which, taken at the flood, leads on to fortune; Omitted, all the voyage of their life is bound in shallows and in miseries. On such a full sea are we now afloat, and we must take the current when it serves, or lose our ventures.'

"Waiting around only allows your power to pass its crest and begin to ebb; if the opportunity is 'omitted' (missed), you'll find yourself stranded in miserable shallows.

"So, my dear, I'm afraid I will have to cancel our arrangement to meet again for the concert, as an opportunity has arisen most unexpectedly to spend a little time in the South of France, where as you know I have wondered where I might live more cheaply and in a warm climate for winter. It seems I should go and see how practicable this unrepeatable opportunity might be, so I do apologise most sincerely for cancelling our plans, and I enclose the tickets so that they won't be wasted.

"I do not know either, whether it may be appropriate for me to stay on a little longer

*there to look for a cheap flat, so I can't be sure
of my plans now.*

*"I am very sorry about missing the concert,
and the party too, but that's honestly how I
feel at the present – to strike now while the
iron is hot. So please don't be upset by my
lack of commitment, Helena. I am just
emerging from my vulnerable pupae and feel I
must fulfil my destiny by spreading my wings,
if only for a very short flight. I have been
trapped for most of my life by mediocrity, and I
feel I must stretch my wings just one more
time. But that does not mean that I don't value
the friendship we had here, a friendship which
I shall always treasure.*

"Your loving friend, George."

Helena's response was a sick feeling in her
heart and guts and tearfulness at intervals
over the next few days as she recognised the
crushing of those little seedling hopes and felt
it was all her fault.

The knowledge he would be going to live in
France didn't help either. It was hard to have a
daughter living in another country, but at least
it was reasonable for one's offspring to spread
their wings. That having met her, only briefly
talking about vague ideas of going to live

abroad, and then promptly to fly away to foreign parts was quite another thing. It stung!

Even his quoting Shakespeare and his kind but distant (in her mind) words of friendship also knocked her out of her usually equable frame of mind, and many were the tears she shed in accepting it over the next busy days, with a bruised heart to hide.

It was not in her nature to be petulant, nor did she easily take offence, but she tore up the two tickets into tiny pieces and dropped them there and then in the porch of the Cottage, not caring about littering.

The mice of course removed them later, but found them unsuitable even for bedding and took them to the River Flitter, to be carried down to the sea, where so many hopes and dreams end.

CHAPTER FOURTEEN

THE SHREWISH WIFE

PRELUDE
♪

QUITE A TIME had passed since the last letting. Helena came up the hill just as a middle-aged woman got out of a car by Turnaround Cottage. She was elegantly dressed in a blue silk dress with an attractive lace panel on the bodice. She came forward with an outstretched hand and a friendly smile.

Helena instinctively smoothed down her own skirt as she responded. She was expecting such a visitor, having been informed of the exact time they were coming, so she went forward to return the friendly gesture, glad that she was wearing her new best dress herself.

"I think you must be Mrs Pam Faulkes?" she said. "I'm Helena Brown."

The woman who had rosy cheeks, a fine mouth and a general demeanour of charm and efficiency, shook Helena's hand warmly.

"Yes, please call me Pam," she said, "and this is my husband, Warwick."

Warwick came forward smiling and also shook her hand. "A proper Wally, that's what she usually calls me!" he remarked, smiling.

For a brief second Helena wondered if there wasn't a slight edge in his voice and it seemed clear that his wife's feelings were hurt.

"I just like to give you a pet name, dear!" she said, turning away. His smile had gone, shoulders drooping a little, as he got the cases out of the car.

Helena therefore focused on her with particular friendliness, helping her over the muddy patch by the gate and solicitously up the path, ignoring her husband who carried in three heavy cases and some bags, having to make two journeys. He seemed to be doing it deliberately to gain sympathy, as Pam, still drooping a little, took it in that he had carried them all in on his own without asking for help.

"Oh Wally!" she cried sympathetically. "I'm so sorry! You should have waited and we'd have helped with the lighter stuff."

Warwick replied in a tone that might have had a belligerent edge to it, "I put all the bags in the bedroom, I thought that's what you'd want." He was puffing and panting as he spoke.

"Wally dear, please try not to breath so heavily. You know it worries me." Pam sounded pathetic, placatory. Warwick only sighed harder. He did not respond and the two women ignored him. After a while his breathing reverted to normal.

Helena thought 'he's doing it just for attention and she knows it', a little surprised at herself. She wasn't usually catty about other people, but there was something that was annoying her about him. 'How does she put up with him?' was the way her thoughts were going, as Pam made very sweet efforts to draw him into the conversation and he reacted in a way that could only be described as sulky.

Helena felt inspired to say to her, "I'm sure you could do with a cup of tea or coffee! How about I make you some while we go through the little bit of paperwork?" Pam smiled again, restored to cheerful sociability as the two women shared this minor task.

Then they began to chat about more ordinary things. Pam seemed amazingly approachable and it appeared they shared many interests.

"Oh yes, I just love Opera – in fact all Classical music!" Pam said enthusiastically as the matter of local culture came up and Helena described the performance she had been to recently. Pam recalled famous opera stars she had heard sing in London in past times.

Asked if she went often now, she replied, "Not really you know. It's so expensive." She looked rather sad, as at a pleasure long denied, with a quick anxious glance across at Warwick, who was drinking his tea without joining in.

Throughout their conversation Pam retained a good humoured smile, but also had a faint air of anxiety as to what Warwick would say or do next. She was clearly very fond of him, stroking his hand when he came near. He reacted as if startled, snatching it away.

She returned her attention to Helena and, said smiling: "I must tell you how I love your dress!

What an eye you have for colour – where did you get it?"

"Oh, thank you," said Helena, very pleased. "Just in 'Dora's', the dress shop in Heathfield," she replied. "These are my favourite colours – purples and blues."

"I love the peacock design," said Pam, "and the way it adds just a dash of turquoise."

In no time they were having a good feminine chat about their wardrobes, as Pam sipped her coffee, talking and laughing with a friendly informality that exactly matched Helena's own approach to life.

"I was on my own for many years before I met and married Warwick. We were introduced by friends and there was an instant attraction, wasn't there, Wally?" Pam asked, trying to draw him into the conversation.

Her face fell, just a little, as she looked across almost timidly at Warwick, who was sipping his tea and taking no notice of them. Her sigh was too gentle to reach him.

Helena's heart was touched and she confided in Pam about her long widowhood and her hopes for her daughter, Jocelyn and family. In fact by the end of the afternoon Helena felt she had made a really good friend, very much on her wavelength, though she felt a certain dislike already for Warwick. She went back to the Cottage full of tea and sympathy for a woman who seemed to have drawn the short straw in the marriage lottery.

The following afternoon Helena decided to accept the invitation to tea again. This was rather against her usual ways, but she had enjoyed Pam's company so much and was feeling particularly low in spirits at the moment.

Her own disappointment at the loss of the longed-for romance with George meant she was feeling sad and a bit at a loose end, so she felt sympathetic to the plight of Pam. It seemed that this charming lady was lumbered with a grumpy and rather stupid husband, though she seemed very patient with him.

Helena went up the lane from her cottage in Flitterbottom at around 4 o'clock and saw Pam coming down the hill, a good 20 yards in front of Warwick, who was going much more slowly. He only caught up with them when

Pam, stopped by Helena, retraced her steps a little, waited and took his hand.

"Come on Wally!" she cried gaily, pulling him playfully up to the gate. Warwick did not seem grateful; he was breathing heavily again and merely grunted. Pam was laughing and chatting cheerfully about their walk up on the Weald as they went into the house.

"Poor Wally! I hope you enjoyed it really, dear. We went rather a long way because you wanted to see the cairn on the ridge, though I knew it would be a bit much for you. I can't walk as slowly as Wally. I always have to go ahead, then wait. It's such a nuisance."

She was laughing rather than sounding concerned, once again tapping his arm and then laying an affectionate hand on it. Wally merely grunted and Helena felt uncomfortable on Pam's behalf and yet somehow uneasy about it today. It felt as if she herself was missing something, under the spell of a constant flow of warm and complimentary chat from Pam, directed at herself and mostly ignoring Warwick.

There was little time for reflection. Pam kept up the flow of interesting topics and had conjured up a nice tea with scones, everything very pleasant and uneventful. As the time passed, though, Helena found herself wondering a little at the way Pam spoke to Wally. She seemed to punctuate their own flowing conversation with brief comments and orders to him, as if he was a little boy, or a servant.

"Sit up straight dear, don't slump. You know it helps you breathe properly, through your nose, not your mouth." "We need more tea." "Fetch the jam from the kitchen table." "No not that jug – find a china one. You know I don't like glassware on the table!" "Why didn't you change your shirt? You know the blue one doesn't go with those trousers."

Warwick reacted by obeying each order, except the last, at which he just grunted, looking down at his beige shorts myopically.

"Doesn't he mind getting up all the time?" said Helena a little doubtfully, as Warwick went out for the third time.

"He knows my back is playing up today, so he doesn't mind doing it," Pam said, serenely.

Warwick came back in and took another slice of cake.

"Oh, you are a greedy gannet, aren't you!" said Pam, laughing and looking at Helena expectantly. Helena laughed too, not sure why.

"Do you know what this silly man did the other day?" said Pam, still laughing. "He got into the back of my friend Val's hatchback, which he'd loaded up for her. Val and I were in the front and she went to the back of the car again, then forgot to put down the hatchback door again, before she got in. She was driving and we went several miles like that and Warwick never even noticed. He just said the engine did sound louder than usual! Oh, Val and I did laugh about that, didn't we Wally?"

Helena smiled, but she was beginning to feel increasingly uneasy. Surely it was up to the driver, with a mirror, to notice that, especially if she'd left the door up herself? It was warm and cosy in the Cottage, but she began to have an uneasy feeling that she was being lulled into something.

She felt she was being presented with more and more evidence of how silly, grumpy and selfish Wally was, but she suddenly felt she wanted to see 'Warwick' instead and make up her own mind.

She got up preparing as if to go, then turned to Warwick, who had earlier expressed an interest in the garden, asking if he'd like her to show it to him. They carried out the tea things to the kitchen and Pam said she would stay in for a nap, so the two of them went out into the garden.

Though small it was bright with flowers and looking particularly charming in the sunshine, but Warwick didn't really look at them.

Warwick broke into Helena's description of why she had planted the dahlias and said abruptly: "She's drawn you in too, hasn't she?" He spoke in a resigned voice.

"But why, why?" said Helena. She meant why do you put up with it, but Warwick took it to mean why did Pam do it.

"It amuses her," he said simply. "When I first met her I thought she was the loveliest person in the world. Couldn't believe my luck that she wanted to go out with me. Picked me out of a lot of other guys who were clamouring for her attentions."

For a moment, an uncertainty crept into his voice. "Mind you, I never met any of them, except one man, strange looking fellow with skinny legs. He came to lunch at short notice, just after I told her I couldn't afford to live with her in the area she wanted, after all. We're only renting, you know," he said a little anxiously. "It takes the whole of my pension to live there, so she buys the food. That's very generous of her, isn't it?

"She told me the man was a previous boyfriend, now a millionaire, desperate to get back with her but she didn't want him back, he was too boring and 'stingy'.

"It made me think I'd better improve my courtship, so I cashed in some shares and we had a lovely holiday."

For a moment a happy smile played on his face, then he frowned, a little puzzled.

"Mind you. I suppose I only ever had her word for all that. I never asked him, of course. How could I?

"She's so in love with me too. The number of times she's said she'd top herself if I ever left her. You don't often get devotion like that do you?" His voice was full of tender pride and Helena sat frozen with horror at what was coming out.

He looked anxiously at Helena, willing her to see it as he now did: Pam was generous, while he, Wally, was stingy for not wanting to rent somewhere beyond his means, with constant anxiety?

"No I don't think that's generous at all!" Helena said, all the more firmly for realising how badly she had misjudged the situation.

Nor did what was being revealed lend itself to one of the usual compromises we love to impose on people – "There are two sides to every story." "She means well." "It's just the way things are." "It's just her way so it's water off a duck's back to me."

"No!" she repeated more firmly. "It's your money, you have a right to say what it should go on and how you want to live."

Warwick looked thoughtful. Other things were coming back to Helena's mind too.

"And by the way," she added, "I think the peculiar way she always walks on ahead of you, then pulls you along, is not nice at all. In fact I think it's horribly rude and it's meant to make you feel how superior she is."

"Well," said Warwick, still self-deprecatingly, "I'm pretty slow. I've got this heart condition. Makes me slow at walking and means I breathe heavily with the least exertion. You see how annoying that must be for her, can't you? She's so fit.

"She says it must be my fault, diet and things, but I'm not sure that's true. My old Dad had the same problem and the Doctor thought there might be a hereditary element. My Dad died early, you know? Not much older than I am now, so I'd like to take it easy sometimes, but she hates that.

"The Doctor says that if my breathing doesn't improve we might have to think of referring me for surgery, or a pacemaker or something. I don't think Pam would like me to do that. I wouldn't be able to get her breakfast and coffee every morning if I was convalescent. So I think I'll just carry on as I am. It's for the best, she says."

Helena almost froze at the memory of how she had judged him to be 'putting it all on'. It was obviously nothing of the sort, as her experienced eye, now knowing what to look for, took in his mottled complexion, and the curious clubbed shape of his fingernails.

"Have you ever heard the term 'walking on eggshells' at all?" she enquired.

Warwick looked quite surprised. "No. I don't think so, but goodness that term does rather describe what my life is like. I'm such a Wally you see! Only half a brain! No wonder Pam finds it hard to put up with me!"

He stared out of the window for a moment and said reflectively, "Yes. Walking on eggshells. Just describes it most of the time!" He paused, then continued hastily, looking at Helena almost pleadingly:

"But she means well! It's just her way, not her fault. I'm very stupid at times. Don't know why she puts up with me! I'm so devilishly absent-minded."

At that moment Pam came bustling out to join them, refreshed and charming from her nap, bringing Warwick his 'wee dram', the consolation of his days, starting earlier and earlier in the day. Helena hastily made her excuses, thanked them both for a lovely afternoon and went back home down the hill, in a state of inner turmoil and distress.

Helena sat for a long time in her kitchen, in the slanting light coming through the climbing rose outside the window. It sent dancing slivers of light over her face, enhancing the pixie look and, if she had known it, adding enchantment and beauty to her features, but her mind was in turmoil as increasingly she replayed the encounters with the Faulkes couple.

She was suffering a quick and unpalatable reversal of all her previous assumptions; it felt like a beautiful piece of embroidery unravelling to show a grinning skull and rotting corpse printed on the canvas underneath.

Suddenly nothing felt safe; no casual assumption of social convention could stand up to the depressed, naked truth in Warwick's eyes and voice.

Helena had known too many situations of manipulation and covert bullying through her work not to recognise it when it was laid right before her eyes and ears.

It felt almost unpardonable that she had been taken in by what she now saw to be a narcissistic woman, who had used every smiling passive-aggressive technique known, in order to appear to be a wonderful forbearing woman married to a – well, to a proper Wally!

Playing back what she knew she murmured to herself, "It's kind of 'smoke and mirrors,' I only saw what she wanted me to see. And perhaps only what I wanted to see! She's worked on him till he really believes he's only got half a brain. And he's convinced he's a laughing stock because she makes him one. Telling other people any silly things he might have done, making them complicit in laughing at him! Oh heaven's – I joined in too!"

She felt deeply shamed as she understood just how she had been drawn into putting him down, and he'd just smiled patiently. What was it he'd said? 'Oh it's water off a duck's back.' No, it wasn't! How cruel it is to anyone over fifty to talk about them having only half a brain or laughing at forgetfulness, as it if was funny! Of course it wasn't funny; it was terrifying and could induce further confusion and forgetfulness.

It would not be hard, with a compliant victim, to get someone to believe they were dementing. It's the great fear we Oldies all have! A sort of Black Death for modern times.

♪

Helena went back a little later, after supper, uninvited and unannounced. Her anger was partly at least because she had been taken in by a clever manipulator, and felt both a fool and ashamed at being complicit in psychological abuse.

However, she also felt a good deal of righteous anger. While she knew there would be little or nothing she could do or say herself to help Warwick, she did know enough about the subject to know that the victims are in effect brainwashed or hypnotised and it takes a lot to make them see what is happening to them. All the same, Warwick had shown some little signs of opening up and he might be starting on the long road to freedom.

Helena had no illusion about being his 'Rescuer', knowing that this role simply exchanges one slavery for another.

Nor did she think she could succeed where others might also have tried – his family for example – till the skilful manipulator alienated them too. 'I could say,' she mused to herself, in words she would later use to her one confidante, Carol, 'I don't know what to do, but

I know a man – or rather a whole Cottage – who does!'

As she approached the Cottage on silent feet, she felt wary and a little uncertain. She could guess how Pam would make her feel given half a chance. There were voices coming out of the open sitting room window and she stopped to listen. It was a tirade from Pam in rasping, whining tones, quite different from the sweet ones she used in conversation.

"I haven't forgotten that you left the landing light on last night. I explicitly told you to turn it off. You're pathetic, you're useless, you can't get anything right."

"But dear," said a trembling voice like that of a child, hardly recognizable as Warwick. "You said definitely to leave it on, so that's what I did!"

"Oh you're just hopeless," raged the first voice, getting louder with each sentence. It sounded as if it was customary for her to raise the volume of her voice if asked to repeat herself, as though the increased volume might better penetrate her husband's dense brain.

"Oh but the night before you said to... you said... Oh, it doesn't matter, whatever you want." Warwick's voice, childlike, defeated, trembled into resignation, but if it hoped for mercy it wasn't getting it.

Helena moved slightly to ease her position but remained where she was, now convinced she was right to hear this, as Pam's whining voice continued:

"You know you've only got half a brain, don't you. What have you got?"

Silence.

"What have you got?"

"I've only got half a brain dear," said a toneless voice. It was not the voice of Warwick but the voice of 'Wally,' the bullied, confused, defeated victim.

Helena had been doing her homework in her old NHS books that afternoon after leaving the Cottage, once having taken an interest in pathological psychology. Such a simple technique, but a Controller can keep an illogical tirade like that up for hours until the confusion is so great that the recipient loses all common sense, agrees to everything. They never even remember what went on or realise that it may have gone on for hours.

Sweeping into the room without apology, Helena said in a cold, authoritative voice: "This has gone on long enough! Warwick, good to see you! And you Pam. It's time for a Story!"

She swept over to the window, which was open, pulling the curtain out of the way. She leaned out, calling loudly:

"Wind, Wind, this is an emergency! Over to you!"

Then, surprising even herself, she put her fingers in her mouth and blew a resounding whistle, something she couldn't remember doing since childhood, but piercingly effective.

Warwick and Pam put their hands over their ears, but whereas Pam cowered down in her chair and looked frightened, Warwick raised his head in delighted anticipation, as a voice that billowed out the curtains called, even sang:

"Listen now, to your story and heed its lesson, both of you."

The top of the Cottage began to grind around to a new position. Pam grabbed the arms of the chair and turned a little green as if seasick. Warwick laughed and clapped his hands as the view changed to the shrubs and copse, as the strong, icy East Wind cleared its throat, preparing to tell a story.

THE SHREWISH WIFE

THERE WAS ONCE a man whose wife nagged him without stopping. "Fetch the water. Cut more wood. I need new clothes! Why did I marry a useless good-for-nothing like you?"

The man held his tongue, fetched the wood and the water and did his best to earn an honest penny, but times were hard.

One day, resting by the fire after a day in the fields, he heard a little scuffling beside his claggy boots. The cat had caught a mouse and was tormenting it. "Catkin, let go!" said the man, pinching the cat's jaws, but gently. It let go of the little creature and he picked it up in his big calloused hand.

His wife came in at that moment. "A mouse!" she cried, "Give it to the cat! Let Catkin have it. She'll scrunch it up and we won't be bothered again!"

She swept out. The man, for once, couldn't face doing what he was told, but nor could he defy his wife. He looked at the mouse with a frown. The little creature nestled in his hand, trustfully and he fed her on milk-soaked breadcrumbs, stroking her gently with his work-ridged fingers.

Then, with a mutinous expression and a pounding heart he found a little box and lined it with soft hay. He hid it up on a ledge behind the wood stack, which only he used and fed the mouse several times a day, keeping her carefully away from discovery by his wife and also keeping Catkin out of the room, with some difficulty. He was not used to subterfuge.

On the third day the little mouse was gone. There was no sign of it, nor any blood and he knew Catkin had not been in, so he trusted it had recovered and gone free and he was thankful.

A few weeks later the man fell ill. For three days and nights he burned up with a fever. Even then his wife didn't let up. "You're lying there on purpose to annoy me. Look at all the work I'm having to do. Get up, you lazy lout, you useless lump of dough, you nincompoop!"

The man said, "Wife, wife, I am sick. Please, I beg you – some water," but she miffed and huffed and flounced, and gave him nothing.

In the third night of the fever the man heard a little voice in his ear, "Open your mouth, my dearest." On the pillow beside him was the mouse he had saved from the cat, holding a teacup. With a silver teaspoon she spooned a bitter liquid into his mouth. "Tansy tea," said the mouse. "It will make you well."

In the morning the man said, "Wife, wife, I am very weak. I beg you, please give me a little bread and milk."

"Can't you see how busy I am?" his wife snarled, "Get it yourself, you hobbledehoy, you bumpkin, you gormless lummox!"

It would have gone ill with the man, but he suddenly felt a touch on his sleeve and there was the mouse. She climbed onto his shoulder and fed him on blueberries and beechmast.

Several times a day the mouse brought him food; a silk bag of biscuit crumbs; a crust of a loaf spread with wild honey; a piece of cheese the size of a guinea piece, and she would twitch her whiskers against his cheek in a mouse-kiss.

Discovery was inevitable. His wife came in complaining as usual, "There's no water for the washing, the leeks need weeding, how am I going to get to market?..."

Her voice stopped. Her husband was sitting up and on his shoulder was a little brown mouse holding a teaspoonful of rosewater to his lips.

"Eeeek!" the woman shrieked, "A mouse! A mouse! Come quickly Catkin, come quickly! Kill the mouse! Kill the mouse!"

She thrust her red, angry face at her husband, spitting venomous words into his ear. The man drew back instinctively and his hand went in a protective curve around the little mouse.

"No!" he cried out. "No! Catkin will not have the mouse. How can you be so cruel?"

His wife's eyes bulged with surprise at being defied. She turned purple and raised her hand at him, holding a ladle.

Her husband was terrified, but held his ground, and brought the little mouse protectively near his breast.

"No!" he repeated. "Your cat cannot have her. It is cruel and I've had enough of your cruelty too!"

He brought the mouse up nearer his face. "We're leaving!" he said to it. "Don't worry. I will look after you!"

The mouse sat up on his hand, twitching its whiskers. Then it made a great leap onto the woman's shoulder and tapped her firmly on the nose with the spoon, squeaking:
"Shrewish wife, shrewish wife,
Too much strife and a misery life!"

There was a flash of light from the spoon and suddenly the nagging wife was gone, and in her place was a sharp-nosed shrew. The shrew was still shrilling, "Slaving away... best years of my life... lazy, useless..." when Catkin, green eyes gleaming, pounced forward and chased the shrew out of the door into the wood – and gobbled her up in one mouthful.

In front of the man stood a young woman, smiling at him and holding out her hand in gratitude and love. She had long mousy hair and was dressed in a brown velvet gown, still holding a tiny silver teaspoon. The mouse-girl looked after the man and never nagged and he looked after her and was always devoted, so they lived

HAPPILY EVER AFTER!

POSTLUDE

♪

AS THE STORY FINISHED Pam stretched and laughed, trying to make it sound sweetly tinkling, but not entirely succeeding. A clenched jaw promised trouble ahead for someone.

"Well, what a silly story! Fairytales eh? It's very late and I'm going to bed and you'd better come up too, dear," she said to Warwick, but the voice of the East Wind said, quietly but with authority:

"You may go to bed as and when and how you wish and so may your husband and all free folk, but you cannot escape the process that has been started. We have only just begun and what spells we are unravelling will take time to bring to a good ending. How much time? Who can tell how long a story will be, before it is completed?

"You can allow the process or hinder it, though it will take longer than the telling of a tale tonight can compass. That may just start the healing and clarification for all who have the kind of ears that can hear a Fairy Story and apply its balm to their hearts and souls."

♪

Both Pam and Warwick were silenced. Helena slipped away and left them, returning quickly to her own cottage at Flitterbottom. She went to bed shivering, in spite of the warmth of the night.

Next morning Helena was up early and found the Visitors, bags packed, ready to go. Pam looked at her with a quick sideways, calculating glance, then started gushing about how well she had slept and what a nice place it was. By this time Helena had realised what a consummate actress she was, able to fake all and every emotion just as it suited her game.

She smiled blandly at both visitors, not bad at acting herself, especially politeness, and very pleasantly helped carry the luggage to the car with them.

She resisted any temptation to wink at Warwick, but she was pleased to see that he was standing quite straight, listening courteously, somehow a little bit more himself today. More Warwick than Wally.

"Thank you very much, Helena," he was saying as he got into the front passenger seat. "Very good entertainment you put on. I never realised Fairy Stories could be so interesting. Not just for children, eh?"

"No," Helena replied, gravely, "Especially not for children."

Warwick smiled. Pam snorted and got into the driving seat. She accelerated off amid a shower of gravel spurting from under the wheels.

CHAPTER FIFTEEN

THE SIN EATER

PRELUDE
♪

IN HEATHFIELD HIGH STREET, Helena was going quietly about her business, having put the latest earnings from the letting of Turnaround Cottage into the Bank account for the mysterious owner and was looking forward to a coffee break.

A voice behind her from a man crossing purposefully over the road froze her to stop dead before she recognised the voice and knew who was behind her. A mottled blush came to her cheeks as if her body knew who it was, before her mind could catch up.

Sure enough, as she swung round, instinctively throwing up her left arm defensively and halting it with difficulty, she saw him behind her. Him, Gerard Forward, not seen in real life since that time in the dock when he got a paltry five years for cheating her husband and her parents and several friends, out of their life savings!

He had done time for that, decades ago, out in three years for 'good behaviour'. All she knew from friends or pieces in the local Derby papers, was that he had been in prison on many other occasions, always for fraud, extortion, misrepresentation. You name the mean scam; he'd done it.

She hadn't heard that he'd been inside for years now, presumably because he had got better at not being caught rather than having reformed his ways, judging by the smirk on his twisted lips. He was older and fatter, obviously, but still had the dashing looks and superficial charm she remembered. 'Of all the people to run into!' she thought, then to her horror she realised it was not by chance.

Somehow he'd found out where she was and even about her job as he said, "Well, Helena. You don't look pleased to see me! Didn't you realise that I'd booked into your holiday cottage for tonight? I'm at a business conference in Brighton tomorrow. Thought it would be good to catch up on old friendships."

Even though his lips were smiling with the boyish charm she remembered, she thought she could see suppressed anger as well.

Stuttering with shock and rage, Helena gave him to understand that had she known who the Mr G Forster really was she would have emigrated rather than welcomed him to Turnaround Cottage and that it was misrepresentation and illegal and she wouldn't give him the key.

His eyes narrowed and he said silkily, still with that smile, "You can't do that my dear. All legal and above board. Never heard of a name change by a reformed character like me?"

Helena could not bear any more. It might be true about the legal name change or it might not, but it was no use invoking the law; he'd outtalk anyone.

"You can have the key at four o'clock, as it says in the letter and please pay in advance at that time," she said and fled to her car, aware that she looked flustered and undignified and judging by his laughter following her he was thoroughly enjoying her humiliation.

In her car she sat breathing deeply for a few minutes before driving, quickly but calmly back to Punnetts Town, a plan at least to spoil his triumph and protect herself forming in her mind.

She stopped a little further up Flitterbrook lane, by the next house before Turnaround Cottage, and thanked providence that her neighbours and acquaintances, Bert and Norah Doveport, appeared to be in. 'And it'll need more than doves to keep the peace over this!' she thought.

Bert and Norah were about to sit down to a country lunch of raised pork pie, green leaves and potato salad, followed by strawberries and cream. All home grown of course, the cream from Pringles Farm, the strawberries from Clover Hill Farm, courtesy of the freezer. Helena was easily persuaded to sit down with them and found them extremely receptive and sympathetic.

Helena had not known before that Norah in particular was an avid follower of soaps and no story was too convoluted or wild for her to follow, but she was also a kindly and sympathetic woman, well attuned to the problem Helena outlined and well placed to help her out.

"We trusted Gerard completely," Helena was explaining. "Harry and he had been at school together. I always thought he was charming. We were close friends for years, and all the time he was cheating in small ways we never realised and plotting this massive Ponzi scheme. Some of our friends and my own poor parents got caught up in it in the end. He persuaded us all, then took the money, all our savings and ran."

Her friends expressed their shock and sympathy and outlined a local scheme on a much smaller scale involving the annual pub outing one year, as well as a recent storyline in a soap.

Helena told them about how it was within weeks of this that her parents and Harry had been killed in an accident, by a lorry on an icy road in the Highlands. Although they knew the bare facts of course, they had not known the details or that it had happened so soon after the loss of all the family money. Helena could not help crying and Norah was extremely comforting, while Bert kept a respectful silence and refilled their glasses with his best elderflower wine.

Helena also realised, in telling them, that in spite of the therapy she had undergone, there was always more to do after such a big series of life events. She was still, somewhere in her mind, linking Gerard's perfidy with the deaths, illogical as that was, and also feeling very guilty that she too had fallen for Gerard Forward's charm and suppressed any fleeting doubts, so that in some way she had still been suffering from a sense of responsibility down the years. She couldn't deal with the guilty feelings that it aroused just now, but there was relief in just bringing them out into the open.

"It wasn't my fault?" she asked Norah, almost like a child, and Norah enclosed her hand in her own big warm one. "No," she said simply.

By the time they had eaten the strawberries – two helpings each and all the cream – they were laughing as they worked out a simple plan to thwart any further nastiness by Gerard. Norah had once before stood in for Helena one winter's day when she suffered a sharp dose of flu, and there was no reason that shouldn't happen again. Indeed, in a country area it is commonplace for neighbours to help each other out with small tasks all the time.

So when that slimy gentleman came up the path to the Cottage dot on 4pm he was met not by a defensive and flustered Helena but by Norah and Bert combined. Bert was well built and strong, as indeed a farmer needs to be, but not a patch on the formidable figure that Norah Doveport could conjure up for herself when necessary.

The legendary lady who, in youth had stopped a runaway bull calf in Heathfield market one day and returned it to its terrified owner, was more than a match for a townie, however smooth an operator he might be on his own ground.

She was exasperatingly vague on why Helena was not there, but suggested she might come over in the morning if he wished to apologise to her. When an apoplectic Gerard asked why he might need to do so, she became positively bovine with vague and dampening comments.

Norah had dealt with such total narcissists before and knew that all the time under their assumed calm was a simmering pit of resentment at a world which never fully appreciated their special perfection and must be punished for it.

She suggested Gerard might enjoy an evening in the Barley Mow up the road within walking distance (he had come by taxi) and he had lost it, almost shouting, "Why should I be spending my hard earned cash on a bunch of drunken yobbos!" He turned his face away as he flashed an embossed shagreen wallet stuffed with notes in order to show off.

Norah deftly took it, extracted the exact fee for one night, which he had hoped to forget, handing it to Bert, and giving back the wallet in one smooth movement. Then the couple went home to next door, where Helena was waiting and where it has to be admitted, they all laughed a lot.

Helena had availed herself of the Doveports' kindly suggestion that she spent at least the evening with them, but said she was sure she'd be alright later in the night, feeling privately that Turnaround Cottage might have its own way of occupying even Gerard Forward. So when the couple accompanied her down to Flitterbottom after 11, they saw no lights and all appeared quiet.

Turnaround Cottage indeed was filled with a sense of waiting, a suspicious calm, unbroken by the Mice who well knew when to stay out of sight completely.

Gerard swore and hurled things about, but with no one to torment he quickly gave up and

– truth to tell – regretted the impulse which had led him to track Helena down in order to see, first, if his charm might still work on her (ever the optimist!) and then to try and torment her.

Thwarted, he sat looking out of the window, where a little wind was getting up, a sound almost as if it was beginning to sob and whine, in tune with his own mood of self-pity. He was vaguely puzzled as to which way the sitting room was facing. He had rather a good sense of direction and was sure he had come in from the South

The wind was now flying up to a gale very fast and the window suddenly burst open, the catch gone. After a short while, his head was freezing in the icy blast.

Leaning out and cursing fruitily, Gerard Forward saw in disbelief that the whole cottage seemed to have turned around and indeed he was looking out to the West, over the sweet flower garden of the Cottage, full of flowering herbs and rich vegetation, and an astonishingly icy West Wind was blowing straight into his face.

"Hear the Story prepared for you, Gerard Forward," hissed a voice, and he found he could not move as his body was held uncomfortably in the West Wind's grip.

"Listen now, listen Gerard Forward and learn, learn, learn from the story of The Sin Eater..."

THE SIN EATER
PART 1

FOR AS LONG as anyone could remember in the village of Worge the villagers and their forefathers had been occupied in the communal care and wardenship of the bands of pigs who roamed the Dallington Forest freely feeding on acorns, 'God's free provisions', as the monks called them. It was a particularly thriving community in its own way.

In those times most of Sussex was covered in forests, in which the isolated villages were almost like separate lands, so cut off they were, with their own customs and ideas. The forests were a haunt of many lawless outcasts and brigands. This little village, like most of them, was suspicious of strangers, tending indeed to distrust anyone who came from 'somewhere else'.

That's not to say the villagers weren't proud of what they had. Each little hovel in Worge stood in a little clearing and had its own piece of land, where they could grow their vegetables, keep chickens and other livestock and store the wood they brought back for the fire.

The pigs provided meat, mostly for sale in Heathfield Market or even further away. They could sell it all, and what they couldn't sell they ate, both pork and bacon, sausages, ears and noses as delicacies, blood for black pudding, chitterlings, trotters, cheeks, crackling, skin for parchment, bones for broth. Everything, as they used to say, could be used except the squeal.

So the villagers had their own ways and customs, but knew much of what went on in the wider world from their market trips, and mostly didn't like it. "We keep to our own ways," they would tell strangers. Even the monks of St Giles Priory hardly ever ventured to this tiny hamlet and their Abbot came only when he had to, requiring most of his flock to come to the church in Dallington.

This isolation meant that a curious custom persisted in Worge, when it had died out in wider parts of the country. Because it was hard to get spiritual help quickly before the deceased passed away, he or she would often die with a burden of unforgiven sin. All was not lost however as an outsider would hang around in the shadows till after the main funeral meal was over then quickly come and take an offering of food and drink specially left apart for him. By doing this, he was taking on the dead man's unforgiven sins and it would be he who would pay for them in the afterlife.

Such a man, the Sin Eater, with his one specific task, would be tolerated, given an amnesty, for the time he needed to slink out of the shadows, but at all other times he was an outcast, a sinner who had done something so grievously wrong that he was destined for hell fire no matter what and might just as well make himself useful along the way.

Joshua Forward was the Sin Eater of Worge. He looked old. Being so bent and knotted, he resembled a branch torn off the tree by a storm, rotting slowly and covered in strange bumps and clumps of weathered skin. He was a small man and was not, in reality, all that old, though no one knew his age, not even himself. He had been the local Sin Eater for long before most of the village could remember. Certainly none now – not even himself – had any idea of the reason why he had been cast out of civilised village society.

All he could remember was that he had a good, common, local name. The Forward families, though long disowning him, were the aristocracy of the district, their name meaning indeed 'Wardens of the pigs', the 'fear' from a 'furrow'. It allowed Joshua, when all else was despair, to somehow keep going. To plough his furrow and pray for release, even into Hell.

In the summer Joshua Forward could eat berries and roots and often small insects. His occupation had the advantage that in the winter when pickings in the forest were poor there would be a corresponding increase in funerals and he would get by quite well on his share.

However, year on year his loneliness increased and other people's sins became a more intolerable burden than he felt he could bear, contemplating a cold future on this earth and the terrifying burning in the fires of hell to come.

INTERLUDE

♪

The Wind seemed for a moment to get personal with his Visitor as it howled in his ear – "Such is the thoughtless burden we can place on the shoulders of our fellow humans. Even though Sin Eating itself may have gone, judgemental practices remain among seemingly Christian people, some of whom affect to know who goes to Heaven and who to a Hell devised by human cruelty, ignorant of the Unconditional Love of an eternal Father."

Gerard Forward blanched and thought of the many things – well deserved though they might be – which had been thrown at him down the years of his life. He put his fingers in his ears, but the Wind continued remorselessly and he could not block out the storm.

"Listen to the story chosen for you, Gerard Forward, and learn, learn, learn from its message. The bud may be bitter but the flower is sweet!"

THE SIN EATER
PART 2

AMONG THE PEOPLE around but not of the village of Worge was a Holy man, who had appeared one season of particularly bad harvests and misery and settled in a little hut some quarter of a mile away. It had quickly became obvious that a Hermit had nothing worth stealing, so the local low life villains didn't bother with him, but a few God-fearing folk from the isolated villages had sought him out asking for his blessing. The Hermit, as was his custom, greeted all comers with equal courtesy and gave to all in their need, whether food or forgiveness.

The Hermit had chosen to be named after St Anthony of Padua, and also seemed to have a particular affinity with pigs. As soon as he had appeared in the old hut the villagers had started bringing him the little runts of each farrowing, those that were born stunted, or too weak to feed and grow properly. It was an understood thing that such piglets, known as Tanthony Pigs, would remain in a Holy man's charge, nurtured and used for breeding if they grew up, never slaughtered. Brother Anthony already had a few semi-tamed piglets around his hut.

It was also not long before Brother Anthony had an opportunity to see the odd old custom of Sin Eating for himself. The local Blacksmith, Job Mathews, had died very suddenly. A full blooded man of great girth and strength, he had been hard at work in his forge, manning the bellows when suddenly his face went even redder, with the fires of Hell (or so his widow Meg thought, remembering her many needless beatings) and down he had crashed with his dog howling at his side.

Full of Ale and a few rip-roaring sins outstanding, never in Church but once a year for Easter – who could be more in need of the services of Joshua Forward the Sin Eater, than Job Mathews, the village decided?

And so it was. Brother Anthony watched from a little distance, noted by the people but permitted as long as he didn't interfere.

When the funeral feasting was over one of the elders gave a sign and Joshua Forward slipped out, hunched and humble, from the shadow of a hazel coppice. He darted forward, stuffed as much bread as he could in his pocket, drank the ale from a pewter cup in one long gulp and muttered a prayer:

"As I eat this bread and drink this cup, so I give easement and rest now to thee, Job Mathews. Come not down our lanes or into our woods. And for thy peace and thy heavenly reward I pawn my own soul. Amen."

Then he was gone again, but he could not walk fast and it was easy for the Hermit following him, to be there to catch him as he fell onto a patch of moss, crying inconsolably. Brother Anthony knelt down beside him and cradled his head from the damp moss. No one had so much as touched Joshua in many years for fear of God's curse. He cried the more.

What was this? Brother Anthony was lifting him up to rest against his knees and speaking a gospel of confession and forgiveness to him. "Indeed Joshua Forward, you are a sinner as we are all," said the Hermit, but he said it with the utmost reverence and love. "Your name is very dear to me," said the Hermit again. "My friend, you too are a guardian of swine, as am I myself, so you are my Brother too."

As Brother Anthony looked with great kindness into Joshua's pale fearful eyes, Joshua suddenly remembered the Sin for which he had originally been thrust out of the village. More than that, he remembered every mean little thought or action he had ever done and added to them all the sins of every corpse he had served to his own advantage by eating their sins, for the payment of subsistence. An unearthly pain of guilt and fear wracked him. He howled aloud and tried to bury himself in the mossy ground.

Brother Anthony continued, not in the least concerned, but kinder than ever. "You, Joshua Forward, both chose and was chosen by God and you are Holy. Know you not who it was that took in and cancelled all the sins of those you served as Sin Eater? Know you not who ate your own sins and so redeemed you of them? You have become like Jesus the Christ and shared the heavy task of redeeming God's so much loved world."

Joshua Forward looked up at him and saw a Man of God in his True Self, an exile from a Southern Country, a warden of pigs and a carer of all living creatures. Joshua knew now how he himself had played an honoured part in the redemptive love that encircles all who remain open with the tiniest crack to let the love in.

He sank down, his mortal body briefly overwhelmed into sleep, his heart eased beyond measure and his Spirit at peace.

In the morning, when he awoke refreshed but hungry in Brother Anthony's cell, the Hermit ministered to him and told him, "Your task is now to continue the mission you took on unwittingly, but no longer as an outcast. You are called to travel the world as a Storyteller for all your remaining years and preach the gospel of love and forgiveness to all you meet. It does not matter if they receive it well or ill. You are and will remain Blessed and a Blessing to all."

Brother Anthony made the sign of the cross on the forehead of Brother Joshua Forward in token of his acceptance into Brotherhood, as they broke bread together.

"I wouldn't want you to be lonely though," said a smiling Brother Anthony, as he packed up a bag of necessaries and food for a few days. "Look – here is your companion and friend, my brother Swineherd!" and he brought out a wriggling piglet, who seemed to realise he was being offered a new master and a good chance in life and jumped into Joshua's willing grasp. They walked tall at last, out into newness of life.

Indeed, the account of Brother Joshua, the Swineherd, became a well-remembered and well-loved story in itself around the fireside in that part of the country for many a long year. Centuries later, historians were hard put to place why something of a pig cult should have spread through a remote Sussex area, but the story remains popular to this day as shown by the Runt In Tun pub at Maynards Green, with its picture of a Tantony pig in a barrel on the pub sign.

POSTLUDE

♪

GERARD FORWARD did not sleep, nor did he benefit from his lesson, convoluted as it was and requiring a need to repent and Turn Around, like the Cottage, if one wished to be forgiven in any way.

Gerard saw no need to be forgiven in his impregnable sense of entitlement. He had not been able to block out the doctrine of forgiving love entirely, but he still resisted it without much difficulty.

"Absolute rubbish," he snarled at his face in the little bathroom mirror in the early morning light. He was still furious that he had somehow been outsmarted after a promising beginning tormenting Helena and he was still spitting in fury at the equally calm and resistant farmer's wife, Norah Doveport. "Bloody Bitches!" he exclaimed.

As he shaved, still fizzing with thwarted anger, he saw a strange change coming over his face. It was almost as if the skin was becoming hard; a darker terracotta colour was overtaking his patrician features. He had always been vain and been able to ignore the jowliness, the signs of aging and becoming fat, but this was different.

The change progressed quickly. When he touched his skin, nothing felt different, but looking in the mirror he could see suddenly that his face appeared to be growing a strange terracotta coloured extra skin, like an earthenware mask. His face was being covered very quickly with a surface that looked just like that of a pig.

He could see his shocked eyes unchanged through the eye holes. His mouth, with its broad lips, no longer suggested a hedonistic and charming playboy but an unthinking ugly porcine creature within which he had become trapped. Every turn of his head showed him, in the mirror, that the unwanted integument extended right round his head, and covered his shoulders too. His face had become indeed an ugly and weird sight!

One might have regarded it as a reflection of his inner state except that pigs are lovable creatures and among the best and most patient of God's creation.

Once more enraged and filled with hate for this pig of a creature, all the more because it seemed to be himself, he brought up his fist and crashed it side-on into the mirror!

He dimly heard a collective cry of horror from the mice but did not know what or who that was. He was busy staunching the bleeding with a hand towel and studying what remained of the mirror in a thousand pieces scattered over the basin.

In confusion he wiped his face on the towel, blood going everywhere. He swore again, binding his bleeding hand up properly. Even without a mirror he knew that the mask was really there but was somehow invisible to all except to him. He knew he would never be able to forget this, his true face!

And somehow he also knew that to get rid of it, all he would have to do would be to crack the earthenware jar enclosing him in his own implacable will and let it drop away.

"Never!" he shouted in defiance to the Cottage. "Never, never, never! I will never crack it. It's mine!"

Gerard Forward was feeling thwarted in a way that prison had never succeeded in doing.

There he had always been able to work the system; here there was no system to work. Just a sense of a strong but benevolent world that would not let him play the villain indefinitely, nor permit him to torment others forever. That inability to satisfy his own cruelty would be the most painful thing he could ever feel; a true taste of an intolerable hell of self will. Would even that stop him in his course?

Who knows. He is not there, not yet at least. "NO!" he shouted defiantly one last time into the wind, now just stirring the curtains. "I said NO!"

He took his bag, slamming in his night things and rang the taxi firm. He was gone, up the lane to meet a taxi and was carried off still in a rage and defiance to catch his train long before Helena decided, with her newly acquired confidence, to see to him with icy politeness but have Norah hovering in the background at the garden gate in full view.

However, when the two women came in, they realised he had already left and very probably after a tantrum.

They found a topsy-turvy bedroom bearing witness to his chaotic haste but no sign of the gentleman himself or his belongings. It was fortunate, Helena thought, that he had been forced by Norah to pay in advance the night before, but at first she was concerned at the sight of the blood. Then she thought that, had he been badly hurt there, he would surely have phoned for an ambulance or knocked at someone's door. People rise early in the country.

She realised she was going have to claim for the broken mirror in the bathroom and arrange for its replacement. Not a problem. Whoever the mystery owners were she had never had any queries over replacements or repairs.

Helena and Norah, with Bert's help too, were soon able safely to get rid of the broken glass, though even with their stoutest gloves and lots of soapy water it was a long job to wipe up every drop of Gerard Forward's spilt blood.

"What a pig of a man he is!" exclaimed Norah. Helena, agreeing completely, added, "Maybe, just maybe he caught sight of his mug in the mirror and couldn't stand what he saw. But it's an insult to all those nice pigs to call him one – he was something much worse!"

Neither had any idea that the Mice, holed up just out of sight behind the wainscoting, were solemnly nodding agreement, and could have told them just how accurate their assessment was!

Helena was not at all put out at this unpleasant task – she was too relieved that she had, if not outsmarted him at last, at least neutralised his power over her. One never 'wins' with such people.

"I'm just glad I need never see him or even think of him again," she confided to Norah as they made up the bed and gave a final extra clean to everything he might have touched or even looked at.

"Tell you something even better!" replied her friend, "He's gone off carrying a good seven years of bad luck for breaking the mirror! What goes around comes around!" And they both doubled up laughing.

CHAPTER SIXTEEN

THE WHITE UNICORN

PRELUDE
♪

THE **NEXT VISITOR** for Turnaround Cottage had booked in, Helena noted, from Eastbourne. On this warm summer's day Helena had come to the Cottage early, to be ready for whenever the new visitor should come, and to enjoy the sunshine. One of the team of gardeners was there, stooping over the dahlias. He straightened himself up and prepared to chat.

Helena liked old Brent. He was reliable, local and always known just as 'Brent.' If he had another name, it seemed even he might have forgotten it and even his wife called him Brent. In spite of the time he spent leaning on a spade or hoe, in time honoured gardener's fashion, he got through phenomenal amounts of work and was inclined to disapprove of the younger members of the team, who came and went all the time, as better jobs beckoned.

Brent's good second-in- command, a tubby middle-aged man, who had the unlikely but true name of Tony Shrub, was in the garden as well and came from the composter at the back, smiling. Everyone liked Helena, though she would have been surprised to hear it. Both men accepted her offer of a cup of tea and they all sat in the sun companionably for a while.

A stranger pulling up in a car was the signal to Helena that it was time to receive her new Visitor. Tony went off on his motor bike with a lot of smoke and noise, while Mr Brent, as Helena persisted in calling him being old fashioned, began turning over the vegetable patch for a new crop of lettuces.

Helena had been intrigued by a booking from Eastbourne, as it was only a half hour drive away, but quickly explained by the man himself. He met Helena on the path as she returned the cups to the kitchen. He was tall and attractive, with a distinguished look, though she also detected a slightly unhealthy pallor and a sort of translucency, shown up by the bright sunlight on his balding head, suggesting less than perfect health.

"Is it Mr Jeremy Cornwell?" Helena asked. He smiled at her and took the proffered hand in a gentle handshake. "I see you're booked in for one night, with the option of having one or two more?" She said it more as a question and he replied:

"Yes. I hope that's all right. It was short notice as we discovered a gas leak." He corrected himself: "I discovered a gas leak, and had to go to a friend's for a few days. In fact it's all being sorted quickly after all, so I just need the one night, if that's all right with you?"

Helena agreed readily. Bookings on a weekday were less usual, but work on a house explained it. Not for the first time she wondered how the mysterious owners of Turnaround Cottage expected it to be a paying business. The usage was low and a little erratic and the price too on the low side. Surely it hardly covered the normal outgoings and her salary?

Well, that was not her business. There had been a time when she had wondered whether it could even be a cover, but dismissed the idea. It was hardly any useful scale of money laundering and there was certainly never any activity to suggest smuggling, though that had been a staple pastime of the Sussex coastal areas in past centuries. She was coming to the conclusion that it must be owned by an eccentric millionaire who didn't need the money and preferred to be anonymous, but maybe had some sentimental attraction to the Sussex Downs. Or to Windmills, and only wanted an excuse to keep it going. Only surely he would have picked a working Mill?

Dismissing such thoughts, which never really mattered, so long as she felt it was all above board and gave her a useful retirement salary, she concentrated on bringing out the towels and showing this Visitor around. She noted that he was breathless on the stairs, which somewhat confirmed her impression that he might have poor health.

For once she accepted a cup of tea, missing George Miller more than she would have believed possible – or sensible. They chatted about Sussex, comparing it with her home county of Derbyshire. Jeremy seemed knowledgeable about many things, which was partly explained by him having spent most of his working life as a Librarian after extensive travel as an adventurous young man.

Helena talked about the friendship she had experienced with one recurring visitor,

George, who had the appropriate name of 'Miller.' When Jeremy asked whether George was likely to visit Sussex again, Helena unconsciously turned her head away. "No," she said, abruptly. "He's going to live in France. In fact he's there at the moment searching for a place to live."

She turned the conversation to the Visitor's family and it was his turn to clam up. Helena must have shown she felt she had overstepped some invisible social mark, as a few moments later he broke off from a discursive monologue on whales to say apologetically:

"I'm sorry. I think I rather snubbed you there. My parents died when I was quite a young man – that's partly why I took ship as a sailor for many years, before going to University. I got my degree and settled in Eastbourne with my partner many years back. He worked in a delicatessen. Very good cook too."

He self-consciously avoided looking at Helena as he said this, so she was able to be quite straightforward with him.

"So your partner is a man?" she said, her tone indicating that this seemed almost commonplace – which indeed it did to her.

"Was. Not is. Jose died five months ago. Oh damn! I'm going to cry! Sorry!" he said, tears already gathering in his eyes.

"Of course you are. It's for me to be sorry. You must still be absolutely raw at such a loss!" said Helena warmly.

"Can I tell you just a little about Jose and me?" he asked, assuming consent and going on to tell her quite a lot about 'Hosay' as he pronounced the name.

He and the younger Jose Diaz had met many years ago, when he was visiting Spain with his shipping line and they had fallen deeply in love. Of course it was even against the law in those day and they had learnt to conceal the nature of their friendship from the start, as all gays of either sex had to do. It had been easier when he was studying and Jose had been the breadwinner for a few years.

Their love had been tested in all sorts of ways, most cruelly when after decades together Jose had fallen ill.

"It just started with him picking up every germ going," said Jeremy, crying afresh at the memory. "Colds, all the time. Flu – every outbreak. He had to give up work – luckily, because they would have sacked him anyway. Then pains in his arms and legs, vomiting in the mornings. We twigged gradually what was wrong, but it was still devastating when it was confirmed."

"The secrecy must have been horribly difficult too," said Helena sympathetically. "No one really talked about the 'Gay plague' early on, except in whispers!"

Jeremy confirmed what she said with a nod, still almost too overwhelmed by the memories to speak, "The worst thing of all was that I couldn't be put down as the next of kin, so all the time in hospital I was just elbowed out. I thought his family had accepted me but they were simple people, peasants, virtually, and they'd never realised what the friendship was. Then of course the shit really hit the fan!"

He continued to pour out his hurt and Helena just listened.

"Their Church was apparently totally against it and the family wouldn't let me be with Jose at the end for fear of being cut off by the priests. I'm sure that wouldn't have happened. All the priests I've met have been very sympathetic. I think his family were a bit jealous, to be honest and made it up.

"But all I really know was that I let him down at the last. I wasn't there when he died, peacefully luckily, but I can never really forgive myself for that even though I couldn't help it."

Helena was very grieved, indeed felt herself ashamed somehow over the prejudices in society, but knew better than try to make him feel better by superficial comfort for his feelings, which risked just devaluing them again.

After that they talked calmly for quite a while more, on every subject under the sun. Then Helena gave him a big hug as she set off for her home, making sure he was all right. Indeed he seemed happier just to have shared so much. She guessed it was not common for him to be able to do so, and the bereavement was still very recent. He was carefully bottling it all up again as she left.

Left on his own in the cottage, Jeremy ate a simple salad supper he had brought with him, drank some hot milk and began preparing for bed. He felt cleansed and relaxed in this place and was, somehow, not at all put out by the appearance of a group of six Mice, in a straight line-up, evidently intent on addressing him formally. He had gone through too much to waste time on being frightened or even surprised these days.

"Hello Jeremy," said the largest Mouse.

It seemed the most irrelevant question to choose but he couldn't help saying, "How do you know my name, Mouse?"

The Mouse raised a paw and waved it dismissively. "Easy! Of course we heard Helena call you by it! The point is we think you need a story. Can we ask the West Wind to tell you one?"

"Certainly you can," said Jeremy, fascinated and astounded in equal measure.

The Mice jumped onto the window sill, pulled back the curtains dramatically and proceeded to call up the wind with a series of Mice chirrups and squeaks and a strangely piercing whistling sound.

Jeremy was not to know that their polite enquiry was mostly for show. The West Wind had already pinpointed Jeremy as a necessary recipient of a particular story. The Mice just thought it was polite to ask, somewhat to the West Wind's annoyance. She blew strongly through the open window, setting the red brocade curtains billowing inwards, but her voice calling him was soft and gentle.

"Jeremy, Jeremy, you are sad because you could not say a proper goodbye to Jose. If you knew what I know you would know what I know, that every tear you shed about this matter, every sigh you have made, every wish deep in your heart has been granted, because there is no Time.

It is all happening in the present. Your present and his present. It is a present for you both and you need never think he did not, does not, will not, know how much you loved him. Your every day together was a meeting and a parting and a declaration of love, even the ones which did not seem so or were marred and quarrelled over in some way.

So accept this story, given you by Time and the White Unicorn itself to show you that time is not real, but Love is so real you can never lose it once given."

Here is the story, so beautifully told by the West Wind, to Jeremy Cornwell, comforted in his grief for his lost love, Jose Diaz...

THE WHITE UNICORN

THE PINE CONES sputtered and spat as their oily content flared, filling the little cottage with their healthy scent. The fire's warmth began to reach out to his cold limbs.

Brother Hugh straightened his aching back, looking forward to an evening at rest after his labours in the forest. Tomorrow he must take the firewood and pine cones to the elderly poor ones in the village for their Christmas.

A sudden tap on the window drew his attention. The shining shape of a horse seemed to be out there, which was strange enough in itself, but nothing could have prepared him for what he found as he opened the door.

He could hardly take in the delicate beauty of the pure white horse, still tapping on the window with its single horn. What immediately drew his attention was the woman, swaying on the creature's back, eyes closed.

"Help me!" she cried. "Please, I beg you for the love of God, help me!"

She was not young, though her careworn face might have been beautiful once, he thought. It stirred some sort of memories within him, exquisite yet unaccustomed and uncomfortable, from a past he had long put aside.

He instinctively moved forward holding up his arms, just in time as she slid down unconscious into them. He caught her clumsily, then instinctively shifted his grip to hold her safely.

Those strong arms which had caught many a new-born calf, or lost sheep, even a lost child, in recent years, seemed to understand the need for tenderness mixed with strength which they had never known in his tempestuous, selfish, youth. That new skill, forged in the years of guilt-ridden pain came unconsciously into his dark eyes as they stared into her white face.

As if called, her eyes fluttered open and for a moment hazel met brown and something was shared, then vanished. "I'm Alysa," she whispered. "I've come back."

Her voice was so faint that he could not be sure he had even heard it. Had he imagined her voice, as he had so often done in those early years?

A sharp kick from a silver hoof made him look round. The white Unicorn looked at him compassionately, as if it might speak, but then dissolved and vanished before his eyes. Woken to practical actions, Brother Hugh carried the unconscious woman into the hut, to lay her on a sheepskin by the fire and chafe her cold hands and arms. His hand, laid diffidently on the wonder of her breast, felt a faint heartbeat.

The little woodland animals who shared his cottage came near, as it was feeding time, but he was preoccupied and the squirrel and the little wild birds came up fearlessly to help him. Only the red fox stood back, calculating, nervous, its head up and alert for danger to his beloved master...

The woman who had called herself Alysa stirred, her eyelids fluttered open and once more her hazel eyes met those of Brother Hugh. He could not help himself, the words burst out of him:

"Why? Why? Alysa? Why did you leave me so suddenly and marry him? It is twenty-one years since you broke my heart!"

"He kidnapped me! The Duke! He had always lusted after me and he seized his chance when his uncle died and he inherited.

As Duke he could do anything he wanted — and he wanted me!"

"But why did you not tell me! Never a word! Did you not know I would have come to your rescue?"

"Yes! And got killed for it too!" cried Alysa. "His men took my parents hostage as well, to ensure my silence. I could not risk all your lives!"

She looked at him with such love in her face that he believed her, as the tears of over twenty years began to pour from his eyes in release. All he had ever really needed, in those agonising early months, was to understand, to know if it had all been lies or if she had ever truly loved him. Somehow he knew now, as surely as if an angel was telling him, that her love for him was as deep and faithful as his had always been for her.

All those years of struggling as a reluctant monk, because it seemed the only way, other than the sin of suicide to add to his sin with Alysa! All the nights that gentle Prior Joseph of his order had listened to his weeping confessions and his terrible grieving, followed by the years of acceptance and peace.

Alysa seemed to be reading his thoughts. She fumbled with a heavy silver ring on her finger and pushed it into his hand. His fingers closed around it and pressed it to his chest, where a familiar pain was rising. Could he reach Brother Oswald's foxglove medicine?

He forgot all pain as Alysa showed she had more to tell. She stretched out her free hand to him and Brother Hugh took it in his. She continued:

"The baby! I must tell you about the baby. That was the worst thing; not being able to tell you. I called him Roderick, after your father."

His mouth felt dry as he stammered, "You had a baby? Did he die?"

"No Hugh," she cried, "our baby! He lived. He lives still and is the heir to the Dukedom! My husband could see that I was increasing soon after the marriage. So could his physician and both knew that he was unable to sire children. But he was desperate for an heir! When I was safely delivered of our lusty boy at full term, seven months after the marriage, it suited him to say it was a seven-month child. Of course the midwife and the physician backed him up!"

Brother Hugh had remained silent, overwhelmed with emotion. "I have a son!" was all he could whisper. Then looking adoringly into her face he corrected himself. "No. *We* have a son, Alysa!"

"He is quite different from the Duke!" Alysa continued. "He is loved and accepted by all the fiefdom. He will marry and have children and rule wisely, Hugh. I know it!"

The pain in his chest was crushing him, but he cared nothing for it. All those years of loss and grief had passed and a great joy and peace were sweeping over him. His last sight on earth was Alysa's face, as beautiful as when they first lay together in a love that would last beyond the grave.

♪

Prior Joseph and Brother Oswald the Almoner found him in the morning. The pine fire had died, but its scent still sweetened the air in the little hut. The little birds and the squirrel were silent in the beams above him, but the red fox lay with its head near to his hand, moaning like a child.

"It could have happened at any time," said the Almoner. "He will be sorely missed for all his many kindnesses. I often wondered at his story, before he came here."

If he hoped the Prior would tell him, he was disappointed. Prior Joseph merely said, "I must admit it is a great relief to me not to have to tell him the news we received at first light this morning."

He was staring with a frown at the heavy silver ring he could just see clasped tight in Brother Hugh's lifeless hand. No monk wore such a thing.

The Prior continued, in reply to the questioning look on the Almoner's face:

"The Duke and his Lady are dead! They were in their carriage and something must have startled the horses badly. They fell down off the mountain and they and the coachman were killed. I think it must have been at about 8 of the clock last evening. We must go and prepare to say prayers for them both, and for our dear Brother. The Duke was a hard man, God rest his soul, but she was as lovely a Lady as ever lived! Thank goodness the new Duke Roderick takes after her, not him!"

As he spoke, the Prior was gently prising loose the ring. He recognised it very well, but had never seen it except on the hand of the Duchess. He stood for a moment in troubled thought, then his face cleared. "God is love," he said, almost to himself, "and who are we to judge who deserves it and who doesn't?"

Turning to the Almoner, who was studying the ring in shock as he recognised the arms engraved on it, he said, "See that this ring remains with our Brother and is buried with him. Please understand that this is under the seal of the confessional!"

And so it was all done, but no one else ever saw the White Unicorn.

POSTLUDE

♪

JEREMY found that as he listened to the story the tears had once again been rolling down his cheeks. The fact that it was a love story between a man and a woman did not bother him, for all his life he had been used to a kind of instant translation, allowing him to live into the heterosexual experience and make it match his own feelings.

He found that the Mice were all sitting on his knees and shoulder, joined by quite a few more and he didn't mind a bit. Indeed he nearly wiped his eyes with one, mistaking it for the handkerchief in his sleeve.

The Mice did not leave him until he had crawled into bed and the main Mouse herself, with heroic effort, tucked a fold of sheet under his chin. He felt loved by the mice and by the Wind and by the Cottage itself and most of all by Jose. He slept better than he had in months.

When Helena came in the next morning she was eager to see if she could find out whether Jeremy had heard a story and if so what had happened? She was beginning to put little clues together as to what happened to some of the visitors.

On this occasion he had a knowing look in his eye as he replied to her query that he had slept very well. Mice activity had been a little distracting, but welcome.

Jeremy's demeanour was happier, quite mischievous even, particularly considering the sad nature of their talk the previous night. He told her, quite simply, that the West Wind had told him a story about true lovers dying, yet it had made him somehow happier. He motioned her to sit down and she did so, with him opposite her in the red brocaded chair.

"I think some time you may need a story," he said, "though I hope not. If you do, just ask the Cottage. The Mice told me you tell them stories yourself?" And she nodded. She felt almost speechless at someone who could see and speak of these strange things so easily.

"Helena," he said to her. "It helped me so much when you listened to my story last night so sympathetically. I hope we can continue friends and meet up occasionally?"

"Of course," said Helena warmly.

"I'm thinking your quick eyes have noted my health problem. Did you realise I am, in fact, suffering from that modern version of the plague that my darling Jose died from?"

Helena nodded. "I worked in the health service," she said. "Only as Admin, but one learns a few things. Even," and she looked at him meaningfully, "when NOT to worry about something!"

"Yes," Jeremy responded. "You have no idea what a relief it is not to have to explain or see a look of fear come into people's faces. I'm not contagious or dangerous and you know that, but not everybody does."

"Will you be all right?" Helena asked, simply. He replied in kind: "I've no means, really, of knowing. I may join my friends, so many of them have gone. Too many to name. Though people are starting to make wonderful memorials to them, even publicly. 'The times they are a'changing!'

"I'm not sure I mind too much, now..." Jeremy continued, thoughtfully, "But still... there are new treatment plans coming all the time, combined drug therapies and lifestyle and so on. The whole scene could be very different in just a few years' time. I think I should like to put some effort into fighting for that, for Jose's sake and for others if not for myself."

"I want you to live!" said Helena warmly and he laughed.

"Yes, I think I do too. There's a lot of work still to do to break down prejudice. The story I heard in here"... He hesitated. "Of course, Jose and I couldn't have a child, like the normal lovers in the story did. But some are even talking of gay couples marrying and adopting children. Too late for me of course, but... well ... what a change that would be!"

"I can't see any reason why not, for my part," said Helena, "though I think there might be a lot of opposition from some quarters. But I don't need to tell you that! You've suffered prejudice all your life, I guess?"

As she prepared to leave he caught her hand and said, mischievously, "That man you're in love with must be an absolute idiot not to see that you're the true Gold and snap you up!

What's he thinking about to go off and live in France?"

Helena blushed deeply. "How on earth did you guess!" she exclaimed.

"Oh, I'm an expert on other people's love lives," he said, laughing. "It was just the way you spoke of that previous visitor – George, was it? And your tone when you said he'd gone to France.

"You know something? Old Uncle Jeremy doesn't believe he'll stay there. And we will all do well when that happens, because I won't be a threat but a friend to both of you."

Helena laughed and blushed again. She didn't believe what he said about George, but it lifted her mood amazingly and they parted with a mutual exchange of details and a warm hug.

INTERLUDE
♪

SPRING IN THE CIVIC CENTRE

The Mayor considered that the gardens ought
To have a share in Spring.
Tulips would be respectable, he thought,
Quiet, and quite the thing.

"Obedient tulips stand in rows," he said,
"And never make a mess,
But to make sure, we'll still fence off the bed."
The councillors said, "Yes."

But oh, if they had only known the truth!
The Spring can't be confined.
Those wild and dangerous tulips, like our youth,
Subvert the civic mind.

The typists, all seduced from sober ways,
Remove their woolly vests,
While golden waves of flowers fall in spray
Around their naked breasts.

The treasurer cries, "How erroneous!
The scheme has fallen flat.
Next year I say, stick to begonias,
And plastic ones at that!"

The stripy tulip-tigers roar, and try
To reach with yellow paws
And swipe the ankles of the passers-by,
Gnashing their crimson jaws.

Pubescent schoolgirls walk in twosomes
near,
Still thinking of their sums.
Those saucy orange tulips wink and leer,
And try to pinch their bums.

Tell all the filing clerks to stay away—
Some things cannot be filed.
With sex and aggro in the park today,
The Spring is really wild!

CHAPTER SEVENTEEN

THE RETURN OF ARACHNE

PRELUDE
♪

LUNCH had been served, eaten and cleared away at Cyclamen Lodge. They were a reduced company this Sunday. The Colonel had been taken out by a great nephew, who tried to keep in touch occasionally when he was in the country. Most of the other residents were similarly out with local relatives or members of local churches, who faithfully fulfilled a felt obligation to keep in touch with them.

Aunty Mabel Dunnett was having a nap, having enjoyed her Sunday roast dinner very much. Her niece Carol had not been able to come for a few weeks, having much to do back home in Derbyshire.

Helena came through the door to make up for her friend's absence and was waiting for Mabel to wake up. Joe had promised that the four of them plus Rosie Cullen could take the van and go for a drive. In the meantime she was watching Dolores Entwhistle with great interest.

Sitting with her little great granddaughter, Dolores was as absorbed as Jenny in what they were doing. Her small fingers seemed not much bigger than the little girl's and their heads were on a level as Jenny perched on a stool beside her, the curling white hair of the old lady showing an uncanny likeness to the soft waves in the yellow locks of the child.

Dolores was a small dumpy woman and Jenny was a quiet, shy little girl, daughter of Francine, her oldest granddaughter, a single mum. Jenny attended a special needs school and speaking did not come easily to her. Every week Francine had taken to bringing her to Cyclamen Lodge on a Sunday for a 'special hour' with Dolores Entwhistle. Both tired easily and had memory problems.

Francine would cry silently inside with a mixture of sorrow and relief at this friendship, some 80 years apart. Her own memories of this grandmother were of Dolores as already seeming to be a very old lady, occasionally sitting in a corner in their house at holiday times, but with very little to say for herself.

Somehow this friendship between the two had happened for Jenny when she had grasped the idea of 'family' and having other people than her mum but no dad. Also, the word 'special' was not an insult, as when the local children mocked her, but a word which meant something different, nice, comforting.

In her mind Jenny 'saw' it like a tangle of fine gold thread linking her to her 'special' people, which included the lollipop lady outside the school in Eastbourne, and the little dog in the corner shop, as well as some, but not all, of her relatives.

Now, Dolores also seemed to come into her own with this special great granddaughter, Jenny, and their soft voices alternated in their precious time together every week. The other old folk were thrilled to have a little girl visiting, as not all had grandchildren themselves, though it was also a treat when the primary school classes came to listen to 'Memory Time', arranged for the benefit of both age groups.

Francine had suggested Jenny call her 'Nana Dolores' to distinguish her from ordinary grannies, but it came out, after great effort from Jenny as 'Nana Doll' – a lovely name for her, with her sweet round face and body. Francine bought Jenny a set of colourful Russian dolls. Helena watched how the pair became absorbed in them, as indeed they did, tirelessly, each time they met.

"See, Jenny," Nana Doll was saying, "you put your fingers round the bottom part, so... and turn the top around and lift – gently now dear! – and see what we have... Oh!"

Jenny laughed in triumph as her clumsy fingers eventually managed to open each doll in turn, each one smaller than the last. In the centre was a miniature rabbit and Jenny cried out in triumph: "Bunny Wabbit today!"

Francine always added different things each week, a sweetie, or a tiny charm or toy. It became a ritual for someone to find one thing each week for a little ceremony of opening the doll. Even the Colonel tried to find things, though his offer of some of his special baccy had to be tactfully deflected.

Meanwhile Helena was watching Rosie. She noted how good the younger woman was at keeping an eye on all the residents while at the same time completely focusing on the one in front of her. She was noting when Jenny got bored, or Nanna Doll got tired and moved in swiftly to offer distractions,

Rosie's rather plain face lit up when she was caring for people and she seemed to come into her own as compared with some of the other young women who were patently bored with being compelled to spend an afternoon with their crumbly old relatives and probably wouldn't be there unless they hoped to be remembered in the will.

Helena took advantage of keeping the endless supply of tea for the visitors by taking the opportunity to mention this to Joe when he came in with the Rumbelow frog mug for a refill.

"Look at Rosie!" she said. "Isn't she kind? After all, she's not on duty today. It's just that she promised Francine to bring in Jenny to see Dolores so she wouldn't have to miss her session with her Nan. What a lovely mother Rosie herself will make one day! And a very practical wife for some lucky man. She cooks like an angel you know! Have you tried her quince and apple tart?"

She offered him a piece and it was indeed delicious, leaving a somewhat thoughtful Joe to consider Rosie in a different light. He'd never really thought of life-long characteristics in the blonde barmaids he normally dated – those being the only girls available at the end of a late shift – but he reflected that he himself wasn't getting any younger and it could be a bit lonely on his days off. He noted she had a very sweet smile which transformed her features and a rather nice full bust.

The afternoon was still young, other staff were in charge in the Lodge and Joe felt it would be good to offer to take Mabel and Dolores out in the Van, if Rosie would care to come with them. He asked if Francine, Dolores' daughter and Jenny's mother, who had stayed quietly in a corner, would like to come too, bringing Jenny of course, and she was very pleased.

Helena volunteered quite happily as well, thinking that helping out might serve to ease the ache in her heart over George a little, as well as being better for her to be in company. At the last moment Colonel Brassington turned up, his outing having been cut short by a local bus strike, so they smuggled him into the Van too.

Mabel voted, as might be predicted, to go to Turnaround Cottage, so Helena laughed and said she would take her own car. Everyone was happy to go there too, especially as it was turning wet so a trip to the seaside would not be much fun.

♪

Once at the Cottage, Joe, with Helena's permission, lit a fire and they all gathered round, the day having turned a little chilly. The older members dozed serenely and Helena and Rosie involved Francine and Jenny in an old fashioned game of snakes and ladders they found in a drawer.

Joe looked up from the fire and was astonished to see a group of six mice, advancing in style as if wishing to speak to him. So strong was this impression that he got down to nearer their level and spoke to them first. On the first official trip to the Cottage Helena had insisted to the Mice that they must stay out of sight. There was more than enough magic around without talking animals.

However, Helena had not thought to repeat the ban and she had missed having the Mice around, so she decided to let whatever happened just happen.

After Joe's previous visit to the Cottage and hearing the Story there he had convinced himself it had all been a dream. Now he wasn't so sure. He noted from the corner of his eye that the rest of the party did not look at all surprised, except for Francine, who only knew rumours of the strangeness of this place.

Jenny was hardly surprised by anything, because in her special world nothing was amiss except when people were unkind to her. The Mice – in her view – looked as if they were kind.

So Jenny smiled at the Mice and said "Hello!" That galvanised Joe.

"What can I do for you, Gentlemen?" he asked

In spite of trying not to be surprised, even he was slightly shocked when the largest one said, "Not so much of the 'Gentlemen', please. Three of us are ladies!"

"I do beg your pardon!" he cried, shocked at his own unthinking sexism. Jenny slipped her hand in his consolingly.

"Mice do not look very different, except to other Mice," conceded the lady Mouse, mollified by his response. They came round in a semi-circle and she continued:

"We think you need a story, but the Winds are having a bit of a temperamental day. They say they're not on strike, just a go slow, but believe me you don't want a go-slow Story from that lot! It will take from here to Eternity and longer!"

"Well," said Joe trying to think logically in a very strange and unusual situation, "what are they on strike about? Pay? Conditions? Do you know what the problem is?"

The lady Mouse looked, if that was possible, irritated. "Yes of course. We are all cognisant of Marxist ideology and the rise of the Trade Union Movement but we cannot see how it applies."

Chastened, Joe could only think of saying, "Well, have you asked them? What do they say?"

Six mouse jaws dropped as one. "Marx never says anything about asking the workers," said another mouse tremulously. Joe was tempted to say something a bit sarcastic about Idealogues and Philosophers, who all knew what everyone wanted without ever asking them, but wisely felt it was not the time.

Anyway, the leading lady Mouse went over to the window and shrieked like a penny whistle out into the garden.

A curious conversation appeared to ensue, of whistles, Mouse squeaks and high-pitched blowing noises. When she beckoned him over, Jo saw a wind-tossed garden, not at all what he had expected because the Cottage had turned around and was facing North, with the view of the bins and the compost and the garden shed, leading to the little River Flitter.

"Listen!" said the voice of the North Wind, not at all slowly. "I will tell you because you have asked nicely and I can see how badly you need an emergency story. It must not be assumed that the Go Slow is over!"

Joe never did discover what the Industrial Action by the Winds was about, but it didn't matter because it seemed that they didn't know either and abandoned it shortly after. I understand this is not unusual even in a post-Marxist world and is deemed to be all the fault of something called a thatcher.

So here is the entertaining Story that the North Wind, risking his Union's accusations of being a 'Black leg', condescended to tell the Mice and their visitors, even though he impressed upon them the importance of Solidarity. Helena couldn't help thinking that a lecture on solidarity was somewhat unexpected, not to mention hardly appropriate from the Wind, but she too snuggled down and listened as the North Wind began to tell about...

THE RETURN OF ARACHNE le NOIR

IN A LITTLE VILLAGE square in Muddles Green, a sort of suburb of Hastings, an oldish, plumpish, untidyish woman with darkish hair was studying the flowers in a municipal flower bed. She sighed deeply and approached one of the Council gardeners, asking questions about a plant with pretty purple and yellow flowers flopping over the fence. You might have guessed from his answers that she was enquiring about its poisonous potential and you would have been right.

"What if you ate some of the flowers?" she was saying. "Or does it have berries – what about them?"

"Well, it do have berries in the autumn. Dark purple ones they be," said the Gardener, who – in case you're interested – had been to Eton and had a degree in Classics, but found it better for his professional prospects to affect a BBC Mummerset accent.

"Oh I just love purple," said the lady, enthusiastically. "After dark, black is my favourite colour!"

The Gardener continued as if she hadn't spoken: "That there plant be called Deadly Nightshade, Ma'am, so p'raps that should suggest it wouldn't be very good for you to eat it."

"Well, I suppose it's better not to make a drink of it," the woman said. "What would happen if you sat under it and the berries just fell into your mouth?"

The Gardener scratched his head, pushing his flat cap back, sighed, and moved away. His training in horticulture, which had largely consisted of watching Gardeners' Question time and occasional visits to the Chelsea Flower Show, not having prepared him for this sort of advanced interrogation.

Anyone observing the strange lady might also have been slightly surprised to see her next move, which was to enter the Benefits Office in this sleepy seaside place. There was indeed such an observer to see this, including the swift furtive look the lady cast around first, as if ashamed to be seen.

The observer, a portly gentleman with a well-scrubbed pink face, had drawn back into the shade of a side alley quickly enough for the lady not to have seen him. He scratched his head, looking thoughtfully at the door, marked usefully South Sussex Benefits Office.

Mark him well, for his name is Gregory from Gloucester, her one-time husband and you will see him again!

The lady, assuring herself – wrongly – that she had not been seen entering the Benefits Office, of which she was indeed ashamed, saw a long row of glass fronted desks behind a screen. The desks held a variety of ladies, and one gentleman, whose role it was to assess the financial state of each claimant who shuffled in and who usually picked whoever looked least intimidating today. (The officials knew this, so had a rota for it.)

The hapless individuals seeking benefits (usually human, though you might occasionally doubt it) subjected themselves to a form of inquisition which left no stone of their lives, family history, health, financial and job potential, or level of misery, unturned. This cathartic process was followed (usually) by a giro, offer of work, or both.

The dark haired lady waited for her turn, as there seemed to be a number of people out of work discussing what might be on offer with the important officials. She hung back in order to choose the youngest and prettiest of the officials, calculating – wrongly – that she might prove a soft touch.

Once in place she discussed her past and her skills with many prevarications, manipulative distractions and outright lies, and came out, feeling triumphant, with a giro for a meagre sum and an offer of work, feeling that she had fooled the system.

Not so. No one fools the system and in a temporary lull the angelic looking young lady who had talked to her looked at her colleagues and they all beamed at each other with an evil and identical smile. "We've found another cheat," the smile said. "We can have some fun here".

The fun had indeed started as they had sent the respectable looking middle-aged lady to try the lowest job they had currently on the books – 'Cow pat turning.' Arachne duly turned up at the farm the following day for her shift at the job.

"Wot's yer name, luv?" said a fat woman at the farm gate.

"It's Arachne. Arachne le Noir," said our dark haired protagonist, no longer anonymous.

Yes indeed! It is our old friend, or rather enemy, of an earlier story, the evil widow who had nearly blighted the lives of so many people in the countryside not so far from this farm, aptly called 'Foul Mile Farm'.

"All these 'ere cow pats need to be turned in the sunshine, like every 'alf hour," said a laconic yokel with a straw in his mouth, showing her the place and putting a big wooden shovel in her hands. "You 'ave to really work at it to get round 'em all in the time," he added, as Arachne studied the huge field full of cowpats, stretching to the far horizon and smelling totally dreadful in the hot sun.

Arachne lasted a bare ten minutes in the job, stalking off in a rage, having told the yokel where he could put his shovel and using a small amount of residual magic to raise a couple of cowpats and dump them on the heads of him and the fat woman.

The secret is out, but how did our evil friend, last seen being carried off in a hurricane vortex, destination the Other End of Nowhere, get back at all?

I'm afraid we may never know! Suffice it to say that a couple of years after her inadvertent journey, back here she is, with only the dregs of her earlier magic powers little more than parlour tricks remaining to her.

Hence her return, reluctantly, the next day to the Benefits Office. The well-scrubbed pink-faced gentleman, who had observed her carefully, including her chosen night shelter of a disused shed out near Ridgeway, watched her go in, waiting to see if she would return out later with another address.

While seated in front of one of the glass windows, Arachne was attempting to explain away her brief attempt at the job of cowpat turner, as delightful honest labour in the delightful open air – but, sadly, cut short by the breakdown of an old wound, nobly sustained in saving the life of a prize dog earlier in her life.

This of course was a blatant lie and was instantly recognisable as such by the middle-aged, comfortable looking official Arachne had chosen this time. This lady, Agnes Toope, had heard them all. She herself was, in actual fact, a witch, and a much better one than Arachne, though thankfully not nearly as evil, confining her black magic to bank holidays and people with red hair who annoyed her.

A poor quality down-on-her-luck other witch was also fair game so she offered Arachne the next least-favourite job from her in tray, astonished – and suspicious – when Arachne jumped at the chance to become a Paper Girl in the South West Sussex district.

This was because Arachne had realised it would give her an excellent chance to find her old adversaries, Simon Wiseman, the philosopher, Roland Ransome and Brian Pudley. Best of all, she could perhaps get her revenge on Betty Brown, the Buxom Barmaid at the Dog and Knackers pub, who had so cruelly thwarted her plans last time around. No punishment would be evil enough for this, Arachne considered.

So Agnes Toope, the benefits manager sent Arachne off to the address of a Newsagent on the High Weald road, to start the following morning. The previous three paper boys had all succumbed to childhood ailments, Chicken pox, Mumps and Rocky Mountain Spotted Fever, in that order, and Mr Patel the Newsagent would be pleased to have an older female in the job, or so Agnes correctly reasoned.

As Arachne started on the long walk to the Wealden district she would have been astonished and extremely worried to realise that she was still being followed by the pink faced man, Gregory from Gloucester, the most boring man in all the world.

Arachne survived nearly a whole week in the paper girl job. This was not because she enjoyed it at all. She wore out her only remaining pair of shoes and it was so poorly paid that she was reduced to begging for left-over chips at the Saucy Sally Piscine and Potato EmPorium [sic!] where kindly Sally always saved a few chip shop leavings for down-on-their-luck passers-by.

By ingenuity and minor magic to do with calling out tickets from a mesmerised bus driver, she managed to pay a couple of visits to the Dog and Knackers, where Betty still worked and where she was able to get a glimpse of the whole group: Simon, laughing and – shyly – holding Betty's hand when no one was looking, Roland still in Horse shape, Brian Pudley still a cat. Arachne was successful at last in finding out where they were living and started to lay her plans.

That involved another visit to the Benefits Office for one last try at honest – well, fairly honest – work. This time another of the officials, a deceptively mild and bored looking lady with no name badge, interviewed her. She was, in fact, the Inspector from Head Office and very knowledgeable. She seemed inclined to dismiss Arachne's carefully rehearsed and dramatic rendering of the early stages of Rocky Mountain Spotted Fever, and an attempt to demand compensation for its onset. Since this was no more than a hasty dabbing of red spots in unlikely places with a red biro pinched from the Benefits Office itself, it was never going to gain any dramatic prizes.

Arachne attempted to use her small residual magic powers, magically inducing an office pencil to shoot a puff of nasty sneezing dust at the official. That lady contemptuously deflected the cloud with a puff from her own pencil, held at an angle, returning the magic dust cloud to Arachne's own nose, so that she suffered a ten-minute bout of sneezing, farting and burping, embarrassingly loudly.

Arachne, enraged, had every intention of starting a War and pointed her pencil at an angle again. Then she looked round. Every official eye was upon her, from eleven women and one man. They all held their office pencils just so, at an angle, primed and waiting, with evil smiles on their faces.

Be honest – you're not really surprised, are you? You always knew deep down, just who are in all official Government Offices, especially those dealing with your Income Tax, always behind the Post Office counters and always on the ends of Advice Telephone Helplines.

Yes, Witches! Male and Female, all waiting to thwart you, laugh themselves silly at you and try and keep from you the wonderful Benefits of Life that Politicians have offered and for which you yourself have always voted.

Arachne made one last brave but foolhardy attempt at intimidation. Looking at Agnes

Toope, who happened to live on High Ridgeway, she tried a threat.

"I know where you live!" said Arachne. She meant it to be sinister, as in the Godfather, but it came out just croaky and didn't have the desired effect on the lady.

"Well, of course you do," she said contemptuously. "You've been delivering my paper all week!"

♪

Arachne had endured a lot of bad luck and no success – largely it must be admitted due to her own ineptitude – but the last job, handed over by a bored Agnes Toope, was as a relief barmaid for a new micro-brewery pub in upmarket Bexhill on Sea. It was named for and under the patronage of St Nicholas, who is also known for conviviality right round the year, not just at Christmas. Inevitably it was known as 'Saint Nick's'.

Arachne had to admit she liked the place the moment she went in, and St Nick was possibly the one saint that did not make her feel uncomfortable as a witch. She liked the fresh yeasty smell of Ale, the look of the kindly young man behind the bar and the red faced and cheery older men all round the place, taking their drinking seriously, but not excessively.

"Another pint of the Skull Splitter, please James!" said one old boy.

Another was asking for "Bishop's Finger", but finding it was out said, "Okay then, needs must. I'll have your Profits of Doom tonight then, man!"

In the cheerful scrum round the bar no one marked the pink-faced man slipping in well out of Arachne's line of sight and accepting a noggin of Parson's Perry.

James, the Barman and pub owner, was very pleased to have help and quickly settled a few points regarding wages and arrangements. He accepted she had limited experience, indeed none, setting her to work at once.

Arachne sneaked back at closing time, using a few remnants of an invisibility spell and slept in the back at night. By borrowing a spare yellow curtain and one of the rather fine copper drip bowls from a cask, she managed to beg all round the villages, pretending to be a Buddhist Monk. Such exotically accoutred people were once a common sight in our country areas, adding a welcome splash of colour. Indeed they can now be regarded as indigenous.

By the end of another week Arachne was almost enjoying herself, having discovered where Betty Brown and the other friends lived during her time as Paper Girl. It was obvious to her (as to everyone except himself) that Simon Wiseman was head over heels in love with Betty and she with him, but he simply didn't know it yet, nor believe she could love him back. How much time is wasted in a woman's life by this common – and maddening – male characteristic!

Betty the Buxom barmaid had a little attic room in the pub where she worked, the Dog and Knackers. When not to be found there, she would be likely to be found looking after Roland Horse and Brian Cat, her two other best friends, but even more, spending time with Simon Wiseman in his own cottage. She did some of his cleaning and cooking, but also curled up in front of the fire trying to educate herself by reading his books and discussing them with him, a pastime he enjoyed very much, having a high appreciation of her intelligence.

Indeed, far from being at all intellectually snobbish, he longed to bring the light of learning to many more people, only enhanced by his tendency, since the enchantment of

Arachne some years before, to becoming literally a standard lamp again in moments of stress or excitement. Simon longed to ask Betty to marry him and she longed for him to do so, but they were both too shy and unsure of themselves.

Meanwhile, Arachne had advanced along her chosen path of forcing Simon to fall in love with her. Although not at all well off, he at least had something to live on and she was sick of trying to find work. Wearing her peculiar false Buddhist costume, with a black woolly hat pulled over her ears, she was even able to engage in light conversation with Betty, without that lady suspecting a thing.

"There you are, dear," said Betty, unloading half her groceries into the copper begging bowl, "! hope that helps." Several times over the next few days, Betty noticed the strange yellow-clad figure and gave her some food, a few coins or at least a cheery wave. All the time, of course, Arachne was plotting her downfall, and for that she realised she needed some powerful medicine.

Modern love potions can normally be obtained on free prescription on the NHS and are superior to the hit-or-miss old fashioned ones, being recipient specific, but you have to know who to ask and she had no suitable connections.

Arachne used her first week's wages at St Nick's pub to get a number of ingredients such as eye of newt and toe of frog that were essential for what she had in mind with her reduced capacity for spontaneous magic, so she was still able to put together a really powerful brew.

Then, still disguised as a mendicant monk, she contrived to get into the Dog and Knackers pub and add a hair from Simon's coat, cunningly snitched one rainy day, to personalise the potion.

On a second occasion she was again able to enter the pub unobserved and pour the love potion into his half of bitter. Simon, unaware, drank it up and got up to go home, reeling slightly and grabbing his coat as he went out of the door. One glimpse of Arachne outside and he was instantly smitten, following her around like a puppy for the next few days.

Luckily Betty was extra busy in the pub so had no idea what was going on, as Arachne led a bemused Simon round and about, making all the arrangements for the wedding. She arranged for the banns, a forged certificate of course, booked the Vicar at St Dogo's Church and also arranged to take Simon there first thing on the important morning, which happened to be a Friday.

After that it was also very easy work to get up very early that day and first lure the unsuspecting Betty to the belfry of St Dogo's Church, by a note purporting to come from Simon. Arachne had thought of everything, including the difficulty for herself of overcoming a noted pacifier like Betty, who was renowned for breaking up any fights that started in the pub or outside it and remarkably strong in handling full casks of beer and difficult men in any and all situations.

However we all have our weak points and Betty was such a friendly and lovable person that she was easily deceived as to people's true motives. Again using a small amount of her residual magic Arachne had written a passable imitation of Simon's writing and signature, begging Betty to meet him in the belfry of St Dogo's Church on that Friday morning. Betty duly came in, up the circular stairs, calling out:

"Hello, Simon! I'm here dear, what is this about?"

A few whiffs of laughing gas, stolen from the pharmacy while enquiring about a missing prescription, was enough to allow Arachne to overcome the poor unsuspecting young woman and leave her tied up securely on the floor of the little balcony around the inner side of the belfry. This allowed full hearing of everything going on far below, and the intention was to leave Betty to lie there gagged and powerless, throughout the ceremony, listening to the wedding of Simon to Arachne instead of to herself – a truly evil plan.

Arachne thought she had anticipated every possibility for error, but one thing she did not know was that the belfry at St Dogo's was full of Mice, who were related to every mouse family in Sussex and all incurably romantic and helpful to humans. Can you hear a little group of them chattering as they crowd around Betty, stuck in the belfry and struggling desperately within her bonds? Will they know what to do? Will they be able to help? – Ah! Time will Tell!

The little church of St Dogo in Bexhill was slightly anomalous, having been founded in the late 14th century by a drunken shipwrecked sailor from Flanders, who was under the impression he had been washed up in France and was very grateful to the Saint who had connections in both places, though none as it happened in England.

This sailor therefore built the attractive little church, of St Dogo in Bexhill on Sea. It can be found in any reputable guide book.

The Saint himself was very cross at this turn of events. The shipwreck had happened just after his 200th birthday, April 16th 1390, and this caused St Peter to rouse poor Dogo out of his tomb in France, where he was sleeping off the party celebrations, in order to relocate him to Bexhill.

However, as in life he had had the reputation of being able to bi-locate (that is, to be present in two places at once); he found this was a way to keep his French nationality and run a few churches there as well as in Bexhill, in anticipation of something that might one day be called a Common Market.

He was also happily evoked right through the centuries by those (mostly men) who wanted to be able to assure Interested Parties, like their Wives or the Vicar, that they had been seen down at the bear-baiting, the jousting tournament, or the golf course at the precise moment they were also in Church, simply by invoking the spiritual powers of St Dogo.

It was in this beautiful and practical church that Arachne had arranged to have her wedding to poor Simon Wiseman, faking getting the banns read and inviting practically the whole of Sussex to be present, including the Benefit Officials at Muddles Green. She had also arranged for all the regulars from the Dog and Knackers pub to join them too, so that Simon's humiliation would be complete.

Of course, you know that in all the many weddings that take place in soap operas, there has never been a single one which didn't end in a massive quarrel, a gunfight, revelations of shocking family crimes, or similar slight bars to matrimonial happiness. These preferably start at that thrilling moment when the Vicar says, "If anyone knows of any just cause or impediment ye are to declare it now or forever hold your peace." Every single person in the audience, I mean Congregation, fights down an inclination to shout 'Yes!' and invent one on the spot.

In this case, you will not be disappointed. At exactly the point when Arachne le Noir puffed herself up in manic delight at regaining her prey and Simon closed his eyes and gave himself up for lost, as the Vicar said those delightful words, which I feel compelled to repeat in all their compulsive glory -

"If anyone present knows of any Just Cause or impediment why these two persons should not be joined together in Holy

Matrimony ye are to declare it or forever after Hold your Peace..."

At exactly that point, I tell you – hold your breaths now! – Roland Horse opened his mouth to shout: "We believe her to be a murderess!" But realising he had no proof of this, he subsided into existential angst at the sheer unfairness and futility of human and equine existence.

At the same moment Brian Cat was fighting the temptation to say "She's a Wicked Witch, what more do you want?" because he realised that this would be a sentiment often felt by the Groom's friends and family, though expressed more delicately pre-wedding, and in any case would come much too late to help.

Simon also wanted to say "I don't, I don't!" over and over again, to cancel out where he had felt impelled to say, "I do!" Ever since his earlier enchantment by Arachne he had been subject to an unfortunate tendency to partially revert to being a Standard Lamp and this was affecting him now. His feet seemed trapped in a metal tripod and he couldn't speak without spitting out sparks.

Being a Philosopher, his other tendency, to intellectualise everything, was also affecting him. He got bogged down in trying to work out if what was holding his feet down and preventing him from running away was his Standard Lamp pediment and whether that could count as an Impediment.

The Vicar luckily didn't seem to notice that the groom was spitting out sparks as he said "I do" and other words – Vicars are used to extraordinary things happening at weddings, particularly if they watch soaps. Simon began to give up in despair, wondering whether anything said by St Benedict in the 6th century had any bearing on his problem and what Descartes might have done. He was rapidly becoming lost in such useless meditation.

As I was saying when interrupted by those compulsions of novelists (which I have resisted so far, but I would have burst if unable to indulge for once) to delay the excitements of action by a lengthy analysis of the exact mental state and secret thoughts of every character – just to show how clever we writers are.

"If any Persons present knows of any Just Cause or Impediment why these two persons should not be joined in Holy Matrimony ye are to declare it Now or forever Hold your Peace" droned the Vicar and everyone shot up in alarm as a voice from the back of the Church roared out:

"Yes! I have an Impediment! She is married to me!"

It was Gregory, and he was not referring to the impediment – more of an inconvenience – of him still being at least 50 percent a Pig, but to the Marriage Certificate held out in his sturdy trotter, I mean hand.

Of course! Arachne le Noir had murdered her first two husbands, but had transformed the third, Ghastly Gregory from Gloucester, into a wild Boar (and my goodness, was he wild about it). The spell, for whatever reason, was now wearing off. Simon was saved!

Simultaneously Betty's saviours, the Mice in the Belfry, finally gnawed through the cords holding her down and removed the gag stopping her mouth. She lost no time in shouting out an endorsement of Gregory's – very unexpected – intervention and had already worked out the best and safest way to get down.

Having a scientific turn of mind and a deep trust in the physics of underwear, she relied on quickly removing her bountiful blue bloomers, tying them with some of the cords, to form a makeshift but effective parachute.

Uttering a heartfelt prayer to St Dogo – who was delighted to leave his boring cloud in Heaven to help a maiden in distress, particularly one lacking underwear – he and the awed congregation were treated to the beautiful sight of Betty the Buxom Barmaid parachuting down from the balcony, her blue bloomers billowing out above and nothing below to help her safely to the ground.

As it happened, her fall was cushioned in any case, by her landing directly on top of Arachne, breaking her fall nicely and rendering the witch slightly unconscious.

Simon, the love potion he had been given by Arachne having worn off, for once acting quickly and decisively – unlike his usual philosophic dithering – used the moment to snatch the certificate of banns from Arachne's hand. Where her name was written he put his finger and called up the residual energy from the lamp. There was a crackly sort of flash from the paper under the name and he could see before his eyes it being rewritten in a fine Italian hand.

"You can marry me to Betty now, to my own True Love!" Simon shouted triumphantly.

He thrust the paper into the vicar's hand. That worthy was protesting that he could not marry someone else to him, Simon, because it wasn't what was written on the paper.

"Read it, Read it!" he protested.

Turning to Betty herself as she stepped off Arachne's recumbent body, Simon took both her hands and said, "Oh Betty, my own true love. At last I can ask you if you are willing to marry me? Please marry me Betty!"

"Oh Simon!" cried an ecstatic and astonished Betty, taken from despair to blissful happiness in a few short moments. "I would love to marry you, Simon! Oh darling!" and they kissed passionately for as long as they could.

Simon, for once, became the practical one. Seizing the moment, he turned back to the Vicar, who was still making gobbling protests like a turkey which has been asked to read a Christmas wish list, and cried out again: "Read it man, read it! Read the name on the Certificate!"

Sure enough, the vicar obediently read out the name. "Betty Brown, the Buxom Barmaid!" it said in a fine Italian hand. The Vicar's elderly eyes widened as he took in the accuracy of this identification. With an effort he dragged them away from the aforementioned attributes, only to drop them towards her hem, where they were arrested by the hint of the blue bloomers beneath the bell of her skirts, Betty having hastily put them back in place.

"Yes, certainly, Mr Wiseman," he said, drawing his eyes back to the job in hand with an effort. "It will be a real pleasure to marry you to Betty."

He proceeded to battle through the preliminaries again and then the whole marriage service, so fast that no one had any time to protest. Not that anyone wanted to. Simon, Betty, Roland Horse and Brian Cat all wore expressions of soppy contentment and the whole congregation were totally thrilled. This was better than any soap on the telly...

Arachne was still out cold and Ghastly Gregory was chafing her hands and her brow, generally looking after her with the greatest love and care.

As the Bridal Pair came down the aisle to the usual Wedding March... "Dah dah, deedah dah dah, dee..." a recovered and subdued Arachne was encircled firmly by Gregory's right trotter.

Outside the church, on the lawn, a hasty wedding party had been arranged and all were welcomed. Betty and Simon felt nothing but kindness for everyone, all past troubles being forgotten.

Even Agnes Toope and the other members of the Benefits Office Coven were included in the party. As was Arachne – what could be more humiliating for a witch than being forgiven without even having to ask for it? Though I suppose being married to Ghastly Gregory ran it close. He was now dedicated to looking after her day and night for ever, sharing with her, over and over again, his wealth of anecdotes which was fast earning him the title of the Greatest Bore in Sussex, as he had once been Prize Bore for Gloucester.

♪

Arachne eventually resigned herself to her horrible fate. It was somewhat mitigated by finding that Gregory has sampled the real ales at the St Nick's Inn and loved it there. James, the Publican, welcomed them, though he never quite believed the story Arachne poured out to him – ironically it was the one time in her life she ever told anyone the unvarnished truth. Arachne and Gregory spent most evenings there.

Her cooking was still a little erratic, so sometimes they were happier with a Dusty Knuckle pizza and a pint of Magpie's Magic. James would often ask Arachne, who had now lost all her magical abilities, to help out behind the bar when things were very busy and she grew contented and even happy. Now that truly is a miracle!

Everyone continued to agree that the wedding of Simon Wiseman and Betty Brown the Buxom Barmaid was the best and most thrilling wedding anyone had ever attended, even those who had been extras at the historic wedding in East Enders when the bride and her sister both drowned. Most, of course, were too young to remember an earlier event when Toadie in Neighbours rolled the car into the river and accidentally drowned his new bride, Dee.

So Simon and Betty's wedding certainly qualified as the best one in human memory and they and all their friends in the village and at the Dog and Knackers pub, lived....

"All together now, folks – HAPPILY EVER AFTER!"

POSTLUDE

♪

THE GROUP had listened and laughed
and greatly enjoyed their story. There had
been little time for tea after, but Helena had
provided a couple of packets of biscuits for
them to take back in the Van and a bar of
chocolate for Jenny.

She had also leant out of the window and
called out her congratulations and thanks to
the North Wind. She was sure afterwards that
a blowy female voice snorted "Phooey!"
blowing straight into her face and into her ear.
"That lazy North Wind!" Helena heard the
South Wind say. "He went on outright strike
when he was told about doing overtime, so it
was me who had to tell you this Story after all,
not him!"

Helena said, in conciliatory tones, "Well it was
a marvellous story and we are very, very
grateful." She was just trying to come to terms
with the idea of Industrial Action – or rather,
Inaction – as taken by any Wind and felt it was
best avoided. Anyway, it had been a great
afternoon for them all.

The South Wind laughed in fitful puffs and caressed her eyelids and cheeks. "We really like you, Helena," she was sure the South Wind said, but by that time it must be admitted she was getting a little sleepy.

Joe was collecting up all the coats and bags and rugs to load into the Van and keeping half an eye on Rosie, who was seeing to everyone's needs, from organising a rota for the toilet to listening to a chaos of comments and helping everyone but Helena into the Van.

Once they were all safely in, Rosie continued listening (apparently intently) to Colonel Arthur telling a tale of his heroism in the War. Mind you, she had heard it often enough to have passed a stiff exam on military tactics, as well as having a soft spot for the old man, so it wasn't too difficult.

She and Francine had developed a real affection and understanding through looking after Jenny together all that afternoon. Jenny had slept through some of it on her mother's lap, but had divided the rest of her time between Nana Doll and her new friend Rosie. The addition of any new people to Jenny's restricted world was a great achievement and a source of joy for her mother. The friendships built that day endured through many years of their lives and had effects that also lasted.

Many, many years later, Jenny, the 'special' woman, would retain only the haziest conscious memory of these times, but they opened up to her to a world of joy and laughter and kindness, not just teasing and shaming and a depressed mother, since Francine and Rosie benefitted each other in many ways.

As for Jenny herself, the lessons she learnt in those times with Nana Doll and Rosie lasted even though she remembered little of them consciously. Ever after, something good always happened when she was faced with a task in her world, a place where otherwise ordinary things were always so difficult.

If she was trying to work, whether to lay tables, speak to a stranger, or wash dishes, she would feel as if her hands and mind were being guided by another pair of hands. A vague feeling of a series of slow, careful, motions would give her the patience to take each little piece of a job in turn. Then, miraculously, she would eventually achieve whatever it was to be done! And she would look up smiling and laughing, tasting a sweetie in her mouth and hearing praise in her ears. No one could resist Jenny's laugh of triumph at each tiny success.

But for now we know nothing about the future and Helena goes back down to the Wheelwright's Cottage in Flitterbottom, sending a little sad thought across the seas to George.

INTERLUDE

♪

GEORGE: THE JOURNEY

HAD SHE BUT KNOWN it George might have sympathised with her. He was at that time on his way to France, rather uncertain as to what he was doing crunched on a cheap flight with dozens of other people. Since his neighbour was his somewhat corpulent friend Nigel, the two of them sweltered and sweated in tandem.

George had slept badly before leaving England with dreams that had disturbed him a good deal. Now the plane was lulling him to sleep. It's humming seemed for a time to be like the little river Flitter but something about this journey was different and he rested uneasily.

Part of him wondered why, with so much that was beautiful and restful about his home country, he was so obstinate about moving to France. It would mean upping his schoolboy French to a better grasp of the language and above all it would mean he was a lot further away from the children. He tried to rationalise it by thinking of how much they and the grandchildren would love to have a grandpa to visit in a foreign country, but he had an uneasy feeling that the sort of place he could afford might not seem so attractive to the younger generation.

So at the very time Helena was resolutely trying to put George out of her mind, he was shifting uneasily around in his seat on the plane, unable to quite get her out of his own mind after all and regretting that he would quite possibly never see her again.

George was even wondering whether there might not be fates much less pleasant for a wandering man – as he described himself in his mind – than settling down in a wheelwright's cottage in a Sussex hamlet. His mind, indeed wandering in the half-sleep state, spun around in contemplation of wheels as bringing progress, of all sorts, good and bad. Wheels used for carts and cannons, water mills, watches, trains, for plying and spinning yarn. Wheels to go long distances from those you love – or to come home to them. Wheels used to break people as a torture, or to grind the corn to make their daily bread.

Sometimes the Wheel gets stuck and someone is needed to get it going again, thought George, in his half sleep. Maybe the lightest touch of a woman's finger, or the stronger shoulder of a man, or even just someone to be there at the right time to move the stuck wheel, to push the story on, to let the corn be ground, to wind up the clock and to allow Time to roll on once again.

Now his thoughts seemed to be wheeling and dipping like birds in the arc of their flight. The noise of the plane's engines became the song of the little river by Turnaround Cottage, but the song was both harsh and mournful:

"We will go down together!" the Flitter seemed to be saying. "Hold my hand and come with me, through Miffed and Flounced, turn left at Betrayal Beacon, straight on to Crash Corner. Then take the road to High Dudgeon and Foul Temper, past Downtrodden Farm, up Deceitful Way, by Tricky Tracks to Lostin Forest. You will find yourself on Weary Mile. Go through Mirage and Lost, to Hungry Gap, where there are no more Stories for you to hear."

Something in George struggled to hear the warning in this chant, but he was very tired and he just put in his earplugs and went to sleep.

INTERLUDE
♪

THE OLD MAN IN THE MARKET PLACE

THE TOWN SIGN of an Old Woman with a basket from which she is letting out the cuckoo, has stood in Heathfield High Street for over 50 years. It is a joyous reminder that spring will surely come again, but that it does no harm for old women and others of goodwill to help in this, by telling us stories to tide us over the Winter and keep us heading forwards to Spring.

On this particular morning Helena had found an urgent need to stock up with fresh fruit and vegetables. The greengrocer's cat, known as Fluffykins, summarily disturbed from her favourite bed on the carrots, ran off across the market place, spitting an imprecation at Helena and the greengrocer, young Fred. Fortunately neither of them heard nor understood, being immersed in discussion of the price of supermarket goods (exorbitant), the weather (taking a downturn) and Derby

346

County's chances in the football (non-existent).

Neither of them therefore, nor indeed the other people in the marketplace saw exactly what happened next, though one or two said they were sure it was a very big dog, almost wolf size, running at the cat which caused Fluffykins to leap for her life onto the sign and cling pathetically to the painted old woman.

The Old Man looked up and even though he had always disliked and distrusted cats, he could not help himself for once running forward to help. He was one person who did see the big dog, for sure, though he never spoke of it. He threw up his arms, flapping them, at its approach and it seemed to pass through him, like a gust of winter wind, powerfully cold, but exhilarating.

He lost his balance and tumbled in the gutter, sprawling and twitching like a puppet whose strings are cut. His meagre bag of vegetables flew into the road, where a car – the driver distracted for a moment by the sight of a large dog – drove over it, before roaring off into the distance, luckily having missed the old man.

Fred shook a fist at the car, then turned to help Helena who had run straight to the old man and had put her arms around him, asking in a shocked voice if he was hurt. In a hoarse quaver like a croak he reassured her, overwhelmed by her attention. Fred also helped him stand up and took him back to the vegetable stall.

The onlookers, finding that, perhaps disappointingly, the drama was quickly over and no one hurt except a few of Fred's misshapen old vegetables, went on their way, arguing as to whether there had, or had not, been a wolf sized dog charging through the marketplace.

(Incidentally, it never was resolved and became something of a standing joke in the Heathfield pub – for at least a week, until the surprising and unprecedented win of Derby County that weekend displaced all other topics.)

Helena was insisting that the old man should take her vegetables, till she saw that Fred, after luring Fluffykins back in, had silently replaced twice the number of squashed ones already with a bag of his finest. It was Fred who helped the old man into Helena's Ford Fiesta so she could drive him back to his home. He was still shaking and she was concerned, but he refused any other suggestions of help, nor did he invite her in. She questioned him gently to be sure he had suffered no lasting injury and insisted she would call again soon, if he didn't mind, just to be sure he was all right.

He refused, but she could see beneath his gruff manner now and knew he was all right. She couldn't imagine why she had ever found him creepy or off putting. Indeed, after bidding him goodbye and stepping towards her car, she turned back and, seeing how forlorn he looked, could not help but go back and embrace him in a warm hug. "Good luck, dear friend," she said, as her cheek pressed his with a kiss and then she was gone.

The old man stood for a while before going into his cold cottage. Now his eyes were pouring out tears aplenty; warm and gentle the drops pattered down onto his hands as he opened the door and they accompanied him as he went about his tasks, washing his mind finally clean of guilt and grief and separation.

INTERLUDE

♪

GEORGE – FIRST DAY IN FRANCE

MEANWHILE, how was George faring? He and Nigel had come off the plane in the early morning at La Môle Airport, some 15 km southwest of Saint-Tropez, and soon found their small family-run hotel down a back street and booked in for the week, all in with the airfare. After a nap and a shave they went out for an early lunch and explored the town, arranging a couple of trips for future days.

It was delightfully warm and fresh and they quickly found the sea. Nigel met up by prior arrangement with an old girlfriend, Beverley Smithson, who was always happy to see him. All three went out for a cheap and excellent evening meal and saw a film.

It was all going well and, even better, when Beverley introduced George to another expat, who 'just happened to be passing', an elegant and sexy woman a few years younger than him, called Melinda Long.

Being naive it never occurred to George that this friend for him might be a 'plant' and indeed he would probably have been flattered if he had known. Expats always want to draw others to their new lives, sometimes out of genuine enjoyment and kindness, more often because they are bored and disillusioned and need fresh meat all the time.

Which was this? Who can say! George was suitably dazzled and appreciative at so quickly finding a woman friend.

When he fished in the inner pocket of his jacket on going to bed a small piece of paper fell out. He unfolded it and realised at once that it was one of Helena's poems that had come loose when he sent her book back, unthought of since...

> I followed the maze, but you were not there,
> Only the daffodils, secrets keeping.
> I brought you dew from the fairy well,
> But under the apple trees you were sleeping.
>
> The path you follow I cannot share,
> And fairy dew are the tears I'm weeping,
> Apple-tree Spring is only a dream,

With a small cold wind on the daffodils creeping.

When he read it he saw a new side of her, resigned and elegiac grief. Feeling unaccountably guilty, as if he had hurt her and then invaded her privacy – as it clearly did not refer to him, having been written long before – he crumpled it and threw it in the bin. In the night something, whether dream or memory, got him up, to smooth it out and tuck it in a deep place hidden in his case, without rereading it.

The two men met up with the women again at coffee next morning. They started well with flirtatious badinage of a type to which George was well accustomed. Melinda pretended not to remember him and to confuse him with another George. "No. I'm the handsome one!" he said and Melinda smiled saucily back and touched his cheek with soft fingers and an invitation in her eyes.

They spent time in an art gallery and visited an exhibition of textiles and quilts, about which Melinda in particular was very knowledgeable.

It seemed a very good idea, even an inevitable one, for the group to visit an agent *immobilier*, or estate agent, and look to see if there were any two-bedroom flats within his monthly means. Indeed there were, and Melinda in particular pointed out one very near her own *appartement,* in a very superior area.

After a bibulous and hilarious evening meal with Nigel and the two women, George had a moment of uneasiness. The two men had agreed to split the bill between them. Far from being cheaper than back home, this meal, though excellent, was extremely expensive and Melinda had begged Nigel to order the best wine on the list.

George, mentally counting the cost of a week like this, had a momentary picture of Helena laughing, with tomato sauce on her nose on the pier at Hastings.

CHAPTER EIGHTEEN

QUESTIONS

PRELUDE
♪

IT **SEEMED** to Helena, going about her duties at Turnaround Cottage in a rather mechanical way, that everything about her short lived friendship with George was full with too many questions and no answers.

The cottage itself seemed to be reminding her of the particular question as to why he should have come into her life and opened up long-forgotten possibilities of love and companionship, only to go again as completely and inexplicably as he had arrived in her world, in an old Mercedes.

He'd never explained his choice of car, come to that, Helena thought, in exasperation as she cleaned and tidied Turnaround Cottage, though there was no one booked in at present.

She thought, not by any means for the first time, that she probably should have kissed him properly – or improperly – when she had the chance. Why should he prefer France to the English countryside? Was it her fault? Who would he be kissing now?

She finished her tea from the Rumblebum mug and looked with loathing at its bulging green stomach and pop-out yellow eyes, staring her down. She drew back her arm and threw it towards the window in what felt to be a splendidly childish gesture. Alas! She'd never been much good at sport and the fat frog flew across the room, missing the window and hitting the heavy brocade curtains. It bounced back safely to land, unharmed, on the cushion, from where it seemed to leer at her triumphantly.

She abandoned herself to tears, for good measure thinking how foolishly her mind had thrown up what must have been fantasies of a tribe of philosophical Mice with a Wind who told stories to heal and comfort. What nonsense!

She lay for a while, consoled by her bout of tears. The Mice stayed out of earshot and she went into the bathroom to look into the mirror

– replaced from Gerard Forward's equally childish rage. She saw nothing but a familiar lady of indeterminate age with red and puffy eyes, so she washed her face in cold water, feeling better.

The odd idea came to her that perhaps she should ask to get a proper story this time. This was the night that she and George should have been at the concert. Perhaps he would have come back here; perhaps he would have shared her bed at Wheelwrights Cottage down the hill? What was the point of speculating, he wasn't here and that was that!

Nevertheless there was some feeling that she must somehow hear a story that was perhaps really meant for him, or even for the two of them, so she went home for supper and then returned to the Cottage and sat in the red brocade chair by the window. She was half-reading a not very interesting novel, watching the clock and told herself she just happened to have with her a small bag of overnight necessities.

At 10 o'clock she gave up the pretence of reading, made herself an infusion of hops and chamomile, with a dash of honey, as prescribed by Dolores – but checked by Rosie Cullen – and got herself ready for bed in a lace trimmed blue silk nightie with matching dressing gown, though there would be no one but the Mice to see the outfit and she sat back in the chair in the sitting room, not exactly asking anybody for anything but feeling somehow ready.

The Mice had, in fact, been very loving, but circumspect, sensing that Helena was not in the mood for telling them stories nor for too much company. They remembered the torn-up tickets, drew their own conclusions and kept their own counsel.

Now however they sensed it was time to come out and lend a friendly helping paw. One of the older Mice – she never knew them apart, but after all they were a collective, going on through generations of different mice - climbed up onto her knee, then as she did not move, climbed up to her shoulder, kissed her affectionately with its whiskers and leaned over to pull aside the curtain.

It was almost as if a wind had been waiting for just this signal, as indeed it had been. The East Wind was blowing gently over her a soothing breath of scented air, coming from all the gardens of Punnetts Town, with their herbs and flowers. The Cottage was pointing her to the copse and the wooded slopes leading to the village and her good neighbours, hidden for the moment but always there for her.

"It does not matter who this story might, or might not, have been meant for," sighed the East Wind. "It is enough that you, Helena Brown, beloved of many, wish to hear it and you are here, now.

"So, hear a story about...

QUESTIONS

ONCE there was a woman who lived with her husband and little son in a clearing in a wood on the outskirts of a small village. They were poor, but he worked in the forest and she sewed and embroidered, and they just about got by. One day the husband and son fell sick. In spite of all she could do they died, and the woman was inconsolable.

She sat for days, rocking herself and crying, and then she got up and walked to the village.

She went to the village Priest. "Why did my husband and child die?" she asked.

"It's a very sad thing," said the priest, "but it must have been God's will, and has to be accepted with patience."

The woman went to the village School Teacher, who didn't believe in God. "Why did my husband and child die?" she said.

"Things like that don't happen for any reason," he said, "they just happen, and they have to be endured with fortitude."

The woman went to the old Wise Woman, who lived on her own deep in the woods.

"Why did my husband and child die?" she asked.

"Who else have you asked?" said the Wise Woman.

"I asked the Priest."

"And what did he say?"

"He said it was the will of God and I must accept it with patience."

"What did you think of that answer?"

"I didn't like it," said the woman.

"Who else did you ask?"

"I asked the School Teacher."

"What did he say?"

"He said things like that happen, and I must endure it with fortitude."

"What did you think of that answer?"

"I didn't like it," said the woman.

Then the Wise Woman said, "I can't answer your question. If you want an answer, you will have to ask Death himself."

"Right!" said the woman, "I'll do that."

"To do that," said the Wise Woman, "you will need both patience and fortitude. Take this nut, and tonight instead of going to bed, build up the fire and throw the nut on it, saying

360

'Death, come and answer my questions', and you will see what you will see."

The woman went home and did as she had been told. When she threw the nut on the fire, a cloud of smoke swirled out and there was Death in front of her, keeping all the heat of the fire away. What did he look like? He looked just like he is. Everyone knows what death looks like.

She began to ask him her question, but he raised a hand to stop her. "You have summoned me, and I have come. You can summon me if you wish every night for nine hundred and ninety-nine nights, and ask me anything you want. After that you will not see me again, until the time appointed for me to come for you."

The woman asked her question.

"Why did my husband and child die?" over and over again.

Death did not answer. He stayed looking at her, keeping away all the heat from the fire, until she felt she was freezing to death herself, and still she kept asking.

"Why did my husband and child have to die? Why did you take my husband and child? Why won't you give me an answer?"

All night she kept rocking and crying and asking her questions, but Death said nothing more, and at the first light of dawn he vanished.

That day she could hardly work for tiredness, but she looked after the cottage and garden and waited for evening.

At nightfall she summoned Death and again he came. Again she asked her questions, over and over. Death kept the heat of the fire from her and said nothing, vanishing at first light.

And so the days and nights went on. After a while she asked other questions. "Who are you? Did God kill my husband and child? Is the School Teacher right? Is the Priest right? Why won't you answer me? Why did my husband and child die?"

She found that, in spite of the cold and the endless nagging questions, she could doze a little during the day, and do her work. She began to embroider again, on little scraps of cloth; simple things, a cross, a gravestone, a child's hand, a spiral, a dark cloud, a teardrop.

Quite often she was tempted not to summon Death, thinking, what was the use? He never answered, but somehow every evening she found herself making up the fire and calling him to come.

Gradually she was asking other things.

"Why is there suffering in the world? Why is there illness? Why do people die? Why do they live? Is there a God? Who am I? Who created evil? Why do people hurt each other? Why did my husband and child die?"

In the daytime she cared for herself and her garden, and she went on embroidering a picture for each question, on a scrap of cloth; a circle, a square, a diamond, a demon, a tiger, a monster, a mouse, a carrot, a bird, a flower, a flame, a knife.

She kept the scraps in a basket, and people coming past wanted to buy them, but poor as she was she wouldn't sell. They asked her questions, and sometimes she answered and sometimes she didn't, and sometimes she asked Death the next night. It made no difference; he never answered.

The days passed into months, one hundred days, two hundred, three hundred. It had become a familiar ritual, and still she asked her questions, and still Death kept the heat of the fire from her, and never spoke a word.

"Why are there rainbows in the sky? Where do swallows go in the winter? Who named them? Why does it bleed when you prick your finger? What is the meaning of life? Why does birth hurt? Why does death hurt even more?

What makes the seasons change? What do cockroaches eat? Why do apples fall from the trees? What's the smallest thing in the world? Where is up? Why did my husband and son die?" and always she embroidered them the next day onto the scraps of cloth

Eventually, nine hundred and ninety eight nights had passed. The last night of all she built up her fire and summoned Death as usual.

She opened her mouth – and found she had no more questions to ask.

All night she sat there with Death, in front of the fire, and now she felt almost companioned by him.

Just before dawn the figure by the fire stirred, and said, "As I told you, this was the last night of my coming, until the day I finally call for you. You have asked me no questions. Is there anything you want to say?"

The woman looked straight at him, and it seemed as if the heat of the fire came through the dark figure and warmed her through and through.

"No," she said. She bent her head and felt great wings sweep past her, then a wind blew out of the cottage and the Angel of Death was gone.

The woman picked up the basket of embroidered scraps. Walking over to the door she opened it wide. The sun was just rising, stitching a golden edge onto every leaf and blade of grass in her garden.

Dipping her hand into the basket she began to throw into the air the embroidered scraps she had so patiently made. The wind took them, and they fluttered up above the trees, flapping and flying and fanning out into a great arc. The susurration of their flight sounded like the chattering of swallows migrating, or the chirp of grasshoppers in summer fields.

She watched till they had all flown purposefully away, out into the world; all her unanswered questions, full of the untried promise of children.

She took the empty basket back into the cottage, and began the new work for the new day.

POSTLUDE

♪

HELENA was crying silently as the story ended, but she felt grateful. She inadvertently picked up a Mouse instead of her hanky, and apologised, but the Mouse just said "You're welcome", and dried her eyes for her, on a scrap of lint from the cushion.

A very small and serious looking female Mouselet came out with what looked almost like lace and presented it to her. It proved to be a quotation from the manuscript of the Philosopher who had stayed there, many tears ago and left it behind. Only, since Professor George Miller had taught them, the Mice had now learnt to value these slips of the written word, instead of eating them.

This one had indeed been bitten but only round the edges, the fine mouselet bites creating a beautiful border with a lace effect.

Helena thanked the Mouselet very gratefully and named her 'Winifred'. She had learnt that to be named personally was regarded by the

Mice as a great honour and they were called by the name for the rest of their lives.

Helena laughed a little tearfully and blew a kiss towards them all, then stumbled up the stairs to bed, where she slept through, with the best night she had had for a long while.

In the morning all was quiet, the window in the sitting room was shut and she went back down the hill to her own cottage, marvellously comforted. She took out the slip of manuscript, which she had not been able to read in the dim light the previous evening. In a fine sloping hand it read:

'From Jalaluddin Rumi. 13th Century Persian Mystic and Poet... "Sell your cleverness and buy bewilderment."'

"I certainly did that," she mused, smiling. "I've been led into a wilderness more than once and I'm the better for it."

INTERLUDE

♪

RESOLUTION

THE OLD MAN was still badly shaken by the fall in the Market place. He could not rest that evening and he found himself once more walking down the chilly paths to Flitterbrook Lane in the dark just before dawn, guided more by the gurgling sound of the river Flitter and instinct than sight. It was so dark that even the familiar ways were almost indistinguishable.

Something had changed in him. As he turned up his collar against the light wind and rain he was murmuring a sort of mantra that had come to him in the night. "My name is Tom Crow. I'm young Tom Crow. My name is Tom Crow. I'm young Tom Crow," over and over again. A sort of instinct was leading him towards Flitterbottom and the Wheelwright's Cottage where his Grandfather, Old Tom Crow had once lived, but he turned off into the garden at Turnaround Cottage, drawn by the drowsy scent of the late summer roses.

He must have dozed again on the bench by the roses because he was suddenly aware that he was standing in a square conservatory that he did not know, created entirely of glass. He could look out of each facet at a different part of the garden and it seemed that this glass construction imprisoning him had replaced the cottage. There were four doors. Stepping up to each of them in turn it seemed that he looked out onto the perfect garden, each in the perfect season.

Bluebells and anemones in the wooded East garden with clematis and winter jasmine out in glory all along the road. Spring appearing in lilies of the valley and anemones edging an untidy lawn, with its untidy spring growth and a riot of African lilies gone wild by the banks of the Flitterbrook

The summer garden of the lawn and a few beds of perennials to the South. An old hunched apple tree, heavy with fruit, leaning perilously into Autumn nearby, over the rockery and neat beds filled with snapdragons, marigolds and dahlias.

Autumn leaves in all colours falling from the trees to the West beyond the garden. A little lawn with lazy bonfire smoke curling up in the breeze. Autumn sunshine picking out the red hot pokers and valerian by the swing and vegetables in neat rows among the flowers

To the North, a dusting of light snow on the red holly-berried bushes and the dustbins, softening the hard lines of sheds and compost beds. Late roses and straggly shrubs filling in hollows and covering clutter discreetly.

He opened the East door to step into Spring, but as soon as he did so all the light vanished in an instant. He was looking out into a dark void, no path, an endless, fatal drop in front of his feet. He shut it hastily and went to the next door, the West, autumn crocus and bonfire scent, and then the next blindly, and the next.

No use, each time the lights would go out as he opened the door. To step forward would have meant a fall dizzyingly into nothingness. With each hasty closure of the door again the perfect, heavenly gardens would appear. He began to cry with frustration and fear, real soft tears dripping down his shrivelled old cheeks and from his nose onto his collar, as a child cries. It came to him that he was being told to trust his vision of the light and step out, in that trust, into the dark void. How could he do that? How many centuries of betrayal lay behind him?

A memory came to him now, not of those times of mutual distrust and disappointment, but of yesterday. That lady from Wheelwright's Cottage where his Grandfather had lived, picking him up from the ground with warm concern and kissing his cheek, like a friend. A memory of the greengrocer, young Fred, replacing his lost vegetables with twice as many, as a neighbour would do, almost as if he himself was Somebody!

He opened a door quickly then, at random, and stepped out before he could change his mind. His eyes could still only see a vast, dark emptiness but his feet were steady and true on some sort of firm path, leading him out into the gardens. Confused but delightful scents of roses and bluebell, leeks, lavender, and leaf mould full of mushrooms, blew over him in a warm breeze. And now there was light in the blackness; a glimmer of starlight by which he could see he was facing South, across the trees and the River Flitter, looking over the downs to where the sea met the stars in the sky.

He seemed to be reliving, rather than remembering, the times when, as a very little boy, no more than four, he would be visiting his Grandfather and be brought out here to see the stars and the sea where they joined each other. He hardly reached to the knee of the old white bearded man with kind eyes; Grandfather Tom, who would bring out from his waistcoat pocket the big silver watch on a silver chain and swing it in front of little Tom's enthralled gaze, chanting, "See Tom, see. Time flies!"

Then he would bring the watch neatly to land in little Tom's chubby open palms. "You've got time on your hands!" Grandfather would chant, to little Tom's uncomprehending but delighted laughter. It was all part of the ritual.

Finally, Grandfather would close all little Tom's fingers over the watch with his own big strong wheelmaker's right hand, saying solemnly, "Now Tom, now! You've got all the Time in the world!"

He could hear his mother in the background, laughing too and taking it up, "Yes Tom, yes, you've got all the Time in the world in your own hands!" and he would carry it very, very carefully till the time came to go home and give back the watch.

Somewhere, somehow in the many centuries between, he had lost all the Time in the world. It had trickled through his fingers or been stolen, or dropped, or somehow dissolved in growing up.

Now for a godlike moment, he knew again that he held in his hands all the Time in all the World. He could see the figures in the garden clearly now, the woman in the white dress rising from the clay, weeping, and the crying child on the swing and Old Grandfather Time himself. Little Tom stretched out his arms in joy and amazement at this gift. It was given him so he could humbly give it back in a blessing. A blessing for this world, that for an eternal 'now' he, little Tom Crow, owned!

He raised his left hand and obediently the sun began to rise in the East. He opened his right hand and allowed the moon to drop down below the horizon. Then, filled with awe and humility and love, he gave the world back to itself and let Time do its work.

The scent of lilies of the valley and bluebells and sweet herbs still hung in the air. He could hear the lark, released into the day singing high above. He could still, for a moment, see the woman and the child and they were not weeping anymore but smiling, then they dissolved into the increasing sunlight in the garden. Old Grandfather Time himself, holding his silver watch and chain, was smiling, as he too dissolved and was gone.

As the Old Man walked back up the hill towards the downs, he saw Helena, in the distance, on an early morning walk and waved to her with friendliness. It was right, he thought, that Helena, who he had once thought snooty and who lived in the wheelwrights cottage, should have played her unwitting part. She, Helena, whose name means the Outsider, the Alien, was the only one who could move the stuck wheel on and free Time itself.

INTERLUDE

♪

GEORGE AND MELINDA

THEY ALL PARTED after midnight amid many florid compliments, kisses and much laughter. The following day Melinda contrived to get George to herself and take him sightseeing on the water bus. She also asked him to come shopping, going to look at several shops, buying expensive candles and napkins "for my dinner parties".

Then they called into a very upmarket perfume shop. "This is a lovely emporium, George. I always get my perfume here; they know me. They match the scent perfectly to the woman, you know, isn't that nice?" she cried, smiling at him with wide-eyed friendliness.

It seemed to George that she was hinting, quite strongly, that he might like to buy her some of her favourite perfume as a memento. He disentangled himself tactfully, as he had been rather shocked to find how quickly his holiday money was already going down.

Melinda chatted on. "I'm determined to cook you a really nice dinner this afternoon," she said brightly, taking his arm and cuddling up close. "Come on darling. We'll go to the market, you'll love it! What's your favourite dessert?"

George did indeed enjoy this very much and was greatly reassured by how cheaply they could get wonderful meat and fish and a variety of fresh vegetables. He got to choose a meal of grilled sardines and rice, with slices of oven-baked aubergine lightly drizzled with *huile d'olive*.

So after the relative cheapness of the food, which she paid for, it seemed churlish to quibble when he insisted he would buy the wine and she once again picked the most expensive.

It was a surprise to him to discover that, after a further longish walk and a languid lunchtime drink, they were once again outside the upmarket perfume shop! By this time George felt relaxed, and mellow. It just seemed right to reward his pretty guide with the perfume she so clearly desired. An ornate bottle of Yves Saint Laurent Opium found its way into her bag and he was rewarded in his turn by a passionate kiss.

CHAPTER NINETEEN

TREASURES FROM THE SEA

PRELUDE
♪

THE DAY had started with a clear blue, crisp morning, when Helena had gone for an early walk on the downs and waved to the Old Man in the distance.

Later it turned blowy, with fitful sunshine and showers as she walked back up Flitterbrook lane to check over the Cottage for another Visitor. He was only staying one night and she was slightly surprised to see that he seemed to be there already, given that he had said he did not have a car and the bus she had assumed he would get was not due for a while. Still, it was not at all unusual for visitors to make the most of the trip by coming early and going for a walk, or to lunch in Heathfield.

The man who came forward to greet her was tall and fairly substantial, of uncertain age, but with white hair and a pleasant expression.

She hadn't read the paperwork dropped through her door only the day before. It was a last minute booking, and it really didn't matter, but normally Helena prided herself on noting the name and any details that enabled her to welcome the Visitors more personally.

Today, her thoughts were so far in the past and tears so near the surface that she hardly trusted herself to say more than a few civilities as she showed him around. She was abstracted and low in spirits, still missing George and her abandoned hopes. As was usual with her, she tried to suppress the tears and act in her normal friendly way, so as not to cause her friends anxieties they could not alleviate, nor voice her concerns to a stranger.

It was also not unusual for a Visitor to offer her a cup of tea, out of friendliness or their own loneliness. Helena was unaware that, in spite of her years, she was a pleasing and inviting friend to many lonely people. Men especially were drawn to her sweetness, lovely eyes, and the impish humour that sometimes, irrepressibly, bubbled through the veneer of formality.

Now, Helena was preoccupied again with her sorrow. She felt she had managed to let go of the romance with George Miller, that had seemed so promising yet apparently came to nothing, and it would probably be a while before she could regain her contentment.

She cheered up a little thinking that tomorrow afternoon was the Barbecue at Three Cups Inn and she was going to help once again with the Oldies. Her dear friend Carol had come down too, and was staying on for a week in Aunty Mabel's own cottage as usual, to keep it aired, but they would have some time together later on she was sure and she would be able to talk about George with her.

As commonly happened the man indeed suggested a cup of tea, but Helena refused, politely but firmly and went on her way. So she did not see the way the mice ran towards this Visitor as he walked through the door and how they clustered round his feet. She would hardly have been able to show him to his room! They chirruped and squeaked in ecstasy, climbing up his clothes to twitch their whiskers on his cheek, while he laughed and stroked any he could reach with his big, gentle fingers. Indeed, the only other person they seemed to treat like this was dear, woolly Aunty Mabel.

Helena spent a quiet evening, crocheting hats for the Sailors Charity she liked to support.

People thought of sailors as hard bitten grizzled men of great toughness, but many were very young men, boys almost, from the Philippines and other third world islands. Homesick and scared, the gift, through the charity of a woolly hat with a kind message inside, was warm with a feeling of somebody's care for them. A constant supply was needed, as many such hats went overboard in the storms, sadly sometimes still on their owners.

"What a price others pay for us!" was her thought as she contained her tears and created a deep greenish-blue expression of a Grandmother's love to give away...

Tonight, Helena found herself thinking of the seas, not as on a sunny afternoon at Seven Sisters Bay, but out in the deeps, waves like dragons snorting foam as they reared higher than the mast. Of mountainous craggy rocks, on which a fragile wooden vessel could crash in a heart-stopping instant, rolling down the trough of the wave to slow, bubbling oblivion.

Even more oppressed by this meditation, Helena set herself to sing an old Hymn for all those poor young men... "Oh hear us when we cry to Thee, for those in peril on the sea!" she sang, but her voice broke into tears of loss and despair and she stopped again.

Later, still troubled, she found her steps leading her on a late night walk past the Cottage. "Helena!" called a voice and she saw it was the Visitor, sitting smoking a pipe out on the little lawn. Reassured by the pipe, she joined him and sat silently for a while. It was a fine warm night she noticed, with a harvest moon enlarging in the sky already. It will be full tomorrow, she thought, just right for the party.

After a while the man put down his pipe and said, "You are sad." It wasn't a question but a statement. Suddenly Helena found herself pouring out her heart in a way she hadn't done for years; hadn't needed to really.

God knows, she thought, how often she had to tell this story before she somehow came to terms with it. How her husband Harry Brown and parents, Stephen and Maria Denton, had both been killed in one day in a big car accident on a snowy main road when cars were crashing like skittles. The horror of the moment when you scream "No, No, No!" as if that could make it not so, because you know that your life too is over.

How the need of the little Jocelyn without a father or grandparents was now both Helena's doom and her salvation, to bring her up and give her as near a semblance of a normal life as a widow, with small means and much pride possibly could.

Of how that pride was gradually pared away to a deeper, more loving thing and how it returned painfully as a beautiful recognition that she had brought her daughter up to live, be happy and move on.

Helena described in happy tears now, how Jocelyn had met Jon Masters, a research Biologist at university and they had got married a few years ago. She had waved the newly married pair off on the flight to Spain to take up a post in Madrid University, her heart breaking with joy, pride and loss.

How she had just been able to afford the fare once, over a year ago, to see the new little baby grandson, Rodney, now nearly two years old, but how the parents, hard up, themselves would send her a ticket soon for another little visit. Soon! Soon! Soon! – the deepest desire of her heart!

The Visitor sat silently, attentively. Helena knew that way of listening from good experiences of caring professionals, enough of them to cancel out the ones who were, let's say charitably, not understanding. Perhaps for the first time she could give herself entirely over to the experience of being cared for and nurtured.

She found herself walking back down to her home, but never remembered quite how she got there, nor how she got to bed and slept deeply, feeling refreshed on waking.

The Visitor put out his pipe, which had never been lit anyway and walked round the Cottage to the East side, as if expecting someone. Sure enough down the road, pausing a moment by the Flitterbrook, came the old Man, Tom Crow. Unable to sleep, through happiness this time, he had come to see again the Cottage that had played such a part in his life and now seemingly in the lives of others.

He stopped short, startled, as he saw that there was a man in the garden. Surely not the gardener at this hour? The old man started a stumbling explanation, but the Visitor smiled and said, "You're just in time to hear another story, if you wish. Are you ready to share your new found peace with another?"

Together they sat on the bench outside the cottage door, smelling the soft night scented stock and rosemary. It seemed warm to the old man who had gone through so much and the Visitor never complained of the cold.

Certainly he listened to the Story presented to him by the chuckling voice of the River Flitter. After all, that little waterway certainly has a vested interest in any story that leads us to the sea and it has heard so many stories from the Winds that it has acquired the taste for them.

Here is the story...

TREASURES FROM THE SEA

THERE WAS ONCE a woman who lived in a tiny cottage on the edge of the Sea.

The front door opened onto the cobbled village street, but behind the house the shingle sloped down sharply, and there was no back door – only a window opening straight onto the beach. When the East Wind blew up a storm the waves lashed the whole house, and sometimes blew the spray right over into the front.

The woman says, "At high tide the water comes right above the windows. I have to keep them tightly, tightly shut," she says, "or the sea climbs in again and takes them away. My family. Shouting and sick and no family anymore. Of course I have to remain tightly shut. I remain tightly shut. Don't ask me why."

She cannot remember who she is or where she came from. She remembers only that other kind people have put her in this tiny cottage and tell her she came from a long way away in a boat one day. Is it true? "I can't remember," she tells them.

The one thing she really knows is how to make patchwork, very beautiful so people say.

They bring her pieces of cloth and buy what she makes. She spends all her time cutting up the fabric into the precise little shapes and then piecing them together into intricate named patterns. "There's Windmills and Bear's Paws," she says, "Robbing Peter to Pay Paul, Pickle Dish, Honeycomb, and Puss in the Corner."

The kind people give her money every week and the nurse says she will get well, but that she's been very stressed. She believes them because they are kind and now she won't have to remember the seasick waves shouting at her and dark, dark, dark, dark... Or was it a train? "Was I ever anywhere else?" she says. "Why can I not speak about it? Where are my family? My parents and children and uncles and aunties and cousins... no, no, no. Never go there. Keep the windows shut against the sea. Don't ask me."

She loves the patches though. She knows every pattern in her book as she fits the pieces together. Sometimes she goes and stands by the little River that comes out into Seven Sisters Bay and hears it reciting the names to her. Then she goes and finds the patterns in her book.

Listen to the voice of the little River Flitter, hidden in the greater waters of the Cuckmere, but singing the strange liturgy of the quilts she makes in her distress...

"Where can your Wandering Feet take you, except on a Wild Goose Chase?" says the brave little Flitter. *"We will go together down Drunkard's Path, take the Underground Railway and the Rocky Road, till a Streak of Lightning from a Storm at Sea, ends in Broken Dishes, a Fool's Pipe and a Lost Ship on Tumbling Rocks."* She puts them together in dark pieces of navy and brown, maroon red and dark grape purple.

In calm weather, however, the sea is smooth as a meadow, and sometimes the woman hears it tapping on the sill. Then the sea is nice to her and she opens the window and "it is giving me a present," she tells the kind people.

Sometimes it may be treasures from the deep, a pearl, intricate coral, a translucent whorled shell. It may be rubbish, broken wood, seaweed, flotsam, and sometimes a dead bird for her to bury in the strip of salt-bitten garden at the side of the house.

It is often when this cold East Wind blows – the wind of the dead men's feet – that the sea brings her the birds to lay to rest.

"I think I might be dead too," she sometimes tells the kind people, but she doesn't say it aloud so they don't hear. It's a comfort to bury the birds. "Maybe they have the souls of my family," she tells the kind people walking past in the street at the front of the house, but she keeps the window shut. Tightly, tightly, tightly shut so the kind people don't hear. Sometimes she thinks perhaps she never had a family anyway.

Everyone seems to know her. She knows no one. She knows that in and around the village live all the farmers and the tradesmen and their wives; the butcher, the baker and the candlestick maker; the tinker, the tailor, the soldier, the sailor, the rich man, the poor man, the beggarman and the thief – all very kind and with respected and time-hallowed places in the community, even the thief.

She knows she isn't anyone. "I'm not anyone," she tells the birds as she buries them in her garden.

There is also one strange man who does not fit in. He is tall and thin; no-one knows where he lives, or how, she tells the sea. He has a thin, sneering white face, white sparse hair, and he always wears a greeny-black suit with flapping tails, so that the children call him 'Mr Magpie'. "I don't like him," says the woman. "He's not kind man."

He sidles along the edges of the village and the edges of the daylight, often passing by at twilight, setting the village dogs howling.

♪

One day, Mr Magpie slid up to her as she stood in the open door of the cottage and gave her a piece of fabric. She felt his smile was sly and malicious, and she didn't really want to take something from him, but somehow she found herself accepting it and he melted away into the shadows as she looked at her gift.

It was a piece of fabric, coloured dark purple, with writing on in stitches, fine stitches such as she used to sew. It felt rough in her fingers and the woman could see it was a Memorial Quilt.

Before she could stop it she had read all the names on it.

All of her own family, and other people's families she didn't know. Some who she had longed to remember, all she had tried to forget. More, these new names must be those who are going to die in the village soon and all... "No... no!... Don't read it, fold it up, shut it up, tear it up, close the windows tightly, tightly, tightly... too late!"

The windows of the cottage stayed shut for a long time. A time of confusion in her mind. People came and went. The kind people came and made her eat, gave her medicine. She sat alone in the cottage, staring out of the window, and saw that the sea was withdrawing. Slowly and inexorably it retreated, until it was just a silver line on the horizon, and then it was gone and she was truly alone.

The children in the street didn't speak to her now, but sometimes about her. One day she heard a little boy just outside saying, "That's the house where the mad lady lives" – and she heard the 'thunk' as his mother smartly clipped him on the back of the head. "Just you stop that, Tommy, you little bastard," she said, "have some respect. I won't have you saying that!"

The lady didn't mind. She thought, "Perhaps I am mad? Perhaps it is someone else? Perhaps it's that other lady who lives in the house and can't sew the patchwork? I have to get back to sewing the patchwork to prove I'm not her, that mad lady who shares the house."

The woman got out her sewing box and needles and scissors and threads again and slowly, slowly, with difficulty began to cut and sew again. She would stare out of the window to where the sea had been but there was no comfort there. The grey silted-up sand stretched to the horizon, showing up the dead creatures, twisted wrecks, bones and oily feathers and dried out jellyfish and seaweed.

Slowly, with her needle and thread she began to piece her life together again. She cut up the cloth Mr Magpie had given her and sewed the little patches together in the pattern called Morning, but she had dyed it all black to obliterate the names, and no-one would want it. What is the point of patchwork all in black?

Sometimes as she sat sadly looking out at the street she would see Mr Magpie sidling past, with a smirk on his face, giving her his malicious smile. She hated him, and would pull the curtains.

Time passed, and passed again, and one day it seemed as if the bitter wind had changed and a new feeling came over the landscape, she did not know how or why.

The birds were passing overhead. She heard their cries and knew they spoke to her if only she could understand what they said.

Tommy's mother came to the door, looking sad and embarrassed with a request. "My mother has just passed away," she said. "She always said she wanted to be laid out with a piece of your lovely patchwork, but I haven't liked to bother you."

The woman smiled and spoke, croakily, for it was the first time in months apart from the kind people. But here was a new kind person who seemed to want something from her.

"I'm sorry," she croaked, then cleared her throat, "I've only got this." She held out the finished black Morning quilt she had made from Mr Magpie's terrible gift. The light sparkled and gleamed in facets, wherever the little seams were and the changed direction of the weave.

Tommy's mother beamed at her. "But that's lovely!" she said. "Look at all the textures. It's all black too. So respectful for a funeral. Oh thank you so much!

"What do I owe you?" she continued, but the woman would take no money, and they shook hands on the transaction.

Going into the back room the woman opened the sea window for the first time in months — for what had been the point in opening it when the sea was no longer there to give her presents? – and there was a sweet West Wind blowing, and it played on her eyelids and her lips and her hair, like a gift. She stood motionless as the dusk spread over the landscape, and eventually saw at the horizon a fine silver line, as slowly, slowly, the sea began to flow back.

It came so slowly and was so calm that all the stars in the sky were reflected in the deep grape-blue surface, changing and shimmering with an occasional ripple. As the sea came to the window and reached the sill, a sudden surge tossed onto the sill a piece of fine silk cloth in the same colour.

The woman washed out the salt, dried and ironed the cloth. She sewed it with stars all over in silver thread, through many days and nights.

When it was finished she took it back to the window and threw it into the sea. She called out: "All these stars are now my family and your family and all the families, especially for all who have no family. I've sewn the stars into it for you, so my family now belongs to you and your family belongs to me, and to all who have no family and we all belong to you, the Sea."

The cloth seemed to multiply and spread until it covered the whole sea, the stars sewn on it glittering in the light of the moon. Then it was swiftly withdrawn over the horizon, leaving the dark sea once more to lap against the windowsill.

♪

The woman continued to live in the cottage, and to piece together fabric the villagers bought her. Now she was able to talk again, to be part of the life there and to take her own place with the kind people.

Now she made her patchwork in all colours and it was a joy making it. It was all reds and pinks, royal purples and greens, jade and turquoise, lemon yellow and buttercup yellow, brown and fawn, peacock blue and aquamarine. It was all of the colours in the rainbow and more, loved by all who saw and bought her work, but still she knew the final, the perfect piece with exactly the right colours and shades and balance eluded her.

As she sat on the beach in the sunshine, sewing and piecing, trying for the colours of storm clouds and wild flowers, the little river within the Cuckmere had a new chant of the patterns for her to follow as she sat on the sand...

"Oh listen, listen!" sang the jubilant voice of the little River Flitter, *"Come with me now and we will follow the Birds of the Air on a Trip around the World. I'm Gone with the Wind, so Catch Me if You Can, while I'm Climbing Jacob's Ladder. We'll go round with The*

Wheel of Fortune to the North Star, on top of the Delectable Mountain, where grows the Tree of Paradise. Come with me! Come with me!"

So all went on smoothly for a long time, till one day when she looked out of the window into the street, she saw Mr Magpie, sidling along, but he no longer smirked or gloated.

He looked utterly ill and miserable. She felt an unexpected pang of pity for him, and went to the window to look for the first time in ages. She saw the full extent of his wretchedness. The rain ran into the holes in his tall hat. The North Wind blew through the holes in the side of his ragged ill-fitting coat. She saw that he was thinner than ever, half starved, with a blank look to his eyes as if he no longer knew who he was. She knew that look well from the inside. Pity for him welled up within her heart.

She held out all the pieces of cloth she had been working on, and called to him: "Wait! I will make you a coat out of these!" As she stretched out her arms to him with the pieces of cloth, they flew in the air, flapping like birds and enveloped him. All the pieces joined up in the glorious pattern of light and dark, exquisitely mixed, that she had always believed would come if she could only fit them together perfectly.

Mr Magpie raised his battered top hat to her and then sent it spinning into the tree tops. He waved and smiled, turned and danced away up the village street. With every step he seemed to become younger and more vigorous, clicking his heels and leaping off the ground. His hair turned chestnut, and corkscrewed in the breeze. The setting sun appeared behind the grey clouds; its misted light sending a river of gold from his dancing feet to the horizon, along which he vanished.

Smiling, she turned back to her house, and heard the sea patting at her window pane. Outside the glass was a white ship, in transparent silk, covered in fine silver embroidery, with silver rosebuds twining the mast and bursting open on the sails. Their petals streamed out in the breeze from the land, and a silver track from the rising moon danced on the waves.

Opening the window, she stepped out onto the deck, and the sea, her friend and ally, released its hold, so that the wind could carry her along, out and away to a new adventure beyond the horizon. That place where the Sun Man, with his flaming hair, and the Moon Woman, with her silver threads, will come together again and all will be well.

POSTLUDE

♪

A S THE STORY came to an end the Visitor noted that the Old Man was asleep and raised his legs to the bench, covering him with a blanket and tarpaulin from the Cottage, against the dawn dew.

He himself sat for a while in the kitchen. The mice who still obeyed his every thought, crowded round him with added joy and if he slept at all for the rest of that night, sitting by the unlit fire, with mice around and all over his feet, we do not know. As the sun rose he went out and saw that the old man had gone, leaving his coverings neatly folded exactly as a good boy always remembers to do.

Helena too woke early, renewed and refreshed, confused and yet knowing something momentous had happened and she contained a deep peace that would feed her forever, walked back up to the Cottage later on to see her Visitor out.

He greeted her smiling. Neither referred to the events of the night. All he said, after a kindly "good morning", was "By the way – do you remember all those thoughts you had a while ago? You know – that the ownership of the cottage might be a consortium, owned by an eccentric multimillionaire? You were spot on, Helena. Except that he owns not only the Cottage but the whole of Sussex, indeed, the world."

While she was puzzling over this, she was only half noticing – and did not think about it till much later – that he had no luggage of any kind. He handed over the exact money in cash, and also his card, the normal slip of white pasteboard, which she had been too sad and preoccupied to take the previous day. As she looked at his card, she was surprised, for no particular reason, to see the name Gabriel, maybe because he seemed so very English and the name somehow exotic.

He put his hand on hers, over the name, lovingly, not imposing himself. As she looked up into his eyes her heart seemed to blossom like a scarlet rose. He bent forward and kissed her strongly on the lips.

Love, confusion and awe, overwhelmed her, at this meeting of their lips, their hearts, their very souls. After that kiss, she watched him turn away and experienced an instant unstoppable impulse to reach out to his arm. Was it to pull him back? Or to hold on and go with him? She did not even know herself, remembering it later that day. Her outstretched hand fell back, even as she knew she would love him and in some way miss him all her life, but must let him go. Her hand had just touched his soft sleeve delicately.

All day the touch of his lips on hers and the soft feel of his sleeve would remain within her body, while she pondered on the encounter. Indeed she knew she would never forget it.

Her glance fell again on the card. Where the surname should be was just a smudge, but she was sure for a moment that it was in the shape not of a word but a pair of wings and even as she saw it, the card slipped out of her hand as a ship leaves its moorings at the start of a long voyage. She watched it flutter away into the bright blue of the autumn morning.

The next morning the Postman's knock on her own door brought her out, bright and smiling, even though it was usually nothing but bills and circulars. Not this morning! Her heart lifted as she recognised her daughter's writing and opened it first.

It was quite short, but so glorious to her that it felt as if time had stopped. Her daughter's husband, Jon, had done so well with his PhD that he had been offered a Research post, at least five years with secure tenure, at Brighton University and they were going to settle near her, to make a home and find a school for little Rodney. Would it be too much trouble if they stayed a while to house hunt when the time came? And if they could find the money they'd first bring her over to them for Rodney's birthday next month.

Almost unable to think for joy she opened the second envelope. Out fell a cheque – she had won £1,000 on her premium bonds.

So happy was she that it was impossible to stay in, though she had things she had meant to do that day. She and Rosie Cullen and Norah Davenport all went up onto the Downs along Tin Kettle Lane.

It was not intended to be a joint walk; indeed, Norah was carrying her garden shears to cut back the worst of the intrusive hedges, and collect flowers and herbs. Helena and Rosie were also under instruction from her and making nosegays of anything that seemed useful. They were enjoying it very much, in spite of sneezing at times.

Helena had told the others about the two wonderful pieces of news she had been sent. "Good things always come in threes," said Norah in oracular mode. "You mark my words. You'll have a third piece of Good luck before sun-up – that's for sure!"

The three of them talked and laughed, at ease with themselves and the world, but as it chanced they all fell into line as they came back across the High Weald just above the Cottage and Old Tom Crow was once again passing down the lane below.

He saw them for one timeless instant, changed and ageless, caught in a shaft of sunlight that shone on their faces and hair.

A young woman carrying a sheaf of flowers, an older woman carrying a ball of twine and an even older woman carrying a pair of shears. Grace multiplied by three. Spinners of life, all of them, yet charged also with the awesome responsibility of cutting the thread in its due time.

INTERLUDE

♪

COULD THIS BE LOVE?

IT SEEMED that the sightseeing and shopping were over for the moment. Melinda took George to her *'appartement'* down a tiny back street. Once there she shed her coat, came close up to him and asked, "George, dear, would you be kind enough to go downstairs and bring up the bundle of wood you'll find there? I forgot!"

He had noticed the open fireplace and was delighted to do this for her. Then, with much smiling and complimenting him on his physique – which indeed he felt was good for his age – she asked for further help in replacing a light bulb.

Since this involved her getting up on a stool and getting him to steady her with an arm around her thighs, he was very pleased to oblige, though secretly he couldn't help but compare her rather thick ankles with some very trim and shapely legs he had recently seen. Then her perfume hit him and made him feel quite defenceless and filled with desire for her.

In between these activities it seemed she was already pouring the wine and he enjoyed a little nap while she went and prepared their meal. It was indeed a marvellous and delicious treat, He enjoyed every mouthful, then helped clear the dishes and load the dishwasher. She seemed very pernickety about what went where, so he left her to it.

"May I light the fire now?" George asked, putting his head round the open door to the kitchen. "I love an open fire!" He took Melinda's nod for assent and started to lay the firelighter down with some bundles of scrunched up newspaper and build a little cone of sticks. He had just lit the paper and picked up the big bundle of wood to move it out of harm's way, when she came in and expressed horror at his fire setting method.

"Oh no!" she cried. "You've done it all wrong. How on earth do you think you'll get it going that way?" Her voice was a whine increasing in pitch with every phrase. She took the poker, broke up his fire and remade it herself.

"I didn't say you could light the fire, because I knew you'd do it wrong!" she continued. "Why are you being so stupid? Have you only got half a brain?" Her voice was hot with anger, yet he sensed something cold about the way she was looking at him, something calculating?

In this loss of temper, in an apparently spontaneous tirade, there suddenly seemed to George something made up, as if she was testing how he would respond. Almost as if she was looking to see how far she could go before he retaliated, perhaps?

Before he could think this through she was all sweetness and honey again and confused him more by coming up to caress him, her perfume once more making his head swim. 'Does she put it on with a ladle?' he could almost hear his practical Cousin Patricia from Canada saying!

George reached out for Melinda's breasts and she giggled. It seemed as if she poured them into his hand. He was consumed with desire for her, drowsy with – with what? Why did the word 'deceit' come into his mind at that moment? He resolutely banished it, succumbing to the waves of lust, but the mood was suddenly and dramatically broken.

From the bundle of wood by their feet came a high pitched squeak, as a little mouse jumped out of it – a field mouse inadvertently picked up and brought in with the kindling. It ran across the floor, stopped and turned, terrified and trembling.

Instantly Melinda's attitude changed again. She jumped onto a chair, snatching her skirts up high, exposing a long length of thigh, and shrieked: "Oh a mouse! A mouse! George dear, deal with it! Get rid of it!"

She smiled at him appealingly and suddenly the something that had been troubling him hit home. It was all so very fake, it was all deceit! Melinda was no more frightened by the mouse than she was sexually attracted to him! It was a show, a seductive façade for a cold and controlling person. He could see she was more truly herself in her whining tirade over the fire than in any of her caresses.

Unbidden, another face swung into view in his memory. Helena's eyes filled with tears and anxiety, but proportionate, concerned for the mice in the cottage, but far more so for him, when hearing of the traumas in his life, not this flirtatious pretence. He suddenly saw Melinda as a toady, a frog like the

Rumblebum mug, pretentious and meretricious, along with many of her 'set'.

How often had he blinded himself to the real personality of the women who had attracted him? Their secret agenda and the calculation behind the winsome smiles? The insincerity of the over-hasty 'love' they seemed to be offering, not backed up by any unselfish actions? The way that, like Melinda, they efficiently drew out from him his hopes and dreams and – again just as Melinda had – fed them back to him as if they shared them, making him believe they were soulmates. All was pretence.

"It's all smoke and mirrors!" was his first thought. This instant bonding, like crack cocaine, was not the very slow build-up of friendship he had experienced with Helena. For a moment he saw in his mind's eye, that dear friend's crinkly, smiling eyes, as well remembering her vulnerability, so like his own, though his was a better concealed sensitivity of soul. He remembered too, achingly, the sweet, fun sound of her laugh.

"What a fool I am!" was his second self-excoriating thought, at the memory of the many times he had fallen for it. He remembered again his feisty cousin Patricia in

Canada, who had shaken her head at him a few times, recognising this weakness – to his extreme annoyance – and using a relative's privilege once to say warningly, "You're only ever one step away from a woman who'll put a spell on you, George!"

He shook his head, as if to clear it and looked again at Melinda. A moment of choice. Yet he knew that this time there could only be the one choice he could safely make. Without really registering it he saw from the corner of his eye the mouse, emboldened, vanish into the shadows of the skirting board, safe.

Turning on his heel he walked out of the door and down the stairs, not looking back even when Melinda said his name and leant over the stairwell calling him.

He went straight round to the hotel. Nigel was not back as it was still early evening, but he left a friendly note, packed his case and booked out. He heard Melinda's voice on the phone, agitated, asking the receptionist if she could speak to him, but he shook his head to the girl taking the call, walked out and hailed a taxi.

The bouncing of the taxi shook him painfully, driven fast as only the French can drive, especially when sensing a drama. His heart was thumping all the way to the airport. 'Don't look back. Don't look back!' he was repeating to himself, frantically, like a mantra. Vague images of those who turned back swam in the choppy seas of his mind. Images of Medusa, turning her suitors to stone, of Lot's wife, becoming a pillar of salt, of Orpheus looking back and losing Eurydice, even the evil White Witch in the Narnia books turning all who opposed her to icy stone...

The loop of images turned into a dreary soundtrack of thoughts: "Why do I keep doing this? What madness got into me to try and escape to France, to repeat the whole dreary charade of flirtation, an affair and an expensive mistake?" He was filled for a while with grief and self-disgust, but his resolution stayed firm.

It carried him through the inevitable arguing and arm waving necessitated by his change of ticket, but it was successful providing he waited for a few hours in the airport. He didn't mind. He had eaten well, was still a little tight and just wanted to be quiet. He had to return to Manchester, because that was where he had left his car after joining up with Nigel.

He could take his dear old Merc and be in Sussex in about five hours, six with necessary breaks. He might even make the tail end of the party.

Perhaps Helena would forgive him if he could do that?

Perhaps she wouldn't and she'd surely be angry! He knew he would have to be very patient and work hard to convince her he wanted to make friends again, Maybe she wouldn't trust him? Well, *tant pis*, he knew that this time it would be different.

"I've got all the time in the world," he thought and wondered where that had come from. It almost seemed to be someone else saying it in his ear. "Time George! It's time. Now's the time. You've got all the time in the world, don't throw it away again!"

PRELUDE

♪

THE PARTY AT
THREE CUPS CORNER

THE DAY of the Tea Party and Barbecue at Three Cups Inn had started with a clear blue, crisp morning, when Helena had gone for an early walk on the downs and waved to the Old Man in the distance.

This eagerly awaited annual treat, put on for charity, was always well attended by the local people from all the villages in that part of Sussex and indeed from far afield, hosted by The Three Cups Inn on its lush lawns. There would be quite a few people from the Hospital or Care Homes at Hellingly, discreetly broken up into smaller groups, along with plenty of folks from further afield, plus lots of tourists.

Of course the Cyclamen Lodge denizens, Mabel, Colonel Arthur and Dolores, tended to stick together, and enjoyed trying to participate in the activities, so they were all there, with Joe and Rosie, who had volunteered to take them and keep a special eye on them. Nothing to do with those two young people wanting to be together, of course. Perish the thought!

They got there quite early in the afternoon. Along with the official Carers, Joe and Rosie, there was Carol, Mabel's niece, who had come down from Derby specially, and Helena who were also helping, as friends and relatives.

Dolores had been discouraged from bringing her special tea cup with her (the one the Cottage had produced on a memorable earlier occasion) but she was eying the craft stalls and bric-a-brac enviously. An avid knitter, she was only able to do simple pieces now, but Carol bought her a lot of beautifully rich and fluffy coloured yarns so she could go on with her Endless Scarf, a piece to rival the famous Doctor Who scarf in length and sumptuous display.

Miraculously, skills overlearnt from an early age are almost always the last to go. Though Dolores could not easily turn a sock or follow a pattern, she could still knit purl and plain and the Endless Scarf could already go the length of the sitting room at the Lodge, so she was delighted, even accepting her tea out of a plastic mug for once.

Like most women of her generation, Aunty Mabel too had been a champion knitter. Now, alas, even her skills could not survive the trauma of the strokes she had suffered and her left hand and arm were still a little weak and almost unable to manipulate the needles.

Country bred Mabel sometimes felt particularly uneasy in the twilight hours, when the voices of long dead critics could murmur in her head, "Never be without something to do with your hands, for the Devil will find work for them." So although she rarely showed it, being of the stoical breed of women who rarely complained, there were times when she felt the loss of her handicraft capabilities acutely.

Carol could sympathise with this and also help, from her own work as an Occupational Therapist. So she had made sure that Aunty Mabel had relearned skills in a different way, teaching her to stitch tapestry on plastic canvas with thick wool and the use of other gadgets, such as a small one-handed loom to carry round with her.

Picking up on this, Helena insisted on buying Mabel a bag for her new work. It caught her eye, with its beautiful rainbow stripes in soft pinks, lemon, greens, pale blue and mauve, all the sunset colours. On the front it had a White Unicorn standing proudly, picked out in gold and silver.

All the ladies were looking somewhat wistfully at the children's 'Bearbecue' where the youngsters were having a Teddy Bear's picnic with a difference. It turned out to be the brainchild of Norah Doveport, presiding over it with some of her numerous grandchildren helping, particularly Andrew Doveport, a no-nonsense Fireman by profession, and her fiercest grandson.

He was supervising the cooking with a specially guarded stove and fending off the jokes about cooking and eating bears with patience and longsuffering as he told the hundredth tourist, "No, It's a JOKE, we don't barbecue the teddy bears!" – silently adding, "But I'll barbecue the next person who asks me!"

There were a couple of Norah and Bert's great grandchildren among the groups. Francine had brought little Jenny, who ran over and hugged Dolores, her Nana Doll, but was persuaded to stay with the other children, who under the guidance of the adults, were beginning to accept her Special status in a caring way.

The party were sitting on plastic chairs a little apart from the crowds. Joe noticed that Colonel Arthur Brassington was shifting about awkwardly and needed to be taken to a toilet. Damn! They had all got a bit carried away by the fun.

He stood up taking Arthur by the arm in a friendly way, and said, "Come along Arthur, let's go pay a little visit." Arthur went from smiling to near rage in one second flat: "Take your hands off me, Private Price!" he exclaimed. "Show a little respect."

Joe was mortified on his behalf and apologised instantly. "Colonel Brassington, please don't be offended, Sir. Can I help you in any way?"

Too late. Though checked momentarily from a full all-out tantrum, Arthur was not to be so easily placated. "No you can't, young man!" The sour smell of urine was already rising. Rosie and Joe, for once, were lost, realising that to say anything would precipitate disaster, but so would doing nothing.

For the two young Carers the world felt as if it ceased to turn for a moment, as Aunty Mabel, clumsy but completely calm, came to the end of her row and stuck the hook in the ball of rainbow wool. All eyes were drawn to her, even Arthur's, as she placidly put it away with her one good hand in her new stripy bag.

Even Helena's calm had deserted her. Frozen with anxiety, she caught sight of the white and gold unicorn on Mabel's bag as if hypnotised. "Help us!" she found herself silently mouthing. "Please, please, help us!"

Afterwards she was never sure if the unicorn really had winked at her or if it was her overwrought imagination.

Aunty Mabel said in her firmest yet kindest voice: "Colonel, I wonder if I could ask for a hand to help me up?"

"Certainly dear lady," roared the Colonel, rising from his chair and helping her up, it must be admitted with a considerable increase of smell.

Peace once again restored, Joe was able to take the Colonel out to the gent's toilets behind the pub. Rosie and Carol took the opportunity for the ladies to retire to the hotel powder room, while Helena looked after all their belongings.

Closing her eyes in the late afternoon sunshine she relaxed, only to become painfully aware of how much she missed having George Miller, who had originally planned to be with them this afternoon. The tears squeezed unstoppably from under her eyelids and she mopped at them angrily, unaware that at this precise moment he was swearing impotently on a back road near Reading at his inability to restart the Merc and surprise her by keeping his promise after all.

Joe had changed the Colonel's nether clothing from the spares of everything he had carefully stowed in his backpack. Arthur stood patiently while he was cleaned and redressed, suddenly almost like a child in his vulnerability. Indeed, as he fixed on Joe his filmy blue eyes that seemed filled with tears, his carer felt to be seeing the frightened youngster he must once have been.

Arthur looked anxiously into Joe's face and when he spoke he had reverted to a sort of shorthand speech pattern, with a slight country burr. "Was at a good school mind! Boarding, in Tunbridge Wells. Scholarship boy. Difficult. Not like them Nobs."

Joe looked at him encouragingly, kneeling before him as he zipped him up and dusted some grass off his clothes.

Arthur continued, "Pissed the bed, di'nt I? For months. Smelly Arthur they called me, them Nobs, and worse. Mum wanted to take me away but I stuck it out. Good Grammar school. Army."

Joe spoke kindly: "You did very well, Colonel, to rise above all that."

Arthur shook his head. "Never was a Colonel or nothin' like it! Made it up when I got out, din't I? Made up the voice and everything. Always was good at voices, taking the micky and that – made them nobs laugh and skipped a few beatings that way. When I got out it was a laugh at first but I got treated right. Respect. So I kep' at it."

Joe was listening raptly, still on his knees. He had known of course that Arthur had only ever been a private in the army, but no details. He knew most of his dementia charges were like this, desperate to cling to what memories they had, real or invented. It seemed that Arthur had invented for a lot longer than most, half a lifetime perhaps, with no one knowing.

Not for the first time he wondered, compassionately, whether, awful as dementia was, for the patient the forgetting might sometimes bring benefits, a release at last into the real person. A phrase came into his mind. 'A cloud of unknowing' – but he could not catch the origin.

Arthur was continuing, with a slight quaver in his voice, "Never got anywhere. Do you know what my job was?" he asked.

Joe shook his head but smiled encouragingly.

"In the Stores, wan' it? In charge of bedding in the end." Joe could hear a hint of pride in his voice. A good core value, he thought.

"I bet you did a good job," said Joe, getting up and seating them both on a bench just outside the loo.

Arthur turned to him eagerly. "Yea. Did a good job. You know all those new lads coming in the army? Nothin' more than children they were. Pissed their beds, din't they? Lots of them. And the men coming back from the front... they pissed their beds too..."

Arthur's voice faltered. Behind his rheumy old eyes memories were passing, guns were booming, dirty bloodstained kit to clean up. Not just blood, sweat and tears but piss and shit, bits of skin, body parts ground into earth, 'vomiting yer guts out' was what your country asked. Shit!

"Pissin' the bed too, and worse, yeah," he said. "My job to change the mattress. Take it away and clean it. Smelly Arthur again, but I din't mind. My mate Fizz – Philip he was really – we had a good laugh. 'His Majesty's Purveyors of pissed on mattresses' we called ourselves."

Joe spoke from the heart. "I'm glad you stuck with it all," he said firmly. "You're worth a dozen colonels. That's the spirit that won us the war!"

A look of panic crossed Arthur's face as he realised the war must be over. Joe corrected himself quickly. "Will win us the war, meant to say! Hitler's on his way out, thanks to you and your regiment."

Arthur relaxed. Joe could see the mists descending again behind his eyes. Probably wouldn't even remember this moment of clarity, Joe thought.

Arthur had one more concern. "Do you think I should admit it to the ladies?" he asked anxiously.

Joe shook his head. "No. No point. Besides ladies... well, you know, delicate plants! Need protecting." A momentary picture of the doughty Norah Doveport, and Aunty Mabel, strength and common sense personified, plus the empathic Helena, crossed his mind,

"Forgive me, Ladies!" he said silently to these three formidable Graces. Although he was laughing a little inside, it was about himself, at the thought of any of those three needing protection from reality. He had nothing but respect for the old man, relict of deprivation, war and ill health.

"Come on Colonel!" Joe said cheerfully, helping the old man up from the hard bench and swinging his own pack over his shoulder. "There's a lot of Bearburgers out there with our names on them," and they set out to join the rest of the gang on the pub lawn.

A short time later the whole party agreed that they had had enough of the crowds and at Helena's suggestion they decided to continue the party in a quieter way on the lawn at Turnaround Cottage for a while. Francine and little Jenny had joined them and Jenny was holding hands with both her and Dolores, her 'Nana Doll'.

As Helena waited to help Joe and Rosie shepherd the party into the van, she heard her name called. It was Jeremy Cornwell, the Visitor from a few weeks back, the man who had heard the Unicorn story. They had spoken on the phone a couple of times; now he was explaining, out of breath, how he'd been delayed this afternoon and only just got to Three Cups Corner.

Helena introduced him to the party and she and Jeremy walked down after the van to join the others, chatting pleasantly. She was pleased to see him. Neither spoke of George.

It was still warm enough in the late afternoon sunlight to sit out on the lawn there, where the older members of the party had a little nap and even the younger ones were yawning. Cups of tea all round were provided.

There were fireworks promised for a little later, which would be easily seen from the lawn and the party could then come to an end with their safe delivery back to Cyclamen Lodge. Joe had privately arranged to drive Rosie to her home afterwards, thinking about suggesting a drink on the way if she was not too tired.

The group had a pleasantly united feel to it, mostly it must be said, cheerfully sleepy. Tea had been drunk and Helena and Rosie were washing up in the tiny kitchen, assisted by their new friend Jeremy Cornwell who was carrying cups and plates to and fro, and providing cake as necessary.

"Would you like another piece of cake, Jenny?" he asked the little girl. She nodded but Joe said quickly, "Just a small piece, please Jeremy. She's had a lot already!"

"I just want a piece to give to Turnaround Cottage!" protested Jenny.

Rosie poked her head round the back door laughing. "So resourceful, aren't they at this age?" she said and Joe and she shared a smile. "What sort of cake would the cottage like, Jenn?" she asked.

"Nana Doll says I'm called Jenny," replied the young lady with a reproving face. "The cottage would like the chocolate cake with strawberries on it. Please!"

"One piece of special chocolate cake for Turnaround Cottage coming up!" said Jeremy. He passed the pretty china plate over to the little girl. Its painted garland of roses enhanced the rosy strawberries, glowing like tiny lamps on the cake.

Someone else seemed to think so too. For the first time Jenny, then the grownups each in turn, seemed to see the large smiley face of the Cottage, high up on its tower, outlined faintly in the shadows cast by the setting sun.

Somehow, no one seemed to feel or show any particular surprise. Perhaps the party were all soporific with sunshine, or just realised that they had always known where the face of the cottage was, facing down South towards the sea, smiling a comfortable smile at all who passed near.

"Mmmm, it looks Delicious," said the voice of Turnaround Cottage. A comfortable dependable earthy sort of voice, rooted in clay, but with a hint of the wild winds going up at the ends of sentences.

"My dear young Jennifer. How very kind you are. No one has ever offered me cake before.

"The only thing is, my dear," the voice continued, "I'm not sure I can eat it very well. I wonder if you would be kind enough to do that for me?"

Jenny came nearer and laid down the plate carefully for a moment on the grass, while she threw her arms as far as she could around the cottage, with one of her rare, spontaneous gestures of love. "Thank you!" she said. "Please Mr Cottage, will you tell me a story too?"

She sat down on a convenient tuffet, snuggling up to the lowest tier of bricks and started on the cake.

All the adults smiled, involuntarily, as the Cottage, visibly moved, with tears in its eyes and a sob in its voice, said, "No one has ever asked ME to tell them a story. Do you hear that, Winds? It's ME she wants!"

There appeared to be a collective sigh and a brief breath of cool wind from every direction at once, as the winds breathed out gently together. All the leaves of the trees shading the group twisted and twirled for a moment and the sunlight came through like moving, dancing flames over the faces of the Listeners. They moved in closer together, attending eagerly, as Turnaround Cottage began to tell its own story.

Turnaround Cottage had a voice sometimes as deep as a quarry, sometimes as strong as a tower, sometimes rising like a breeze in the sails or the coo of a dove in the sky...

"Listen, listen, listen, to my Tale. The true Tale of the making of the Mill and those who loved me!"

The Cottage could see, what no one on the lawn could, that the audience had been joined by a few others in a magic circle, to last as long as the story.

In the trees leading to their own cottage the Doveports were sitting, as they had once done, some fifty years before when Bert had proposed to Norah under the sails of that self-same Mill.

Just inside the copse, there was a small figure just visible to the eyes of the Cottage. Yes, Old Tom Crow was back, smiling up at the Mill that had been such an important part of his life and of his family! The Cottage seemed to be smiling back at him, and sending him a solemn, secret wink.

CHAPTER TWENTY

THE MILL'S OWN STORY

"I WAS CONCEIVED at a time of strife and starvation," began Turnaround Mill. "The great Emperor of those Frenchmen over the water had tried and lost in his attempt to conquer this unconquerable land of the South Saxons. Many had tried and failed to do so, and would try again and again."

'Colonel' Arthur Brassington unconsciously sat up straighter and squared his old shoulders, as at the click of a gun.

The Mill continued. "There was a desperate need for bread after the war was ended, so two years later men came to this field and in that year of 1817 they went deep down into the earth. They dug up great spades full of the clay, rocks from the quarry to make the bricks that form my body. There were iron fetters and bands to hold me, from the smelters of Crowhurst, tree trunks from our own woods, the Wealden forest. Everything we needed was here. So I was truly born of the strong, rich clay, washed by the rain, my sails blown round by Sussex air and mastered by the Men and Women of Sussex to feed their own people.

"Feed them I did. In me the Corn which had grown in the same earth from which I came, and been nourished by the same sun and rain and winds, was ground into corn to feed all my children, all the children of Sussex!"

The pride in the voice of the Mill caused them all to smile and unconsciously square their shoulders like the Colonel for a moment.

"The need for bread is always there," continued the Mill. "Men came and went, the building fell, but it rose again and in 1835 we were back in business – me and the Winds! That was when they rebuilt me to turn, turn and turn again, always to face the wind. Those were hungry times, glory times for a mill with strong sails and a tower that can always stand and face the wind, as it grinds, grinds, grinds the corn!"

Jenny had even forgotten to finish the cake, so attentively had she been listening, but she did so now and patted the bricks nearest to her. The Mill squinted down at her and smiled.

"It was always for the children!" it continued. "The children need their daily bread, to grow and flourish."

In the momentary silence the little River Flitter could be heard, excitedly joining in:

"It's for the children. Come with me to feed the children. Give them butter from the churn, give them meat from the farm and fish from the sea, give them milk from the cows, clean water and good ale and watered wine and when they grow older the sweet smuggled brandy from France. Give them herbs and vegetables, carrots and cabbage and chipped potatoes. Give them jam from the hedgerow and honey from the bees, but always, always give them corn and oats and rye and wheat as bread. Give them their daily bread!"

The Mill continued: "Some Ninety odd years I worked, grinding everything brought to me, but I took a rest for upwards of ten years till the end of the war they called the Second World War. We hunkered down, we Mills and buildings and houses of Sussex. Direct line of fire, and of bombs, everything bad that could be thrown at us – but we prevailed!

"Then my best master was here. Edward Windham and his daughter Maria. The daughters of Sussex have always been as good as the sons!" – said the Mill, and Norah and Bert Doveport turned to each other from their hidey hole under the trees, smiled and did a quiet high five, learned from their grandchildren.

"Maria married Josiah Gammerling from up Crawley way, but he came to work in the Mill and his son Steph Gammerling was born and brought up in me, and he was the one who rebuilt me, all over again. He and the grandchildren. It was after the war again, you see? The children needed bread! But we never again managed to feed all the children. My machinery was all sound and good still, other foods came and went, we made bread for the local people but we were never as successful or necessary again.

"Then came my tragedy. The summer of '55 was the terrible drought. Everything dried up and dried out. I felt myself shrivel in the heat and when the Big Wind came in from the Sea in the autumn it was a freak of nature. She blew so hard that chimneys in Punnetts Town came down and my own dear, precious sails were ripped off and blown far away, good only for matchwood.

"It was the last straw for the Gammerlings and Windhams. They packed up and left Turnaround Mill, for ever. Went to Manchester and foreign parts like that I did hear. They couldn't bear to set up anything near and see my ruins. I watched them go. Only the Mice were left. Generations of Mice, to keep the traditions going, living on the corn that had blown into the crevices of my rooms. Ah, it was so sad a day!"

At these words, Rosie saw Aunty Mabel crying, quietly and with dignity as old ladies of her vintage do. Mabel remembered so well the day of the great wind and the Mill which she had worked in as a girl and loved so much, torn apart and left to decay.

Rosie unobtrusively passed her the paper hankies, but Joe, who had kept something of an eye on Rosie since Helena had pointed out what a lovely person she was, noticed and felt an increase of tenderness, even love forming in his heart.

"That was a bad time. A very low time," the Mill continued. "No one seems to know who took me over, but a few years later I was all repaired and turned into the cottage as you see me now. Never a Mill again though. They took out the machinery and repaired the floors; the Mice didn't like that, but they stayed. Generations of them, very intelligent little mice, collectively remembering everything about me – I told them. I wouldn't let them forget our glory days."

The Mill fell silent for a moment then continued: "When we had the big Wind again in 1976 I thought she'd come to take me away for good, but there was nothing for her to take.

Just after that the thing happened that changed my life – made we what I am now!"

Perhaps surprisingly, for she was not noted for a good attention span, Jenny was still listening eagerly. She sighed and stood up again, putting comforting arms around the few bricks within her reach, but the Mill felt it and was touched. A big tear splashed down near her.

"I'd felt so useless, all those years not grinding the corn, but one night a family came to stay. They had a teenage boy, a sulky looking lad called Justin. He was rude to his parents, but when he was on his own in the little bedroom at the top he put his head down on the windowsill. His thoughts were black and I was really afraid for him.

"A little West Wind breeze was passing and I appealed to her. I think she may even have felt a little guilty about the breaking of my sails, because she blew round me till I was a little dizzy. That was when I discovered that the winds could turn me around and we changed that boy, Justin's outlook, from the bins and the bonfire to the flower garden and then to the Channel.

"The wind started to tell him a story and he was thrilled, listening, questioning and somehow growing through the listening. That was when I knew that we had to go on doing this. Changing the lives by just a few tiny degrees of turnaround to see a new perspective. The winds and I – we worked on it together, then and ever since!

"So now I once again grind a kind of corn to feed the souls of all who come here needing a Story and willing to listen. The corn that makes the holy bread of the stories is still being ground here and always will be! So, now you know my own story, as I know many of yours and we are all even better friends, as all can be when they share their stories!"

POSTLUDE

♪

THE VOICE of Turnaround Cottage fell silent. The face faded away. The party was over and a group of old people and their carers had to pack up and go 'home' to Cyclamen Lodge, from where Francine would take a dreamy eyed and deeply happy Jenny, who felt more truly 'Special' than she had ever felt before in her life.

As they were about to get into the van, the first of the fireworks went up in splendid style above Three Cups Corner and they waited long enough to enjoy the fantastic rockets and flares for a short while. For once even the Colonel was not put on his personal alert by the bangs, but remained in a state of peace and neutrality. Jeremy was dropped off back by his car, feeling he had a good new life and new friends, slowly but surely accommodating to the loss of his partner, Jose. He gave Carol a lift too.

Joe took Rosie home, again stopping off at the pub for a drink and a deepening relationship that was forming naturally. The

Doveports had vanished into their own cottage. Even Tom Crow went home rejoicing to his own place on the Heathfield road.

Only Helena went down alone and secretly tearful to the Wheelwright's Cottage in Flitterbottom, still unable to come to terms with the loss of George Miller, but nonetheless marvellously comforted.

"There is always a turnaround and a new view," she thought to herself, "Always a new Story to hear and to tell."

Meanwhile, what of George himself? He had been decanted from the aeroplane at Manchester Airport, mid-morning on the Saturday of the Three Cups Party and was reunited with his car. He was still certain that he was doing the right thing, in spite of the problems. He was determined to get to Helena, the real Solution to his sorrows, if only he had realised it sooner. His obstinacy, which had nearly made him succumb to the meretricious charms of the Great French Adventure now helped him drive doggedly on down to Sussex.

He was making good time, even still had faint hopes of reaching his goal in time for at least the end of the tea party. By taking the minor roads via Reading he had hoped to avoid the horrors of the M25.

He stopped briefly in a corner of a nowhere village in the afternoon and alas, when he returned to the car park his trusty Merc had sprung an unexpected leak and there was oil running across the tarmac.

He never thought of abandoning his quest, but by the time he had managed to arrange a place where his Merc could be safely left, and a hire car had become free, he had not only missed the party but it was getting too late for an arrival with an uncertain welcome, so he booked into the nearest Premier Inn for the night.

Even though he was very afraid Helena would be angry and reject him, and even worse, be hurt and tearful, as indeed he realised he deserved, he knew he had to see her himself. He must try and explain, even if she raked him over or slammed the door.

He had certainly been in that position before and couldn't bear to phone her and then be alone after her reaction, whatever it would be.

As a gentleman George had taken the blame after both of his divorces, a nice characteristic but perhaps one which was not always justified and contributed to his diffidence and depression.

He had a meal of sorts and paid for the room in advance, falling asleep very quickly. Consequently, when he woke in the small hours his restlessness could only be satisfied by setting off at once, counting the hours, no the minutes, before he might reasonably call at the cottage.

He reached Heathfield in the early dawn light, passing Turnaround Cottage on his way down Flitterbrook Lane. He somehow couldn't help stopping momentarily outside.

It was dark and seemed deserted so he called quietly: "Hello Cottage! It's me, George Miller. I've been an absolute idiot, Cottage, and I've come to apologise to Helena and ask if we can be friends again. I know you care about her. What do you think my chances are?"

No sound or movement came from the cottage, but he felt its very silence to be gracious and friendly as he continued to speak his heart in safety.

"I really am sorry and your stories taught me such a lot, Cottage! All my life I didn't really understand what love was about. Of course it's of the body, but it's so much more! It means letting someone into the deepest thoughts of your heart and mind. If they're your true love, they understand, but if they're not and they hurt you it's intolerable and you have to close up again or die."

George concluded, "I don't think I ever let anyone in, Cottage; it was too much of a risk. But look what a mess I've made of my affairs without that love!"

The dawn light was strengthening all the time, like a welcome. The River Flitter was splashing past cheerfully and he could see a light in the kitchen window of Wheelwrights Cottage down the hill. He took a deep breath of resolve and slid quietly down without needing to start the engine, to pull up outside the back door at precisely 6 a.m.

The night after the party Helena slept badly and got up just before six o'clock for a cup of tea. She was surprised when a car stopped beside the cottage and peeping out did not recognise it. She put down the kettle again and went to the door. When she saw who it was she blushed deeply and could not help the sunshine within her breaking out, unable to conceal it behind the defence of even the smallest cloud, so loving and generous was her heart.

"George!" she exclaimed, hair tousled, smiling her crinkly smile as she opened her lovely eyes wide in surprise. "How wonderful to see you! Have you come to stay at the Cottage?"

She hardly knew what she was saying, she was so filled, suddenly, with happiness. George, exposed to the full extent of her loving, caring, undefended self, felt dazzled as if the sunshine within her was shining straight into his heart. No longer did he see her just as the woman with the pixie smile and the pleasantly ordinary face and aging body. She seemed universal, ageless, eternally beautiful, eternally desirable.

How could he not have recognised her until now? It seemed that the Soulmate he had always longed for, always believed he would find in France or La la Land, had been quietly inserted into his life in a little country hamlet, found in a newspaper advert for a cottage to let. He had simply not recognised her till now!

All his hesitation and uncertainty of whether he loved her or could be true to her had evaporated like dew at the sun's rising.

"No, I haven't come to stay in the Cottage," he said, his diffidence gone, "I've come to stay with you, for as long as you'll have me. Please!"

His own smile showed all the love he could never really say in words but only in action and went straight to a soul able to read him. Helena's smile responded to his and they kissed in a rapture that neither had even believed possible.

Breakfast somehow got bypassed or gave way to lunch. There was a lot to talk about but none of it seemed necessary. By tea time they had rested as well and were hungry enough to create omelettes out of the Doveport eggs and other oddments of food.

When George tried to explain and apologise, Helena put her finger on his lips and said lovingly, "We can say all that to each other tomorrow, can't we? For now, I don't need anything but your presence, here with me, George dearest!"

♪

By twilight George was reading her his favourite poetry and broke off to say abruptly, "I think we should go and tell the Mice!"

Helena laughed delightedly. "It's like the bees perhaps? You have to tell the bees every major change that happens in your life, or they swarm off and leave you!"

So they strolled hand in hand up to Turnaround Cottage in the Owlight and whispered through the letterbox in the door of their happiness and the plans that they hardly knew themselves yet.

Helena was sure she heard the excited chirruping of the Mice and especially the Mouselets, overawed by this addition to their knowledge and understanding.

George was convinced in the darkness that the top of the old Mill had turned around and the wise old face was looking down at them on the West side, as they sat companionably for a while on the bench.

FINALE

♪

OUR **DEAR FRIENDS**, George and Helena, do not need to speak any more for now. Around them, they feel or almost see, from the corners of their vision, all that was, all that is, and all that shall be.

There is a special privilege of vision that is granted to those who manage to love someone better than they love themselves, whether for a lifetime or only for a moment. When you are able to fall and sink and lower yourself, to do this, there and then you become acquainted with your twin Soul, and truly and forever find Love, both within and without.

So George and Helena, sitting hand in hand in that blessed time that is no-time at all, are between two worlds. They see the true Turnaround Cottage, the Mill which grinds the corn of our lives, Each individual seed is precious, but is not fully able to be used until it has been bruised, broken, crushed, combined with others into one cloud of nourishing flour. Until the sun has shone on it, the water drowned it, the scythe has cut it down and the Bread Maker has stripped it of all that pollutes or is unnecessary.

Then it must still be bruised again, pummelled and kneaded and pulled into shape, and scorched with more heat, before it can become the holy bread of the Stories which will be given out freely and generously to nourish the world.

Does this sound hard? Oh no, no, no! For those privileged by that knowledge, the pain lasts but a moment and the Joy is everlasting!

The little Flitter is still chanting like a liturgy now and the lovers hear it as a background to their own private thoughts and the visions arising before their eyes...

"We will go down together!" the Flitter seems to be saying. "Hold my hand and come with me to the Big Water, to the Glory beyond the Horizon. Come down through Gentle Green and Kindness Corner, through Sweetness and Joyful, to join Dancing Waters, past Angel School and Everlasting, and then through Generous Gap to the Beach at Bountiful, to hear the most wonderful Tales that have ever been told. Please say yes! Please say yes!"

There in the garden they are all to be seen, like figures going round on a clock tower, at the chiming of the hour...

The Bride, smiling on the swing, in her white silk velvet dress, her child looking up at her from the safe haven of her arms; they gaze joyfully into each other's eyes as if they can never get enough Time together to cancel out the past.

Past, present and future all together at once. All in the 'Present' which has been gifted to them. Look – here come the millers – Edgar Windham, Maria and Josiah Gammerling, and Steph Gammerling himself, last of the millers, all reunited with their Mill.

Here too are all those others who have worked in or for the Mill. Young Tom Crow and old Tom Crow, Bert and Norah Doveport, turning around the central pillar like figures on the great clock; now you see them, now you don't...

Old Father Time himself, dancing a stately round dance with Auntie Mabel, who is almost unrecognisably young, laughing as she dances in the way of her youth. Here is her niece, Carol Baker with good friend, Elsa Zeibig.

'Colonel' Arthur Brassington has a smiling Dolores Entwhistle on his arm, as he tries vainly to keep in step with the music, now playing sweet old country airs like a fairground carousel... Here are Francine and sweet, special girl Jenny... Here too is Jeremy Cornwell for a minute, his eyes fixed with love on a shadowy Jose Diaz.

Joe Price is there to help them as the wheel turns, turns, turns around. Rosie Cullen is there too, a china shepherdess with all her lambs and piglets, cats, dogs, and geese around her skirts. Oh look! Leading the animals with her are shadowy children, now you see two, no three, no four! Laughing and larking around, and the carousel plays Old Macdonald had a Farm and other nursery tunes...

So then, for a moment it looks like a fairground Carousel, as we see friends, Roland and Brian, the Vicar, Agnes Toope from the Benefits Office, and even St Dogo, Arachne and Gordon, all as colourful and exotic as a pantomime. Here are Simon and his lovely Bride, Betty the Buxom Barmaid, with all the regulars from the Dog and Knackers cheering them on, perilously perched on top of the brightly painted carousel. Then they are all gone again, as the wheel turns, turns turns...

Passing by so quickly we hardly have time to recognise them as the wheel spins faster, Ebenezer Bartwhistle, holding on precariously but grinning and urging it on. There's another young couple, Nate and Jilly smiling into each other's eyes... and Eliot with a Mermaid in his arms... Two smiling children, Rachel and Pearl, hand in hand with their mum and dad and another baby on the way.

A procession of mediaeval Monks goes round more slowly, to the rich sound of chanting, while a Friar shades his eyes with his hand, looking out without impatience to see if his Love is near at last on her white unicorn... Yes, the next turn brings the beautiful lady Alysa, riding fast to catch him up, her glorious golden robe streaming behind, like the sun which lights up the path through the woods, where Joshua Forward strides forward, his friendly pig trotting at his heels.

Look! There is even a frieze of excited mice to be seen at every turnaround, between and above and below the moving figures, miming their very own cheesy commentary on the bigness and littleness and silliness of life...

Here are all life's lovers and all who love life, in the prime of their lives, reunited with those they thought lost. Their parents, their brothers. their sisters, their friends, their lovers, and above all their own true selves. All of them living their own true life: the stuff of flesh and blood incarnate, or of fable and myth imagined. Does it matter which? Of course not!

As the platform turns turns, turns, can we even see a figure hunched in the shadows, almost trodden under the feet of the dancers, fingers in ears yet peeking out at us with pain and longing? Now it's turning slowly, slowly... maybe... perhaps?... I'm not sure? Could there be a place even for Gerard Forward, the Swineherd, coming to his senses at last, tired of eating the husks the swine eat and longing to return to the Father's house? Can he humble himself to ask?... Who knows...

Now he has gone again, but who knows when and whether the Mercy might at last get to him? The clock face turns, turns, turns, and we have lost him again, without the answer.

All we can see now is Gabriel, bringer of Good News, pacing slowly around the clock, under the sails, with infinite patience like his Master.

Our two lovers, Helena and George, draw together in another passionate kiss because, like our story, true love has

NO END

LIST OF CHARACTERS

List of Main characters

Helena Brown, widow. Employed to look after Turnaround Cottage. Lives in Wheelwrights Cottage, Flitterbottom.

Prof. George Miller. [Visitor to Turnaround Cottage.]

Neighbours

Bert and Norah Doveport. Retired farmers. Live next door to Turnaround cottage. Friends of Helena.

Old Man [Tom Crow] lives on the Heathfield Road, Punnetts Town.

Linked to Cyclamen Lodge Care Home, Hellingly

Mabel Dunnett, [nee Wilkins] Newest arrival to Cyclamen Lodge.

Carol Baker. Helena's friend, lives in Derbyshire. Niece of 'Aunty' Mabel Dunnett.

Colonel Arthur Brassington. Lives in Cyclamen Lodge.

Dolores Entwhistle. Lives in Cyclamen Lodge.

Joe Price, Careworker at Cyclamen Lodge.

Rosie Cullen, Vet's assistant in Heathfield and Community Liaison worker at Cyclamen Lodge.

Francine Entwhistle and Jenny her daughter. Granddaughter and great granddaughter of Dolores Entwhistle.

Visitors to Turnaround Cottage.

Ebeneezer Barthwaite.

Nathaniel Jenkins.

Steven Johnson, Gloria Gunnersford, Rachel and Pearl. A family.

Elsa Zeibig. From Austria.

Pam and Warwick, 'Wally' Fawkes.

Gerard Forward.

Jeremy Cornwell.

Gabriel.

Others

Nigel Stubbs, Friend of Prof George Miller.

Melinda Long and Beverley Smithson. Expat women in St Tropez, France, friends of Nigel Stubbs.

The Mice. A large collective family of small furry rodents who have lived in Turnaround Mill for many generations.